Books by Fern Michaels (*cont.*)

Published by Kensington Publishing Corporation

Coming Home for Christmas

FERN MICHAELS

ZEBRA BOOKS
KENSINGTON PUBLISHING CORP.
http://www.kensingtonbooks.com

Contents

Silver Bells

Chapter One

Amy Lee stood at the railing on the second floor of her palatial home in Malibu, staring down with quiet intensity at her guests, mostly employees and a few acquaintances. The occasion was her annual Christmas party. Why she even bothered she had no idea.

It had taken a crew of four three whole days to decorate the house from top to bottom. Another crew of three to decorate the outside. Christmas trees in every room, huge wreaths with red satin bows over all the mantels. Gossamer angels floated from ceiling wire, while a life-size stuffed Santa complete with a packed sleigh and a parade of elves circled the floor-to-ceiling fireplace that separated the great room from the dining room. The focal point of all the decorations.

The mansion was festive to the nth degree, and she hated every bit of it. She could hardly wait for midnight, when she handed out the gifts and bonus checks, at which point the guests would make a beeline for the door, having done their duty by attending the festivities.

Amy rubbed at her temples. She'd had a raging headache all day, and it looked like it was going to stay with her throughout the night. She knew she had to go back downstairs, paste a smile on her face, and somehow manage to get through the next hour. For the hundredth time she wished she was anywhere but here.

Here was California. While she lived in Malibu, she worked in Hollywood, where she and all the other movie stars worked. Phony and superficial Hollywood—just like most of the people she worked with. But she'd learned how to play the game, and it was a game. If you wanted the star status that she had, you learned quickly what the rules were. And then you stuck to them.

Amy had always told herself she would know when it was time to get out. She wasn't sure, but she suspected the time was *now*. At thirty-three she was fast approaching has-been status. New, rowdy, outrageous, flamboyant starlets were giving the paparazzi a run for their money in their bid for stardom, and it was working. It seemed like the world couldn't live another day unless they read about one of the starlet's underwear or lack thereof, or getting busted for drunk driving while underage or of age, then signing autographs for the arresting officers or going to jail for ignoring the law. Autographs to the highest bidder as they were being finger-printed. Translation—big bucks at the box office.

She wasn't a prude, but she'd always prided herself on a certain decorum befitting her celebrity. She didn't flit from affair to affair, she didn't drink and drive, she didn't do drugs, and she absolutely refused to do nude sex scenes in her movies. One of the tabloids had recently called her dull and said she wouldn't know what excitement was or an adrenaline rush if it hit her in the face. They were right.

Amy looked down at the dress she was wearing. It was a plain Armani scarlet sheath befitting the holidays, with a slit up the leg. It draped perfectly over her body. Just the right neckline, just the right amount of sleeve. She'd walked the red carpet enough to know she looked glamorous in her sparkling gown. Just like all her female guests looked glamorous. Once she'd heard a rumor that if you wanted to attend an Amy Lee party, you had better dress *down*. At the time she'd thought it funny. Now, it wasn't funny. Why was that?

Her head continued to throb each time she put her foot on one of the steps. Thank God she'd made it to the bottom without her head splitting open. She walked among her guests, chatted, patted arms, smiled, and even giggled at something one of her employees said. She risked a glance at her watch. Fifty minutes to go. Three thousand seconds. It felt like a lifetime.

It dawned on Amy that she'd been so busy with the party details that she hadn't eaten a thing all day. Maybe if she ate something, the headache would go away.

Amy made her way over to the buffet table. Earlier in the evening it had looked gorgeous, with a Christmas tree ice sculpture nestled in a circle of bright red poinsettias. The matching red candles had long ago burned down. Red candle wax pooled on the white tablecloth. The lobster and shrimp in their ice bowls, what was left of them, looked watery. The turkey and roast beef looked dry. The champagne fountain was as dry as the turkey and roast beef. She felt a surge of anger. Where were the people she'd hired to take care of the table? Outside smoking cigarettes, that's where. Did it even matter? When the last guest left, maybe she'd scramble herself some eggs.

Forty minutes to go. Two thousand four hundred seconds. What she should do was go to the sleigh, pretend her watch was fast, and start handing out the presents and the bonus checks. There were expensive token gifts for the other guests, so they wouldn't feel left out. Boy/girl gifts. Tomorrow it would be all over *TMZ*, Page Six, and anywhere else the gossips gathered. It was all part of playing the game.

Amy moved closer to the sleigh, touched her secretary's arm, and whispered. Word spread, and the guests started to mince their way toward the sleigh.

Twenty minutes later it was all over, and she was standing at the door wishing the last guest a Merry Christmas. Two weeks early, the last guest pointed out. "But then, my dear, you always were ahead of the curve." Amy forced a smile and stood in the open doorway until the last car pulled away from the driveway. The valet boys waved and walked down the driveway.

Amy turned to go inside when she looked at her oversize magnificent front door. She loved everything about the house, but the front door was special. She'd had it made of mahogany and gone to great lengths to find a lumber mill to round it out so that it looked like a cathedral door. Anytime she had been interviewed at home, the reporters had taken pictures of her front door. A memory. She was going to miss it. Her eyes burned when she looked at the huge silver bells attached to a glorious red satin bow. The bells were hammered silver, specially made. The tone was so pure, so melodious, it always brought tears to her eyes when they rang. Another memory. Maybe she'd take the bells with her.

Amy closed the huge door and locked it. Now she could relax. First, though, she walked about, turning off lights. The buffet table had been cleared and carried away. There was still noise in the kitchen, but she ignored it. She kicked off her heels and made her way to the sofa. She sat down, leaned back, and closed her eyes. It took a full minute to realize her headache was finally gone.

The multicolored lights on the artificial tree winked at her. How pretty it looked in the dim light of the great room. In broad daylight it looked like just what it was—a fake tree with a bunch of junk hanging off it.

As a child, back home in Pennsylvania, there had always been a floor-to-ceiling live tree that scented the entire house. Until that fateful Christmas when she was fourteen and allowed to go to the mall alone. Three days before Christmas, she'd gone to the mall with two of her friends. An hour into her shopping the police had come for her to tell her a gas explosion had rocked their house and killed her parents.

The days afterward were still a blur. She knew she'd gone to her parents' funeral, knew she stayed at her friend Katie's house until her aunt Flo, a writer of travelogues, could be found. A week later she'd been located in Madrid, Spain. She'd rushed home, swooped Amy into her arms, then swooped her out to California, where Amy had lived ever since.

There had been money, lots and lots of money that her aunt Flo invested for her. Huge insurance policies added to her robust nest egg. And the house was hers, too. The town had pitched in to repair the damage from the explosion, then closed up the house. Flo paid the taxes every year and said from time to time that they would go back, but they never did.

Neighbors mowed the lawn in the summer and shoveled the snow in the winter. Kind people, caring people who had loved her parents. Flo said people in small towns looked out for one another. Amy believed it.

She'd cried a lot back then because she missed her parents. Not that Flo wasn't a wonderful substitute. She was, but it wasn't the same as having a *real* mom. Flo had enrolled her in everything there was to enroll in—gymnastics, soccer, choir, art classes, music classes, the drama club—everything to keep her hours full. But at night, when she was alone in her pretty bedroom, which Flo had decorated herself, she would cry.

Her world changed in her senior year when she had the lead in the school play. She'd given a rousing performance or so said the critics. A movie producer had shown up at the door five days later and asked her if she'd be interested in an audition with a photo op. Flo had raised her eyebrows and hovered like a mother hen in case it was some kind of scam. It wasn't. Flo continued to hover, saying college was a must. Amy had agreed, and the studio worked around her studies. Back then she did two movies a year, not little parts, not big parts, but big enough for her to get noticed. And then the plum of all plums, the lead in a Disney movie. Her career took off like a rocket. Flo still hovered until she convinced herself that Amy could take care of herself. The only thing Flo had objected to was the name change from Amanda Leigh to Amy Lee. But in the end, when her niece said she was okay with it, Flo stepped aside and continued on with her own career, which she had put on hold to take care of Amy.

Thanks to modern technology, aunt and niece stayed in touch daily. Time and scheduling permitting, they always managed at least one vacation a year together.

Amy closed her eyes again as she ran the last phone call with Flo through her mind. Flo had called just as she was getting out of bed. She'd flopped back onto the pillows, and they talked for almost an hour. The last thing she'd said to her aunt before breaking the connection was, "I don't want to do this anymore, Flo. I want to go home. I *am* going home. Tomorrow as a matter of fact. I bought my ticket two weeks ago."

"Just like that, you're throwing it all away?" Flo had said.

"Well, not exactly. I have two more pictures on my contract, and I don't have to report to the studio till April of next year. I don't know if I'm burned out, or I just need to get out of the business. Come April, I might be more than ready to go back. I will honor the contract, so that's not a problem. Before you can ask, I am financially secure. You know I never touched my inheritance. I've got fifty times that amount from my earnings, and it's all invested wisely. I'm okay, so don't worry about me."

"Mandy, I just want you to be happy," Flo said. She'd never once called her by her Hollywood name. "I want you to find a nice man, get married, have kids, get a couple of dogs, and be happy. It's all I ever wanted for you. I'm just not sure you're going to find happiness back in Pennsylvania."

"We should have gone back, Flo."

"Woulda, coulda, shoulda. I did what I thought was best. For you. So, you're going to open up the house and . . . what . . . put down some roots?"

"I don't know, Flo. Maybe I'm looking for something that doesn't exist, and you're right, if I had wanted to go back earlier, I would have made your life miserable until you took me. The best I can come up with is, I wasn't ready to go back. I'm ready now, and I'm going. It would be nice if you could find a way to join me. Hint, hint."

"Darling girl, I met *a man*! He has the soul of an angel, and don't ask me how I know this. I just know it. He loves me, warts and all. He's a simple man, never been out of Madrid. He lives on a farm. Owns the farm, actually. Never been on an airplane. I'll ask him if he wants to spend Christmas with my movie star niece. He's seen all your movies, by the way. He thinks you're a nice-looking lass."

Amy laughed. "You getting married?"

"The minute he asks me, I am, but he has to ask first. I have to run, Mandy. I have an appointment I can't break. I'll call you tomorrow."

"Love you, Flo."

"And I love you, too."

Amy sighed. Flo had a boyfriend. At sixty-five,

Flo had a boyfriend. Here she was, at thirty-three, without a prospect in sight. How weird was that?

Amy gathered up the sequined shoes that matched her gown. She walked out to the kitchen to see if the caterers had cleaned up thoroughly. The kitchen was spotless. She locked the back door and turned out the light. The great room had a master switch that turned off all the tree lights as well as the overhead lights. The outside lights were set on a timer that would turn everything off a little before dawn.

As she walked up the stairs to the second floor she found herself wondering if Hank Anders still lived back home. Her first boyfriend. The first boy who had ever given her a gift. Hank had been the first boy to kiss her. On the lips. She hadn't had a chance to tell him good-bye. Where was he right now? What was he doing? If he still lived in Apple Valley, would he remember her? Not likely, thanks to Flo and her transformation from small-town girl to glamorous Hollywood star. She'd had her nose done, gotten braces, wore contacts, and her hair was a different color. Flo had seen to it that her past stayed in the past. She'd never been able to figure that out. As far as her bio went, she was born and raised in California. Went to UCLA. End of story.

Or was it the beginning?

Chapter Two

Henry Anders, also known as Cranky Hank Anders, hefted his oversize suitcase off the carousel and looked around for his sister-in-law, who had said she'd meet him in the baggage area. When he didn't see her, he made his way to the closest EXIT sign. And then he saw her pushing a double stroller with the year-old twins, who were howling at the top of their lungs. He wondered if their high-pitched screams had anything to do with the way they were bundled up. Their mother looked just as frazzled as her offspring.

Alice Anders stopped in her tracks and threw out her arms. "Hank! I'm so glad to see you! I'm sorry I'm late. There was traffic, and my two bundles of joy here are overdue for a nap. I had to park a mile away. I'm sorry. I left hours ahead of time just so I wouldn't be late, and what happens, I'm late! Ohhh, I'm just so glad you're here. I was dreading going through the holidays without Ben. I had an e-mail from him this morning, and he warned me not to be late; that's why I left early. He said you hate to wait around for people."

Alice was a talker, he'd give her that. "No problem. Relax, Alice. I could just as easily have taken a cab or gotten a car service. I'm here, you're here, that's all that matters. The twins really grew since Easter. Ben said they're walking now."

An anxious note crept into his voice when he said, "He's okay, isn't he?"

Alice shoved a lock of dark hair under the bright red wool hat she was wearing. "As right as someone who's in Iraq can be. He said you're the only one he trusts to step in for him at Christmas. He was supposed to come back in September, but they extended his tour. This will be our first Christmas apart." Tears welled in her eyes as she gave the stroller a shove to get through the door Hank was holding open for her.

A blustery gust of wind whipped across the walkway. The twins howled louder. Alice dropped a light blanket over the top of the stroller to keep the wind at bay. One of the twins ripped it away, one pudgy fist shaking in frustration. The wind picked it up, and it was gone, just like that. Hank was about to chase it down when Alice stopped him. "It doesn't matter, it was an old one. Like I said, I parked a mile away, so let's get going. The sooner I get these two guys in the car, the sooner they'll calm down."

Hank didn't know what to say. He was certainly no authority on kids, babies in particular, so he just walked along, dragging his suitcase. He wondered if the twins slept through the night. Probably not from the look of the dark circles under Alice's eyes.

Out of the corner of his eye he watched his sister-in-law. Once she'd been slim and trim. Once she'd worn makeup and had a fashionable hairdo and she'd dressed in designer clothes. Today she was wearing a down coat of some sort that made her look forty pounds overweight. She was wearing jeans and sneakers, and her hair was up in a ponytail, the tail sticking out of the back of the bright red hat. Maybe marriage wasn't all that wonderful. Maybe he was lucky after all, even though at the time he thought his world was coming to an end when his fiancée had left him standing at the altar on their wedding day. He looked down at the twins, who were trying to poke each other's eyes out. Yeah, yeah, maybe he had dodged a bullet.

A twin himself, he wanted to tell Alice her nightmare was just beginning when he remembered some of the things he and Ben had done growing up. Always in trouble, always fighting, always making their parents' lives anxious. Then again, maybe he wouldn't tell her.

Fifteen minutes later, Alice stopped in front of a dark SUV. He whirled around at the furious sound of a dog barking. Alice stopped, a horrible look on her face. "That's Churchill, the dog. Ben got him before he left for Iraq. He said we needed protection because we couldn't afford an alarm system." Hank thought she sounded like she would have gone into debt for the alarm versus the dog. "I think it might be a little crowded, but you'll be in the front seat. The dog sheds. And he poops everywhere. The twins step in it. He pees, too. I can never seem to catch him at the right time to let him out. He's a good dog, great with the boys. The lights are still up from last Christmas. Ben never got a chance to take them down before he had to return to Iraq. I have to get a Christmas tree. Ben wants me to send him a picture. Like I don't have enough to do without going out to get a Christmas tree. I wasn't going to get one. The boys are too little to know what a Christmas tree is."

"Uh-huh. Give me the keys, Alice, I'll drive and you can relax."

"Relax! That word is not in my vocabulary. The last time I relaxed was on my honeymoon, and even then I'm not sure I relaxed. It was *stressful.*"

Hank decided he wouldn't touch that statement with a ten-foot pole. No sireee, not even with a twenty-foot pole. He offered to help strap the twins into the car seats, but Churchill had other ideas and growled at him. He slid into the driver's seat and turned on the engine. He hoped the heat would kick in. He was freezing.

The dog barked, and the twins howled and yowled as Alice walked around to the driver's side of the car and opened the door. She looked Hank square in the eye and said, "I can't do this anymore. I don't *want* to do this anymore. It's all yours! The key to the house is the big key on the ring. You can get the damn Christmas tree, and you can decorate the house and you can clean up the poop and the pee and you can cook and clean and do the laundry and rake and take care of the yard. And you can tell your brother for me that I wish he had left me standing at the altar. There isn't much food in the house, so you'll have to go shopping, and let me tell you, that's an experience from hell. Good luck. The boys get a bath at seven. That's another experience that is right up there with hell. See ya!"

Churchill leaped over the seat to land in the front next to Hank. He threw his head back and howled, an ungodly sound that made the hair on the back of Hank's neck stand on end.

She was walking away! Actually walking away! "Hey!" he bellowed. "Where are you going? Come back here, Alice!" Obviously, she hadn't heard him because she kept right on walking. Must be the wool hat over her ears. He jammed the car in reverse and barreled down the aisle, coming to a stop next to her. He pushed a button and the passenger-side front window rolled down. "C'mon, Alice, you can't leave me with these kids and this dog. I know you didn't mean that; you're just venting, and I can understand how hard it's been. Get in the car. *Please*," he added as an afterthought. The

twins had started to howl again the moment
the SUV ground to a stop. Churchill leaped in
the back and started to lick at the twins' faces.
"Stop that," he shouted, to be heard over the
din.

Alice was on the move again. He inched the
SUV along to keep up with her. "Where are
you going?"

"To get a manicure, a massage, and a pedicure. Then I'm going someplace where I can
sleep for a week and get room service. Don't call
me, I'll call you." She tossed her cell phone in the
car window. Churchill leaped over the seat again
and grabbed it before returning to the back.
He started to chew on it. It chirped in protest.
A moment later Alice ran between the rows of
parked cars and was lost to him.

Hank sat for a full minute, the reality of his
situation hitting him full on. Alice was gone.
She'd meant what she said. He was stranded with
year-old twins and a hundred-pound golden retriever that pooped and peed all over the place
and chewed up cell phones, and there was no
Christmas tree or food in the house. "Shit!" he
said succinctly.

"Ben," he muttered under his breath, "when
I see you again I'm going to kick your ass all the
way to the Canadian border." He knew he'd do
no such thing; he was just venting the way Alice
had vented. He loved Ben even though he'd
never understood why he'd wanted a military
career. Major Benjamin Anders. It sounded so
professional. When he got back from Iraq, he
would be Colonel Benjamin Anders. Hank felt

his chest puff out with pride at his little
brother. Little brother because Ben was two
whole minutes younger than his older brother.

As he tooled along Route 30, his mind raced.
He knew squat about taking over a household.
He lived in a town house, had a housekeeper,
and never worried about grocery shopping.
Hell, he didn't even know what to buy. And, he
wasn't much in the kitchen department either,
which meant he could boil an egg and that was
it. And he could make coffee. He was a bachelor, for crying out loud. Now, in the blink of an
eye he was suddenly a stand-in dad, a dog
watcher, a chauffeur, a grocery shopper, and a
cook. There was something definitely wrong
with this picture.

Maybe he could get some help. The kind
that lived in and did all those things. He could
afford it. Or, he could send the bill to Ben. No,
skip that idea. Not even majors make enough
to pay for that.

Forty minutes later, Hank slowed for the red
light on the corner. In five minutes he would
be driving through the center of town. As always,
he took a moment to savor the small-town
warmth of Apple Valley. He cruised past the
town square, noted the sleigh, the eight huge
reindeer, and all the other Christmas decorations. Glorious wreaths with huge red bows
were on all the sparkling white doors of the
town's official buildings. The square was where
the midnight candlelight Christmas service was
held. The whole town turned out. Kids in paja-
mas all bundled up, even dogs attended, with

antlers on their heads and colorful green and white collars for the season. He loved Apple Valley and the people he'd grown up with. Right now, though, this very second, he hated it.

Churchill started to bark the moment Hank turned off Apple Valley Road, the main thoroughfare in town, onto Clemens Ferry Road, where his brother and he had been born and grew up. The old homestead. He blinked at the commotion going on at the house next to his old home. A fire engine, an ambulance, and the sheriff's car. Something must have happened to Albert Carpenter. Ben had just mentioned Albert in his last e-mail, saying he would be ninety-three the day after Christmas. He wanted Hank to invite him for Christmas dinner and make sure he got some presents. Albert Carpenter had been a substitute grandfather to both boys when they were growing up.

Hank felt a lump the size of a golf ball form in his throat. For years, Ben and the other neighbors had looked after Albert because there was no one else to do it. In fact, a few years ago, Ben had given him a puppy, a little white lapdog that Albert carried around. Ben said it added years to the old gentleman's life. He couldn't help but wonder if Alice had taken on caring for Albert along with her other duties. More than likely.

Hank pulled into the driveway, turned off the engine, and debated his next move. Churchill watched him with keen intensity. Would the dog bolt? How was he supposed to get two kids into the house at the same time? One under each arm. That had to mean the dog would bolt. Maybe. Out of the corner of his eye he saw the ambulance pull away. Out of the corner of his other eye he saw a white ball of fur streaking toward Alice's SUV. Churchill let out a high-pitched bark of pure happiness. Albert's dog. Who was going to take care of her? He knew it was a her because he remembered Ben saying Albert named the little dog after his wife, Sadie. Officially known as Miss Sadie.

Hank opened the door so he could get out without letting the big dog out of the car. He had to find a leash or something. Like that was going to happen. He looked around in a daze, the white fur ball yapping and yipping at his feet. Churchill continued to bark, growl, and howl at what was going on. The twins woke up and started to cry. "Oh, shit!" Maybe if he opened the door to the house, dragged the dog in, and shut the door he could do it that way. He'd have to come back for the kids. He was on his way to the door when he saw the fire engine and the sheriff's car leaving the neighborhood. That was when he saw the Range Rover in the Leigh driveway. The house must have been sold. He felt sad at the thought. Ben hung a Christmas wreath on the front door every Christmas even though the house was empty. First Albert, then the Leigh house. No, first Alice's fit. A trifecta of misery. Flo must have finally sold the house. He wondered why—

it was in such perfect condition. He knew that for a fact because Ben told him that the sodality ladies did a spring cleaning once a year.

The front door slid open. Hank walked into the kitchen and grabbed a dish towel, which he carried outside and looped into Churchill's collar. With his homemade leash, he dragged the recalcitrant canine into the house. The fur ball followed and made herself comfortable on one of the family room chairs. Churchill took the other chair, but not before he lifted his leg on the bottom of it.

Hank lost it then. He marched over to the big dog, who looked at him defiantly. He stuck his finger to his nose and barked, "Do that one more time, and your ass is grass. You hear me? That means you sit out on the deck and look through the window. And I won't feed you either. Oh, Christ, the twins!" He raced to the door and back out to the car. It took him a good five minutes to figure out how to unbuckle the harness on the childproof seats or whatever they were called. A kid under each arm, he marched to the door and opened it. Alice said they could walk. He set them down and off they went. "I need a beer. Please, God, let there be beer in the refrigerator." There was no beer. He had to settle for a Diet Pepsi. Did all women in the world drink Diet Pepsi? He counted twenty-four cans. Alice must be addicted.

Hank looked around for a place to sit down. He was tempted to shoo Churchill off the chair, but one look at the retriever's face squelched that idea. Obviously, the chair was his. Miss Sadie looked at him with adoring eyes and yipped softly. "You just moved in, didn't you, you little shit?" Miss Sadie yipped again and put her head down between her paws. Yep, she had moved in.

Hank looked over at the twins, who were trying to crawl into the fireplace. He realized they still had on their winter gear and were sweating profusely. He removed it, closed the fire screen, then flopped down on the couch after he dumped a ton of toys on the floor. "I can't do this. I don't *want* to do this."

The sudden quiet alerted Hank that something was wrong. One of the twins, he didn't know which one, was trying to take off his pants. And then he smelled it. "Please, God, no. I've never changed a diaper in my life." Churchill jumped off his chair, trotted out of the room, and returned with a diaper clenched between his teeth. He let it drop at Hank's feet. Then he hopped back on his chair. Hank wanted to cry.

The TV suddenly exploded with sound. Churchill had the remote clutched between his paws. A cartoon show appeared. The twins squealed their pleasure.

"Alice Anders, you are a saint," Hank said as he prepared to change his first-ever diaper.

Chapter Three

Amy Lee, aka Amanda Leigh, walked through her old home. Everything was just as she remembered it. All these years later, nothing had changed. Thanks, she knew, to Flo, who stayed in touch with her parents' old friends.

Amy was glad now that she'd had the foresight to call ahead to a cleaning service, which had cleaned the house and turned on all the utilities as well as doing a week's grocery shopping. It was worth every penny in comfort alone. She was toasty warm, and there was even a load of wood on the back porch and a stack of logs and kindling perched on the end of the fireplace hearth. Maybe this evening she'd make a fire the way her parents had always done after dinner.

Her memory of that terrible time when her

world had changed forever surfaced. This time
she didn't push the memory away. Flo should
have let her stay, at least for a while. She
should have cried and been given the chance
to grieve instead of being dragged across the
country where every hour of her day was occupied so she wouldn't think about *that time.*
Now, where had that thought come from? Had
she secretly blamed Flo all these years for the
person she'd become? Did she really want to
look into that? Probably not. At least not right
now.

It just boggled her mind that everything in
the house looked the same. The furniture was
outdated, but that was okay. The oak staircase
had the same old treads and gave off the scent
of lemon polish. The furniture looked comfortable but worn. The house gleamed and
sparkled, and it didn't smell like it had been
closed up for years and years. Even the kitchen
curtains had been washed and starched.

All the bedrooms and bathrooms were closed.
She wondered why. One by one she opened
them. The spare bedroom had a yellow spread
on the big four-poster and crisp white curtains
hanging at the windows. Flo had always slept in
this room when she visited back then. A colorful braided rug was in the middle of the floor.
Her mother had hooked rugs in the winter.
Framed posterlike pictures hung on the walls—
scenes from different cities that Flo had traveled to.

Amy backed out of the room and opened
the door to her parents' room. Tears burned

in her eyes. How many times she'd run to that bed and jumped in with her parents to be hugged in the middle of the night. She thought she could smell either the perfume or the talcum powder her mother had always used. How was that possible? She walked into the bathroom. All her mother's things were still on one side of the vanity, her father's things on the other side. She looked around as though time had stopped and never picked up again.

In one way, Amy was glad that Flo had left things the way they were. In another way, she wished she hadn't. She ran to the high four-poster and jumped up on it. She flapped her arms and legs this way and that like she was making snow angels.

Amy frowned when she heard a high-pitched siren. It sounded like it was right next door. She bolted from the room, which was at the back of the house, and ran to her old room, whose windows faced the Carpenter property on one side and the Anders property on the other. She watched as frantic EMS workers ran into the Carpenter house. She swiped at the tears forming in her eyes when, a while later, she saw the same EMS people wheel a gurney out to the ambulance. Not too long ago Flo had told her Albert Carpenter was in his nineties and in frail health. Such a nice man. His wife had been nice, too, to all the kids in the neighborhood. They'd always been partial to Hank and Ben. She was about to move from the window when she saw movement through the window facing the Anders house. She walked over to the other window, which afforded her a better view, and stared down at the man getting out of the SUV. Ben? Hank? It was hard to tell from where she was standing. Her heart kicked up a beat as she watched the scene being played out on the ground. Kids. Big dog. Little white dog. She burst out laughing as she watched the man run into the house to return and drag the dog into the house with a towel as a leash. She laughed even harder when she saw him straddle each child under his arms. A novice for a father. Ben? Hank? Her heart was beating extra fast. Not a good thing. So much for hoping that maybe . . .

Amy walked across the room to the rocking chair her mother had painted bright red because red was Amy's favorite color. She'd even made the cushions out of red velvet. Amy sat down and started to rock as she let her gaze sweep through the room. It was all just the same. Her boots were in the corner, her yellow muffler and matching wool hat, knitted by her mother, were on the coatrack by the closet door. Her navy peacoat with the gold buttons was still on the rack, too. Guess Flo thought I wouldn't need winter clothes in California, she thought.

From her position in the rocking chair, Amy could see the photos she'd taped to the mirror over her vanity. Most of them were of her, Hank, and Ben. Several of her friend Libby, who had moved away a few months before her parents' death.

Amy got up to check out her closet and dresser

drawers. Everything was neat and tidy even after all these years. A lifetime ago. Time to let it all go. Time to lay all her old ghosts to rest.

Amy looked outside, surprised that it was already dark and it was only five o'clock. Time to think about a nice hot shower, some dinner, and a nice fire and a little television before she retired for the night. Tomorrow was another day. Tomorrow she'd go up to the attic and get down all her mother's Christmas decorations. Maybe she'd venture forth and get a real live Christmas tree. Not a glittery Hollywood tree but one that would smell up the whole house. Then she'd have that Christmas that never happened. The one she'd missed when Flo took her to California.

Maybe Christmas would be forever tainted. Maybe she couldn't get the old feelings back. Well, she'd never know if she didn't try.

Was it Hank or Ben in the house next door? She wished she knew. Maybe she should go over and knock on the door. People in Apple Valley did things like that. Most times they brought food to newcomers. She couldn't help but wonder if anyone would bring her something once they knew she was back home.

As she walked down the steps, Amy crossed her fingers. Let it be Ben next door. Let him be the married one. Maybe she could discreetly ask where Hank was. Find out if he, too, was married. She crossed her fingers tighter.

Back on the first floor, Amy opened the doors of the fireplace, laid some kindling, then stacked the logs the way she'd seen her father do. She had a fireplace in her California home, but it was gas. She'd used it once and was so disappointed with the effect it created, she'd never turned it on again. Within minutes she had a nice blaze going. In the kitchen she prepared a small salad to accompany the frozen TV dinner she popped into the oven. She uncorked a bottle of wine to let it breathe before she headed upstairs to shower.

Her first day home.

Home. Amy closed her eyes and almost swooned at the way the one word made her feel. She literally ran up the stairs, her heart bursting with happiness. She knew, just knew, coming back home to Apple Valley was the best decision of her life.

In the shower, she sang "Jingle Bells" at the top of her lungs as she washed her hair and showered with her favorite bath gel, a Vera Wang scent she'd been using for years.

Thirty minutes later, Amy walked through the family room, where the fire was blazing cheerfully, and on out to the kitchen, where her dinner waited for her. She turned on the radio that was mounted under one of the kitchen cabinets. Holiday music invaded the old kitchen.

She was home. Eating in her old kitchen, using her mother's old place mats, using the same silverware with the green handles. It seemed the same, but it wasn't the same. The sugar bowl and creamer weren't in the middle of the table. Both her parents had always had coffee with their meals, even at lunchtime. Suddenly, Amy wasn't hungry anymore. She reached for the wine bottle and poured it into her glass. Flo had drummed into her head over the years that "you can't go home again," then went on to say some famous writer had said that. It wasn't until she was in college that Amy learned that the writer was Thomas Wolfe.

Amy sat down on what had once been her mother's chair and stared at the fire. She supposed you could go home again physically, but when you got there, you had to be realistic enough to know that time had passed, and it could never be recaptured. And recapture time was exactly what she had hoped to do by making this trip. How foolish she was to even think she could make that happen. The past was prologue.

Now what was she supposed to do until it was time to go back to California? Should she just eat, drink, sleep, watch television? Should she pretend it wasn't the Christmas season and ignore everything? Wouldn't that be a cop-out?

Maybe she should go next door and talk to Ben or Hank or whoever it was that lived in that house. There was nothing wrong with dropping in on old childhood friends. Was there? She tried to talk herself out of the idea by convincing herself that either Ben or Hank's wife wouldn't appreciate an unknown female dropping by—she looked down at her watch—at seven o'clock in the evening. Maybe she would do it tomorrow.

Before Amy could change her mind, she

raced upstairs for her old peacoat. She was surprised that it still fit. She pulled the yellow hat
down over her ears, wrapped the muffler around
her neck, and was ready to go. A walk to the town
square would be nice. She could take her time,
look in the shop windows, and by the time she
got home, she'd be wiped out and ready for a
good night's sleep in her own bed. Her own
bed. Five minutes later she was out the door,
the key to the front door in the pocket of her
sweatpants.

It was icy cold, the wind blustery and pushing her along as she walked down the street to
the corner. Her feet already felt numb from the
cold. No wonder, she thought, looking down at
her feet. She wasn't wearing socks, and she was
still wearing slippers, for God's sake. Stupid,
stupid, stupid. Maybe she wasn't really stupid.
Maybe she was just overwhelmed with being
home and wasn't thinking clearly. She continued walking to the next corner, then she decided, yes, she was stupid, and turned around
to go home.

How bleak and lonely Mr. Carpenter's house
looked. Every other house on the street fea-
tured colored Christmas lights on their porches
and shrubbery. Correction. Every house but
Mr. Carpenter's and her house had colored
lights. She made a mental note to get them
down from the attic and hang them tomorrow.
Maybe she'd hang some on Mr. Carpenter's
house, too. She rather thought Mr. Carpenter
would like that.

The Anders house was lit up from top to

bottom. It looked like every room in the house was lit up. She looked around. The other houses on the street looked the same way. Families needed a lot of light, she decided.

Amy heard the sound when she walked across the lawn in front of the Anders house in a shortcut to her driveway. She stopped and pushed her hat above her ears to see if she could hear better. It sounded like a baby was crying. She listened hard, then heard a whimpering sound. She turned around and there by her front door was the beautiful dog she'd seen earlier. He looked even more golden under the porch light. She whistled softly, and the dog bounded over to where she was standing. "Hey, big guy, what are you doing out here all by yourself? Did you get loose? Like you're really going to answer me. I think you belong over there," she said, pointing to the door of the Anders house. "C'mon, I'll ring the bell, and before you know it, you'll be warm and cozy inside." The big dog walked alongside her as she made her way to the front door.

Amy rang the bell. Once. Twice. On the third ring she thought she heard a voice bellow, "Come in."

She looked down at the dog and shrugged. She opened the door and stuck her head in. "Anybody here?" she shouted.

"I'm upstairs giving the twins a bath," came the reply.

"I brought your dog home. I think he might have jumped the fence. It's freezing outside.

It's not right to leave an animal out in weather like this," she shouted again, anger ringing in her voice. As an afterthought she yelled again, "If you can't take care of an animal, you shouldn't have one. I'm leaving now," she said, backing toward the door, partially blocking it with her leg so the big dog wouldn't bolt.

The voice from the second floor thundered down the steps. "What are you, some know-it-all? If the dog jumped the fence, it doesn't mean I can't take care of him. Stop that! Right now! Now look what you did!" Two high-pitched wails of misery traveled down the steps.

The golden dog immediately raced up the steps, a white fur ball on his heels, yapping every step of the way.

"A thank you would have been nice. Doesn't sound like you're any great shakes as a parent either." Amy screamed out her parting shot as she closed the door behind her. "Stupid ass!" *And to think I couldn't wait to see you. Ha!*

Back inside her own house, Amy raced to her room for some heavy warm socks. She could barely feel her feet, that's how cold she was. Back downstairs, she tidied up the kitchen, poured more wine, then went back to the family room. She pulled at the cushions from the sofa and propped them up by the fire, her legs stretched forward. She added two more logs to the fire and sipped at her wine.

Two revelations in one day. 1. You can't have expectations when you go home again. 2. Ben or Hank Anders was not the boy of her youth. Screw it, she thought as she set the wineglass aside and curled up on the old cushions. Moments later she was sound asleep.

She slept soundly only to be awakened hours later by the sound of her doorbell. Groggily, she looked down at her watch. It was after twelve. Who would be visiting at this hour? She ran to the door, turned on the porch light, and was dismayed to see the huge golden dog slapping at her doorbell. She opened the door, and he bounded in like a whirlwind. He ran over to the fire and lay down on the cushions.

Amy threw her hands in the air. "What's this mean? You moved out? What?"

The dog barked as he squirmed and wiggled to get more comfortable on the cushions. "Does this mean you're staying here for the night?" The dog barked again, laid his head on his paws, and closed his eyes. "Guess so. Can't say as how I blame you. He sounds like a . . . like a . . . big jerk."

Before she made her way to the second floor, Amy bent over to look at the collar on the big dog's neck. CHURCHILL. "Okay, Churchill, see you in the morning."

Chapter Four

Hank Anders staggered down the stairs a little before midnight. He was beyond exhausted from the past few hours with the twins, and he now had a newfound respect for his sister-in-law. Where in the name of God was she? Probably sleeping peacefully in some five-star hotel after being pampered by a trained masseuse.

The two dogs looked at him warily. Churchill ran to the sliding glass doors off the kitchen that led to a little terrace in the back. Earlier he'd seen the area was fenced, so he let the dogs out. His nerves were twanging all over the place as he prepared a cup of hot chocolate the way his mother had always done when things got dicey. Well, as far as he was concerned, things didn't get any dicier than this.

Dinner had been a disaster. The twins didn't

like hard-boiled eggs. They didn't like toast either. When they wouldn't eat, he'd belatedly checked to make sure they had teeth, and sure enough they each had six. Then he'd tried peanut butter and jelly, but they didn't like that either. All they'd done was smear it everywhere. The two dogs licked it up, to his chagrin. Milk from a cup was spilled on the floor and on the walls, leaving a sticky residue. The dogs licked that up, too. He finally found a can of ravioli and handed out spoons. Probably his tenth or eleventh mistake. At least he didn't have to worry about the dogs'dinner.

Bath time had been a total disaster. He wondered if Alice would notice, if she *ever* returned, that the wallpaper was soaking wet or that the linoleum on the floor was buckling where the splashed water had seeped under it. Probably not. Why should she? She had other things on her mind. God, where was she? Was she going to leave him here *forever* with her kids or until Ben got back? He shuddered at the thought. She'd be a fool not to. A five-star hotel, a pedicure, manicure, hairdo, facial, massage, certainly couldn't compare to this experience.

And who the hell was that person who'd brought Churchill back? And how had the dog gotten out in the first place? "Please come home, Alice. Please," Hank muttered over and over as he poured the hot chocolate into a cup.

Earlier, after the dinner the twins didn't eat, he had called the market and placed an order that the clerk promised to deliver early in the morning. He'd lucked out when he called the only employment agency in town. The woman who operated it was running late and was still in the office. She'd promised a "day lady" or possibly a male nanny depending on availability and sir, we do not discriminate, who was capable of minding children and doing light cooking for $750 a week. He'd blinked at the amount but agreed. At that precise moment he would have paid triple the amount she quoted.

Hank was so hungry he thought he was going to pass out. He'd used the last of the bread, so he ate peanut butter and jelly right out of the jar. All of it. Though still hungry, he was too tired to rummage or try to cook something.

When Miss Sadie scratched at the door, he went over to open it. The little fur ball pranced in and looked up at the giant standing over her. She yipped and did a circle dance that probably meant something, but he didn't know what. He whistled for Churchill, and, when nothing happened, he turned on the outside light and whistled again. The small yard was lit up brightly, but there was no sign of the golden retriever. He ran out to the yard calling the dog's name, Miss Sadie yapping and nipping at his pant leg as he raced around. Pure and simple—the dog was gone. "Aw, shit!"

Miss Sadie leaped up, snagged his pant leg, and held on. He tried to shake her loose, but she wasn't budging. Somehow he managed to get back into the house in time to hear one of the twins wailing upstairs. "I hate you, Alice Anders," he groaned as he made his way to the second floor. By the time he got to the boys' cribs, whichever one had been wailing, had stopped. Both toddlers were peacefully sleeping, thumbs in their mouths. Ben had been a thumb sucker.

Hank went back downstairs and opened the front door. He whistled and called the golden retriever's name. He felt like crying when the dog didn't appear. It was so cold and windy and he could see light flurries of snow in the lamplight at the end of the driveway. Miss Sadie was still protesting whatever it was she was protesting by yapping and whining. He told her to shut up in no uncertain terms. She growled, a funny little sound that made the hair on the back of Hank's neck stand on end. He'd read somewhere that little dogs could be killers.

Back in the kitchen, Hank looked at the hot chocolate in his cup. "Good for the nerves, my ass," he mumbled as he searched the cabinets for something a little more powerful. He finally found a bottle of scotch behind a giant-size bottle of ketchup. He removed the cap and swigged directly from the bottle. One gulp. Two gulps. Three gulps. "Where are you, Alice?" he singsonged as he made his way into the family room. "Please come home, Churchill." He immediately retraced his steps to the kitchen and made coffee. He stood in the middle of the kitchen as the coffee dripped into the pot. What kind of child-care provider was he? The worst kind, the kind that drank on the job, that's what kind. Well, that was never going to happen again.

Hank opened the door again and whistled for Churchill. He looked down at Miss Sadie, who just looked sad, like she knew Churchill wasn't coming back. He bent over to scoop the little dog into his arms. She cuddled against his heart, and he could have sworn that she sighed with happiness. At least someone loves me, he thought. Either that or she's desperate for attention. More than likely she missed Albert.

The clock on the kitchen stove said it was one o'clock. What time did the twins get up in the morning? Not that he was going to be any more prepared for them when they did than he was when he arrived. He just knew Alice was sleeping soundly and peacefully on thousand-thread-count sheets while he was afraid to close his eyes.

Somehow he managed to pour his coffee and drink it without disturbing Miss Sadie, who appeared to be out for the count. Who was his earlier visitor, the one who brought Churchill back? Maybe the chick from next door, the one with the fancy set of wheels in the driveway.

As he walked around the well-lighted kitchen he felt sad that the Leigh house had finally, after all these years, been sold. And, without a doubt, the Carpenter house would go up for sale, too. This house, Ben's now, would be all that was left of the old childhood neighborhood. All the other houses on the street had recycled themselves, and, once again, small children played in the yards and even on the road because there was no traffic on the cul-de-sac. His memories seemed like they were a hundred years old.

Hank finally locked the door when he realized Churchill wasn't coming back. Obviously, the dog had jumped the fence. The best he could hope for was that the dog wasn't freezing somewhere. Miss Sadie squirmed, stretched, and licked at his chin before she went back to sleep. He just knew that Albert Carpenter had carried her around just the way he was doing.

Good Lord, how was he going to go to Albert's wake and funeral? He made a mental note to order flowers first thing in the morning. He'd have to find a babysitter. Suddenly, he wanted to cry all over again. How was he going to get the news to Alice? If she ran true to what she was doing, she wasn't going to be watching the news or reading papers. Ben needed to know, too. Tomorrow he would figure out what he was going to do about that.

The coffee had sobered him up, but he knew he couldn't sleep, so he switched on the television and watched a rerun of the daily news on Fox. Eventually he dozed, his arm around Miss Sadie.

Dawn was breaking when Hank finally stirred. Something had woken him. What? Miss Sadie was no longer sleeping in his arms. The house was silent except for a scratching noise on the sliding glass door. Miss Sadie wanted to go out. Then he remembered that Churchill was still missing. He ran to the door and opened it, but

there was no sign of the golden retriever. What
he saw made him blink. A good inch of snow
covered the ground. Miss Sadie was no fool—
she took one look at the white stuff, stepped
over the threshold, squatted, and raced back
inside.

Hank ran to the front door to see if the golden
dog was waiting outside. He whistled and called.
No dog prints could be seen in the snow. Shoulders slumped, he closed the door and went
back to the kitchen to make coffee. While it
dripped, and the twins were still sleeping, he
used the first-floor bathroom to shower and
shave. He wanted to be ready when the groceries
and his new day lady arrived to take charge.

Fifteen minutes later, Hank was ready for
whatever the day was going to throw at him. To
pass the time until the twins woke, he checked
out the little computer station Alice had set up
in a small alcove off the kitchen. He was surprised when he clicked the computer on that it
opened up to Alice's e-mail on AOL. At least
he wouldn't have to worry about a password—
it was all here, right in front of him. And there
was an e-mail addressed to him.

Hank gawked at what he was seeing. Well,
that certainly took a lot of nerve. He clicked
on the e-mail and saw a to-do list. Not one
word about where she was, what she was doing,
or that she was sorry. A damn to-do list. He
lashed out with his foot to kick the side of the
little desk and was instantly sorry. He looked
down at his bare feet and howled in pain,
knowing damn well that he'd broken his big

toe. What the hell else could go wrong? This was way beyond Murphy's Law.

Hank read the list.

- Twins get up around 8. Diaper change. Dress.
- Breakfast. Oatmeal with milk and a little sugar. Applesauce.
- Lunch is soup, crackers, cheese cubes, and peaches.
- Milk as often as they want it.
- Dinner is whatever you want, cut up small or mash all food.
- Churchill gets fed at 4. His food is in pantry in a bag. Do not let anything happen to that dog or Ben will kill you.
- Do the grocery shopping. List is on the fridge. Money is in the tea canister.
- Buy Christmas tree. Set it up. Decorate it. Buy wreath for front door. Hang wreath.
- Put gas in car, it's on empty.
- Give Churchill a bath today. His stuff is over the sink in the laundry room. Keep him warm. Build a fire and do NOT let him outside. Walk him. He can jump the fence.
- Twins get bath at 7. They like to play in the water. Do NOT flood the bathroom. They go to bed at 7:30. Give them a treat, ice cream will be fine if you buy it. They will scream for hours if they don't get it. Churchill gets a dog treat at the same time.

- Do laundry twice a day. Fold neatly and take upstairs. Do not leave in laundry room.
- Do not, I repeat, do not, drink while you are taking care of my sons.

Nursing his broken toe, Hank looked around wildly for something to hit, to smash. "In your dreams!"

Miss Sadie hopped up on his lap. She whimpered softly against his chest. "I can't do this, Miss Sadie. I wasn't cut out for this. How could she leave me here with this . . . this mess? Do you see how ill equipped I am to handle this? I don't even *want* to handle it. I bet ten dollars she's frolicking in some hot tub somewhere having a grand old time while I'm here . . . suffering. What's wrong with this picture, Miss Sadie?" The little dog licked his chin in sympathy.

Hank was on his second cup of coffee when the doorbell rang. Clutching Miss Sadie to his chest, he ran to the door just as the twins started to cry. He pulled it open to see the grocery delivery boy and directed him to the kitchen. He'd charged the food to his credit card when he ordered it, so all he had to do was tip the delivery boy. He took five dollars from the tea canister and handed it over. The boy looked at him in disgust, so he popped another five into his hand. "I used to get fifty cents for going to the store for my mother."

"Yeah, well, that was then, this is now. That's so like, some dark-age time. I have to buy gas, use my own car, and drive through snow and hope the person I'm delivering to isn't going to shoot me dead."

The kid had a point, Hank thought as he ushered him to the door just in time to see his new day lady/man walking toward the door. He groaned. Miss Sadie was yapping her head off, and the twins were bellowing at a high-decibel level. There was no sign of Churchill anywhere.

Hank sighed as he introduced himself to his day lady, who just happened to be an older man who said he was Mason Hatcher. He had quirky-looking hair that stood up in little spikes. Rosy cheeks, wire-rim glasses, and a mouth pursed into a pout. He wore a heavy black coat, sensible shoes with laces, and it looked like he had thick ankles. He was thick all over, Hank decided when Mason removed his coat, hat, muffler, and gloves and folded them neatly on the bench next to the door. Mason looked at him and said, "I don't much care for dogs."

"Yeah, well, the dog goes with the deal. And one is temporarily missing. I'm sure he'll be back soon. He's . . . a little bigger. I'll pay you extra for the dogs." Hank hated how desperate he sounded.

"We'll see," was Mason's response. "Now, where are my charges?"

"Huh?"

"The children. Where are they?"

"Upstairs, second door on the left."

Mason stomped his way up the steps as

Hank made his way to the kitchen, where he started to unpack the groceries. There wasn't one thing fit for the twins. Obviously, broken toe or not, he was going to have to go to the market himself with Alice's list. Damn, his toe was killing him. And, to his horror, his whole foot looked swollen. He also had to go out to look for Churchill. *Don't let Churchill out. He can jump the fence. Ben will kill you if anything happens to him.* The words rang in Hank's ears until he thought he would go out of his mind.

It suddenly dawned on him that the house was very quiet except for childish laughter wafting down the stairs. Even Miss Sadie, her head tilted to the side, was aware of the sudden silence. A minute later Mason was walking down the steps, a twin in each arm. The little twits were gooing and laughing and tweaking the man's nose. How was that possible? He'd turned himself inside out to please them, and all they did was pinch, cry, and fight him every step of the way. Obviously, he didn't have the touch. The right touch.

"I have to go out," Hank said. He was stunned at his belligerent tone.

"I'd put on some shoes if I were you, Mr. Anders. It's freezing outside."

"I don't know how that's going to work, Mason. I broke my big toe." If he hoped for sympathy, he wasn't getting any from this guy.

"Soak it in Epsom salts," Mason said without missing a beat. "When will you return, sir? By the way, is there a lady of the house?"

"When I'm done doing what I have to do is

when I'll be back. I can't give you a specific time. There is a lady of the house but not right now. She's . . . well, what she is . . . she isn't here."

"I see. And you're in charge temporarily, is that it?"

"No, no, I'm not in charge. Well, I am, but I'm not. I know that doesn't make a whole lot of sense but . . . you, Mason, *are in charge.*"

"Very well, sir."

"Call me Hank."

"I can't do that, sir. You're my employer. The company frowns on familiarity. Will there be anything else before I feed these little angels?"

"Nope, that's it. See ya, Mason."

Shoes on, his toe throbbing, Hank dressed and left the house. His game plan was to ride around the neighborhood to look for Churchill before doing anything else. He'd start first by warming up the SUV and brushing the snow off the windshield. He turned around when he heard banging sounds coming from Albert Carpenter's house. Someone on a ladder was banging with a hammer and stringing lights, and who was it standing next to the ladder but Churchill!

"Hey!" he shouted.

A female voice responded, "Hey, yourself!"

"Do you need any help, other than my dog?"

"Your dog! This is your dog! I don't think so! He's mine now. Possession is nine-tenths of the law. I walked him. I fed him. And he slept at my house last night. That means he's mine. It was freezing out last night. He could have died out there. You just try and get him back and I'll . . . I'll . . ." The hammer drove a nail into the post with deadly precision.

"That's private property. What do you think you're doing anyway? Mr. Carpenter died yesterday."

"I know he died. God rest his soul. I'm hanging Christmas lights. What's it look like I'm doing? Furthermore, it's none of your damn business what I'm doing. Don't even think about stealing this dog from me. Just try calling him. I betcha five bucks he will ignore you."

Hank felt befuddled. That was a sucker bet if he ever heard one. Who was this person? She had yet to turn around, and she was bundled up like Nanook of the North.

His toe throbbing like a bongo drum, Hank whistled for the dog. Churchill ignored him. He called him by name. Churchill ignored him. He called out, "Good boy, come on now, I'll give you a treat." Churchill plopped down and put his head between his paws.

"I'll take that five dollars now."

It was like a lightbulb went off in Hank's head. "I know who you are. You're that know-it-all who brought Churchill back last night when I was giving the twins a bath."

Amy banged in another nail with the same deadly precision. "Wow! You figured it out. Guess you have a brain after all. He's mine, and he's staying with me."

"You're trespassing, you know. The old guy just passed, and you're hanging Christmas lights on his house. That makes you some kind of ghoul in my opinion. I wonder what the cops will do if I call them. I want my damn dog, and I want him now."

"Why don't you try taking him and see how far you get." The hammer swung again. The sound was so loud, Hank winced. "Go ahead, call the police. I'm just being a good neighbor. I know for a fact that Mr. Carpenter always had Christmas lights. In his later years he probably had someone do it for him. And just for the record, these are my lights. I didn't steal them, nor did I break into Mr. Carpenter's house in case that's the next thing you're going to say. Furthermore, you . . .you . . . buffoon, don't you think it's a little strange that a woman is doing this when someone of your . . . ilk should be doing it? Go bother somebody else. I'm busy."

Buffoon. Someone of my ilk. What the hell did that mean? His toe was throbbing so bad he wanted to bang it on the porch railing. Anger at his circumstances rippled through him. "Listen to me, you . . . you dog snatcher, I want my dog, and I want him *now.* He's a boy dog. Why'd you put that stupid red ribbon with a bell on him?"

The voice that retaliated was syrupy sweet. "It's like this, you clown. The bell lets me know where he is. This is the Christmas season, and red goes with the silver bell. For the last time, I

did not snatch your dog. He came to me. He
doesn't even like you. I can tell. Look at him,
he's petrified of you. That's pretty bad when a
dog doesn't like his owner. Did you abuse this
poor animal?"

Outrage rivered through Hank at the accu-
sation. Hank bent over to peer at the golden
dog, who growled. "I would never harm an animal. I might have been a little sharp with him
when he deliberately lifted his leg on a chair.
He pees a flood. It took two towels to clean it
up. He jumps the fence. I didn't know he
could do that until this morning."

The voice was still syrupy sweet. "And I suppose you think I'm going to believe that . . .
that ridiculous story. Let's get real here."

Hank was at his wit's end. His toe was killing
him. "Are you always this nasty so early in the
morning, or were you born this way?"

Four things happened at that precise moment before Amy could respond. Mason opened
the front door to get the newspaper, Miss Sadie
beelined out the door and ran at the speed of
light to the Carpenter front porch, at which
point Churchill leaped up to greet his new best
friend and toppled the ladder. The know-it-all
slipped and fell.

"Oh, shit!"

"Oh, shit, is right," Nanook of the North
said as she rolled over in her down coat to sur-
vey the damage. Somehow or other the two
dogs were now tangled in the string of Christmas lights that were twinkling off and on.

Churchill growled, his ears going flat against his head, a sure sign that he was perturbed at something.

Hank took that moment to stare at the woman on the floor, who was laughing hysterically. So this is what she looks like. Something teased at his memory then, something he couldn't put his finger on. She was so pretty it took his breath away. And she had the nicest laugh he'd ever heard in his life. He knew that laugh. Or he remembered it from somewhere. The question was where? "Do I know you?"

Amy was on her feet when she looked up at her old childhood friend. "I don't know, do you?" She bent down then to try to untangle the string of lights the dogs were bent on chewing.

Hank wondered if a buffoon-slash-clown would do what he was doing, which was holding out his hand. "Hank Anders. I'm visiting next door for the holidays."

Amy stopped what she was doing, stood up straight, and looked him dead in the eye, hoping she wasn't giving away the delicious feeling coursing through her. "Mandy Leigh. It's been a long time, Hank." She crushed his hand in hers and saw that he tried not to wince.

"Mandy! It is you! Well, damn! In my wildest dreams I never thought we'd meet up again. You broke my heart when you moved away. I wanted to write you a hundred times, but no one knew where your aunt took you. California, we all thought."

"That's right, California," Amy said. "I've lived there ever since."

"Mom said your aunt Flo was a world traveler. We just assumed . . . no one ever came back. I thought the house was sold. Hell, I don't know what I thought. Look, I'm sorry about . . . about calling you names. This . . . it's a long sad story. Can we go for coffee or something? God, you're beautiful! You look just like I remember."

Amy laughed. "Is this where I'm supposed to say you're handsome?"

"Wouldn't hurt. Mom always said I was good-looking. So, can we do the coffee? I'll help you with the lights when we get back."

"Why not?" Why not indeed. Oh, be still my heart, Amy said to herself as she tidied up the porch, then replied, "Let's go to my house. I can make coffee, and I have some sticky buns. The kind Mom used to make when we were little."

As they walked toward the Leigh house, a light snow started to fall to the dogs' delight.

"Then you aren't mad at me?"

"Nah. I was just venting. I've been upset about Mr. Carpenter's passing. He was so good to us kids growing up. It's always especially sad when a person dies during the Christmas season. That's why I wanted to string up the lights. He used to love Christmas. Remember how we always made him a present?"

"Yeah. Yeah, I remember," Hank said softly. "I remember everything about that time. You really did break my heart, you know. By the way, Miss Sadie, the little fur ball, belonged to Mr. Carpenter. Ben gave the dog to him after his wife died. Churchill is Ben's dog. You're probably right about him not liking me. I was more or less thrust on him out of the blue. I might remind him of Ben. By the way, Ben is in Iraq."

"Sounds like you and I have a lot of catching up to do," Amy said, opening the front door of her house. *And he has no clue that I'm a movie star.* How wonderful was that? Pretty damn wonderful, she decided.

Chapter Five

Amy felt like she was walking on legs of Jell-O as she shed her outerwear on the way to the kitchen. Hank wasn't married. He was right behind her. In her very own kitchen. And he looked every bit as good as she dreamed. He was here. She was going to make him coffee and sticky buns. How good could life get? But the absolute best was, he had no clue that she was a movie star. A mighty sigh escaped her. She whirled around, not realizing how close he was. They literally butted shoulders. She looked into dark brown eyes that she remembered so well. She could smell minty toothpaste. In a liquid flash she could see something in his eyes, the same thing she was feeling. He blinked. She blinked, then Churchill broke the moment by jumping between them. Flustered,

Amy backed away, and Hank sat down on one of the old wooden kitchen chairs.

The exquisite moment was gone. Hopefully it would return at some point.

Amy reminded herself that she was an actress. She could carry this off until she saw which way the romantic wind was blowing. "You know, Hank, I can make you a full breakfast if you like, or we can go with the sticky buns and coffee. Your call."

Hank looked up at the stunning woman towering over him.

He wanted to reach out and grab her. The old Mandy would have smacked him for taking such liberties. He'd almost kissed her. And his heart and his eyes told him she would have been receptive to the kiss. This was a new Mandy. Maybe he should step back and not be so . . . pushy. *Pushy?* He cleared his throat. His voice sounded like a nest of frogs had settled in his throat. "Whatever is easiest. Let's just talk."

"Great! Then it's sticky buns, juice, and coffee." As Amy prepared the coffee and turned on the oven, she threw questions at Hank. "So bring me up to date. Do you come home here to Apple Valley every Christmas? This is my first time back." Was her voice too breathless, too giddy-sounding? Maybe she should be more cool, a little aloof, instead of this flighty person she'd suddenly become.

As Hank talked, Amy set the table with her mother's old dishes. Plain white crockery with huge red strawberries in the middle. Her mother had had a passion for strawberries for some reason. Everything in the kitchen had to do with strawberries: the cookie jar, the canister set, even the place mats were in the shape of strawberries.

"I remember these dishes. Your mom always served us cookies and sandwiches on them. You always said if you had to eat something you didn't like it made it okay because the dish was so pretty."

Amy stopped what she was doing. "You remember that!"

"Well, yeah. I guess I considered it an important thing in my life at the time. I don't have one bad memory of growing up here in Apple Valley. Ben doesn't either. You never said good-bye," Hank blurted.

Amy turned around as she fiddled with the pot holder in her hand. "Flo . . . Flo whisked me out of here so fast I didn't know what happened. I guess she thought I might . . . I don't know what she thought. I used to cry myself to sleep. I wanted to come back so bad, but there was nothing to come back to."

"Do you like living in the land of perpetual sunshine?"

"Yes and no. I really miss the change of seasons. I love autumn, and I even like winter. The holidays here in Apple Valley are my greatest memory. How about you?"

"I live and work in New York. I'm an engineer, have my own business. I have nine employees, and we're doing pretty well. New York isn't that far away from Apple Valley. I came home once a month up until my parents died. Then Ben and Alice took over the house, and I came less and less. But I always came back for the holidays. Ben's in Iraq. He's a major in the army. He was supposed to be home by now, but they extended his stay over there. He's getting out when his twenty years are up. He has another ten years to go. Alice is . . . upset. She was so sure Ben would be home for Christmas. The last time he saw the twins they had just been born. The army allowed him to come home on compassionate leave just before Christmas, when they were born. They're toddling around now, and they *have teeth*." This last was said with so much amazement, Amy burst out laughing.

Hank wanted to confide in Amy, to tell her about Alice's great escape, but he decided against it because he didn't want to be disloyal to his sister-in-law. He decided to change the subject. "Are you going to go to Mr. Carpenter's funeral? I imagine the wake will be this evening. I'm going. I can pick you up if you want." Assuming Mason would babysit. No need to tell Amy about that either, he thought.

"I'd like that very much. I was going to order some flowers after I finished stringing the lights. Then you showed up . . ."

"I guess I came on a little strong. I'm sorry. I've been . . ." He was going to say upset with the way things were going, but at the last second finished lamely with, "Upset with Albert's death. He was special."

Amy poured coffee and removed the sticky

buns from the oven. She let them cool as she poured juice into her mother's old jelly glasses. She hated the tremor in her hands.

"So tell me about you. What do you do in California?" There was horror in his voice when he said, "You aren't married, are you?"

Amy grinned. "Not even close. How about you?"

"I got close, but she left me standing at the altar. Best thing that could have happened to me. 'Course I didn't think that at the time."

Amy blinked, then she said, coolly, "You told me you would wait for me forever. Guess you didn't mean it, huh?"

Hank immediately picked up on the chill in Amy's voice. "I know I meant it at the time. I think by the time I turned twenty-one, I realized you weren't coming back to Apple Valley. I did try Googling you a while back. Nothing came up. I figured you got married, had a new name, and were living happily amid the orange blossoms and sunshine." It sounded so stupid even to his own ears, he couldn't imagine what she was thinking. He gulped at the hot coffee to cover his discomfort.

Amy's voice was still cool when she shoved one of the strawberry plates across the table along with two sticky buns and a napkin. "Guess you're a bachelor then. I thought you would have a bunch of kids by now."

Hank frowned. "Why would you think that?" What the hell was going on here?

Amy shrugged as she sat down. "Well, Ben is married. You're twins. Twins usually do the same thing. I'm sorry, I guess I shouldn't have said that. So, how do you like these sticky buns?"

"Quite good." They tasted like sawdust.

"No kidding. I think they taste like cardboard."

They looked at each other across the table. They were kids again, sharing a joke. They burst out laughing at the same time. Hank spoke first. "I was going to say they tasted like sawdust, but I didn't want to hurt your feelings. I missed you, Mandy. When you left I thought about you every day. Ben used to tease me, said I was in love with you. You know, puppy love."

"I was so crazy about you I couldn't see straight. Back then I believed we would get married after we finished college. I think that's why I was so upset when Flo took me away. I felt so lost and angry, but I was just a kid. I couldn't do anything about it. Every day I used to run to the mailbox thinking you'd find out where I was and write me a letter. I wanted to write to you, but I guess I didn't have the nerve. That might be more than you need or want to know."

"No, no, not at all. I was a mess myself after you left. My mom was good about it. She tried her best to explain what she thought happened. Even Ben did his best not to nag me, but he was getting off on it. You know how kids are."

"Yeah, I know how kids are. If you're not busy after we string the lights, I can make you lunch, or, if you like, maybe we could go to Andolino's for pizza. When I first got here I drove through town. Tony made the best pizza. I'll buy."

"Well, that's an offer I can't turn down. Pizza it is, and let me tell you, Tony's pizza has not changed; it's every bit as good as it was back when we were kids. His sons run the parlor now. So, are you ready? I'll meet you at Mr. Carpenter's. I want to check on . . . on the twins."

"Okay, go ahead. I'll clean up here and meet you on the porch. If you don't mind, I want to stop and get a big wreath for Mr. Carpenter's front door. We can order flowers at the same time. You okay with that?"

Hank shrugged into his jacket. "Absolutely. I just need ten minutes. Damn, I'm glad you came home this year." He was almost to the door when he turned around and came back. "Hey, if I want to ask you out, you know, dinner or something, should I call you up or what? I don't have your phone number. I need a phone number. Those tin cans we used to string between the houses aren't going to work. You know, a date."

A date with Hank Anders. That was the stuff dreams were made of. "Sure. It's 310-200-9999. What's yours?"

She wanted his number. Suddenly he felt light-headed. Hank pulled his wallet out of his pocket and handed her one of his business cards. He felt a jolt of electricity racing up his arm when his fingers touched hers.

Amy smiled.

Hank smiled.

And then he was gone. Amy sucked in her breath as she danced around the kitchen as the dogs pawed and yapped at her. "You don't understand, guys. I think I've been waiting all my life for what just happened. I am just so happy. So very happy."

The dogs yipped and yapped as Amy moved between the table and the dishwasher. When she started to sing "Jingle Bells," they howled. She laughed as she slipped into her heavy down jacket. "Hey, guys, it's snowing again!"

Amy, the dogs behind her, walked across the lawn to the Carpenter property. Hank was nowhere in sight. What was he doing? She looked at her watch. He'd said ten minutes. Now it was more like twenty. She shrugged. If he was blowing her off, then he was blowing her off.

Hank Anders watched Amy from the front window. His heart was beating so fast, he thought it was going to leap right out of his chest. The minute he'd gotten inside, he collapsed against the door. How was it possible that now, right at this moment, his childhood dream was coming true? He'd been *that* close. Close enough to kiss her. And not the kind of kiss he'd planted on her lips when they were thirteen years old either.

Mason, the new nanny, took that moment to enter the foyer. Alarmed, he raced to his employer. "Are you all right, sir?"

"Mason, my man, I'm about as right as a guy

can get. How's everything going? I'm in love. Are the twins more than you can handle? Did I tell you I'm in love? Did they eat? They're kind of sloppy. This is such a great feeling. By the way, I found the dog."

Mason stared at his new employer. He met all kinds of people in his line of work. "I'm certain Mrs. Anders will be happy to hear that. Perhaps she's the one you should be telling. I'm happy for you. The boys are fine. They ate ravenously. They're playing in the family room. They've been changed, and I'm considering what to make them for lunch. About dinner . . . is there anything in particular you fancy?"

Hank gaped at the nanny. What the hell was he saying? "No, no, not Mrs. Anders." He motioned Mason to join him at the window. "Her. I'm in love with her."

Mason pursed his lips and glared at Hank, disapproval in every line in his face. "I see! Then my advice is *not* to tell Mrs. Anders."

"Dammit, no. That's not . . . I guess I didn't explain. I'm not the husband or the father of the twins. I'm their uncle. I live in New York. My brother is Mr. Anders. He's the husband, but he's in Iraq. I'm just visiting. Don't worry about dinner. Fix something for yourself. I have to go to a wake this evening. Can you stay past bath time? I'll pay you extra of course. Did anyone . . . you know . . . call?" Please, oh, please say Alice called.

Mason looked befuddled. All he could think of to say was, "I see."

"You already said that. What is it you see, Mason?"

"That things in this household are topsy-turvy. Or as my old mum used to say, at sixes and sevens. There were no phone calls. But, your e-mail has been pinging ever since you left. I assume that means you have messages."

Alice. Alice must have e-mailed again. "So can you babysit this evening?"

"Of course, sir. I charge twenty-five dollars an hour."

"Fine, fine!" Hank said as he leaped over the gates that held the twins prisoner in the family room. Just one big playpen. The minute the boys saw him, they started to cry. Mason was on the job immediately. A second later the boys were laughing and playing peekaboo with their nanny.

Hank clicked on the e-mail and was chagrined to see it was from his brother, Ben, and directed to Alice. He told himself he had to read the e-mail. Told himself he wasn't being sneaky. He had to find Alice for the boys' sake. It was such a sweet e-mail, Hank felt his eyes burn. Ben apologized again and again for not being home for the holidays. He thanked his wife for the recent pictures of the boys she'd sent him. He asked about the tree and who she was going to get to put it up. He said how much he loved her and couldn't wait to get back to her waiting arms. Then came the clunker that made Hank's back stiffen. *I know you said I shouldn't do it, but Hank will under-*

stand. He won't hassle us to repay the loan sooner than we're able. Hank's my brother. I'd do the same for him. I can see the stress and strain on your face. Photos don't lie, Alice. I know you're killing yourself with all you have to do. Start looking for someone to come in to help. With Hank coming for Christmas, he'll give you the money. This is no time for either one of us to be too proud to ask if we need help. I didn't get an e-mail from you yesterday or today. I hope nothing is wrong. Write me, honey. I love you. All my love, Ben.

Hank clicked off the e-mail but saved it. "Mason!" he bellowed at the top of his lungs.

"Yes, sir."

"Can I hire you for six months?"

"I would think so, sir. Contact the agency and arrange it. I need to warn you, I'm in demand. I say that with all due modesty."

"Even with the dogs?"

"I suppose I can get a book on dog training."

"Good, good. Okay, I don't have time right now to call the agency. Will you do it and reserve yourself for the next six months. I'll . . . what I'll do is . . . throw in a bonus. Name it and it's yours," Hank babbled as he backed out of the door.

"Very well, sir."

A blustery gust of snow flurries slammed Hank in the face the moment he stepped outside. He laughed when he saw Churchill and Miss Sadie trying to catch the elusive flurries.

"Damn, I'm sorry, Mandy. The twins . . . and

then there was an e-mail from Ben I had to read. You hung all the lights! You didn't need me at all."

"Sure I do. I waited for you to plug in the lights. Cross your fingers that they work."

Hank inserted the plug. Amy clapped her hands in delight. "I have a package of extra lights. It's amazing that they still work after all these years. Well, our work here is done. You can carry the ladder back to my house and put it on the back porch. Should I keep the dogs, or do you want to take them to your house?"

"Yours. The nanny doesn't have a dog book yet. Yeah, yeah, your house. My car or yours?" Then he remembered Alice said the SUV needed gas. "Yours. Alice said hers is low on gas. I'll fill it up later, but since I don't know how much driving we're going to be doing, let's use yours."

"Okay," Amy said agreeably.

Ten minutes later, the snow still swirling and twirling, Hank and Amy settled themselves in the big truck. "Pretty fancy set of wheels," Hank said. "Is it yours, or is it a rental?"

"I bought it when I got here. Mom and Dad's old cars are still in the garage. I didn't want to take a chance on either one of them. I knew I was going to need a vehicle. I might decide to stay on longer than I originally planned. I might even decide to drive cross-country when it's time to leave."

Leave. She was talking about leaving. Hank felt his loss. Well, he couldn't let that happen, now could he? "It's really snowing. Looks like it's going to keep up. If it does, maybe we could go sledding like we used to. We could pull the twins on the sled. I think our old sleds are still in the attic. You could use Ben's if you don't have one."

"Sounds like fun. I'm game. But not until I get the house set up for Christmas. You any good at setting up a tree?" She twinkled.

"The best tree-setter-upper there is. Takes two people, though. Ben and I always did it. It's the lights that are a killer. The tinsel can drive you nuts. Ben always insisted on hanging one strand at a time. It took all night."

"Really? Mom and Dad always did it after I went to bed.

When I woke up, there was this magnificent tree all lit up, with all the junk I made through my school years. We didn't have any fancy heirloom ornaments. How wonderful for you," she said sadly.

"I didn't know that, Mandy. What did you do for a tree in California?" Hank asked.

Amy bit down on her lip. "Flo wasn't big on cleaning up pine needles in July. She said that's how long it took to get them out of the house. We always had an artificial tree, and it glittered with shiny ornaments and white lights. The wreath on the door was artificial, too. It got a new red bow every year. We used to go swimming on Christmas Day and have a turkey. I did my best to sleep through the whole season."

"I upset you, didn't I? I'm sorry, Mandy. That wasn't my intention." Hank stretched out a hand to pat her arm.

Amy blinked away tears. "Well, we've arrived. Does Karen Powell still own OK Florist?"

"Yep. She expanded a few years back, added a nursery, and sells outdoor plants as well. Even trees. The parking lot is always full in the spring and summer."

A bell tinkled over the door when Amy opened it. She looked around. It was just the way she remembered. New merchandise, but the old beams were still there, with greenery and decorations dangling downward. "It looks like a Wonderland with all the trees. It's so festive, with all the greenery and red and white Santas. My gosh, I don't know what to buy. I want a little of everything."

"Then let's get a little of everything," Hank said happily. Damn, he was getting a large dose of Christmas spirit all of a sudden.

"Okay, but first I want to order the flowers for Mr. Carpenter so they can deliver them today. How about if I order a large arrangement and put your, Ben's, and my name on the card?"

"Sure. Sounds great. Oh, and will you include Ben's wife, Alice? Just tell me how much our share is."

"No problem."

Amy walked over to the counter and spoke to the girl behind the computer. She explained what she wanted, signed a card, and handed her a credit card. "I'm going to want a dozen or so of your poinsettias. All red. Shall I pick them out and put them by the door?" The frazzled clerk nodded as she punched in the order.

Amy and Hank spent the next hour picking out just-right poinsettias, knickknacks, and whatever pleased Amy. The clerk rang everything up while a young boy loaded the cargo hold of the Range Rover. She ripped off a tape and slapped it down on the counter in front of Hank along with Amy's credit card. "Sign on the X."

"No, that's not my card," Hank said, picking up the credit card. "Hold on, I'll get my friend to come in and sign the slip."

Hank walked over to the door and tapped on it. Amy turned around and smiled. He held up her credit card and motioned her to come inside. Without meaning to, he looked down at the platinum card in his hand and saw the name Amy Lee. He frowned. Who the hell was Amy Lee? What was Mandy Leigh doing with someone else's credit card?

Hank's stomach crunched into a knot as he stared at his old childhood friend as she walked toward him, a smile on her face. He realized at that moment he didn't know a thing about Mandy Leigh. All he knew was she was home for the holidays and lived in California. Otherwise, all their conversations were on the generic side. He'd been loose as a goose and opened up and confessed to loving her.

The name Amy Lee sounded so familiar. Did he know her when they were kids? Was she a client or a client's wife? Nothing was ringing a bell for him.

Who the hell was Amy Lee?

Chapter Six

It wasn't until Amy finished her third slice of pizza and drained the last of her root beer float that she realized she'd been doing all the talking. Hank had only eaten one slice of the delicious pizza, and his root beer float was basically untouched. He also had a strange look on his face. Like he wanted to say something or possibly ask her something and didn't quite know how to go about it. The words "moody" and "sullen" came to mind. She shook her head to clear her thoughts. She didn't need this, no way, no how.

Maybe he thought she'd spent too much money at OK Florist. He'd commented on her Range Rover, calling it a pricey set of wheels. Maybe he had a thing about women spending money. He'd been fine before they got to the florist, so whatever was wrong had nothing to do with Mr. Carpenter or the dogs. It had to be her. Something about her was suddenly bothering him. She racked her brain to try to recall what she might have said or done that would have made him so quiet all of a sudden.

Well, she certainly wasn't going to worry about Hank and his moods. She had things to do and places to go. She fished some money out of her pocket and laid it on the table. After all, she'd invited him to lunch, so it was up to her to pay for it.

Amy got up and slipped into her jacket. The waiter approached and asked if she wanted change. She shook her head. "Are you ready, Hank?" she asked coolly.

"What?"

"I asked you if you were ready to leave. We came, we ate, I paid the bill, and now it's time to leave. Are you ready?"

"Yeah. Sure. My mind is somewhere else. I'm sorry, Mandy."

"I am, too," Amy said as she headed for the door. She slammed through the door, not caring that Hank walked right into it as it was closing. She ignored his yelp of surprise and headed straight for the car. Midway to the Rover, a young woman in a Girl Scout uniform rushed up to her. "Would you care to donate to Mr. Carpenter's funeral expenses?"

"What did you say?"

The young girl repeated her question.

"I didn't know . . . of course." Amy emptied out her wallet.

"How about you, sir?"

"I didn't bring my wallet with me. Tell me where I can drop off my contribution. I'll do it as soon as I get home."

"Mrs. Masterson. She lives at 82 Cypress Street. She's in charge of the fund-raiser."

"Okay, thanks." Hank climbed into the Rover and buckled up. Amy peeled away the moment the door was closed securely. She clenched her teeth. If he thought she was going to start babbling, he needed to think again about his rude behavior. Some things were just not meant to be. So much for dreams and long-lost loves.

"The snow is really coming down," Hank said, in an attempt to make conversation.

The snow wasn't a question. So she didn't have to respond.

Hank eyed Amy out of the corner of his eye. He tried again. "That's pretty sad about Albert Carpenter. I knew he didn't have any family left, but I would have thought he had some savings, enough to bury him."

That wasn't a question either. So she didn't have to respond to it either. Instead, Amy concentrated on the falling snow and driving on the slick roads.

The rest of the ride home was made in silence on Amy's part. She swerved into her driveway, turned off the engine, and hopped out of the Rover. "Don't bother yourself. I can unload the truck later. I have other things I need to do now. Do you want to take the dogs, or should I keep them?"

Her voice was as cold as the snow falling all

about him. Hank did a double take. He knew a brush-off when he got one. He'd had more than enough in his lifetime to know the signals. He took a moment to wonder if Mandy was bipolar. One minute she was on top of the world, and the next she was doom and gloom. She hadn't said a word on the drive home. "I'll take them," he said curtly.

"Fine," Amy snapped. She opened the door, and both dogs ran to her to be petted. Hank did everything in his power to get Churchill to go with him. He finally had to give up when the big dog bared his teeth. "Guess that's your answer, Mr. Anders."

Mr. Anders? "Yeah, guess so."

Amy moved to the door to close it. Then she added insult to injury, Hank thought, when he heard the deadbolt snick into place. He felt lower than a skunk's belly when he hightailed it back to his brother's house.

What the hell is going on?

The house was exceptionally quiet. Instead of calling out, Hank walked out to the kitchen to see Mason puttering around at the stove. "Is there any coffee, Mason? Did anyone call?"

"I just made fresh coffee. No one called, but your e-mail is pinging again. I just put the boys down for their naps. My agency has booked me for the next six months. All you need to do is call to confirm and give them your credit card information. Is something wrong, Mr. Anders? You look . . . dejected."

Was something wrong? This guy was really astute. Hank wondered what kind of confidant he would make. He poured coffee. "What are you making?"

"Stew. I always make stew when it snows. The weatherman is predicting six inches of snow by morning. Did you go to the market, Mr. Anders? We need milk for the boys."

"Stew is good. I'm going to go to the market when I finish this coffee. I have to get gas, too. What I said earlier . . . you know . . . about me being in love. That wasn't true. Well, it was at the time, but it isn't now. I overreacted. Women are so . . . what they are is . . . hell, what are they, Mason?"

"Complex. Fickle. Manipulative. Selfish. Mind you, I don't know this for a fact, but I do read a lot. So, I guess what you're saying is the lady next door spurned your advances. Would that be a correct assessment, Mr. Anders?"

"It will do. I didn't do a damn thing. She froze on me. She goddamn well kicked me to the curb is what she did. What do you think about *that*, Mason?"

Mason opted to take the high road. "I think, sir, before I can comment, I would need to hear the young lady's side. As you know, there are two sides to everything."

"There must be something wrong with me. I was left standing at the altar a while back. The twins don't like me. The dogs don't want to come home. I don't get it. I'm a stand-up guy. I'm nice to old people. I've always liked kids. I'm generous, never ask anyone to do anything I won't do myself. My employees gave me a plaque that said I was the best boss in the world. I don't have dandruff. I use a top-notch deodorant. What the hell is wrong with me?"

"I don't think I'm qualified to comment on anything other than the boys. I think they sensed your uneasiness. In other words, you have little experience with toddlers. They sense your fear. I can't be certain, but I imagine it's probably the same thing with the animals."

"What should I do?"

"Try to repair the damage. Relax. Flowers might be an option. You need to be comfortable with yourself. I really think you should go to the market now before the roads become hazardous, Mr. Anders. The boys drink a lot of milk."

Hank looked over at the computer. He had the rest of the day and evening to check e-mails. Mason was right, he needed to get to the market and gas up the SUV. "Do you know how to bake a pie, Mason?"

"Of course. Doesn't everyone? What kind would you like?"

"Berry. Anything berry. I don't know how to bake a pie. I don't know how to cook. Period."

"Let me check the larder to see if the lady of the house has all the ingredients. I'll make a list for you, Mr. Anders."

Antsy with his inactivity, Hank walked into the living room so he could look out the window. He gasped when he saw Mandy and the dogs on Albert Carpenter's front porch. Mandy was stringing wire on the back of the giant wreath she'd purchased at the florist shop. Even from here he could see how huge the big red bow was. He'd wanted to hang the wreath with her. Was she making a statement of some kind?

Hank felt guilty and knew it showed on his face when Mason came up behind him with his list. He held out Hank's wallet. "I'm thinking you might need this."

"Thanks. I wasn't spying, Mason."

"If you say so, Mr. Anders."

"All right, I'm spying."

Mason cleared his throat. "Have you given any thought to speaking with the young lady and telling her whatever it is that's bothering you? It's entirely possible that she's reacting to something you did or said. For every action there is a reaction, Mr. Anders."

Hank snorted. "Try this on for size, Mason. Why would the lady in question be using a credit card, a platinum one no less, with someone else's name on it?"

"I'm sure there are many reasons why and how that could happen, Mr. Anders."

"Oh, yeah, name me one," Hank said belligerently.

Mason squared his shoulders. "Very well. Perhaps the card is in her maiden name. Perhaps it's a corporate card. Perhaps the young lady uses a pseudonym. And, Mr. Anders, is it any of your business to begin with?"

"I'm outta here," Hank barked as he opened the door. Slipping and sliding, he made his way to the SUV and turned on the engine and the heater while he cleaned the snow off the truck. He kept looking over at the Carpenter house, hoping Mandy would acknowledge him. She didn't. The dogs were so intent on romping in the snow, they weren't even aware of him.

"Screw it," Hank muttered as he backed out of the driveway. His first stop was the Masterson house on Cypress Street.

Ten minutes later he was ringing the doorbell. A pleasant woman opened the door and smiled at him. He reached for his wallet and explained that he was there to give a donation for Albert Carpenter's funeral.

"That's very nice of you but some very kind, generous person is paying for the funeral. Mr. Dial just called a little while ago. This same person, who I'm told wishes to remain anonymous, also paid for the church ladies to prepare a dinner after . . . after the burial. Everything has been taken care of, but thank you for stopping by."

Hank nodded and shrugged as he jammed his wallet back in his pocket.

Two hours later, Hank was back at the house, with the SUV gassed up and enough groceries to feed an army for a month.

He looked across the yard and saw that the colored Christmas lights had been turned on. Wise move. This way Mandy wouldn't have to get dressed and slog through the snow when it got dark out. The huge evergreen wreath on the door looked festive. He craned his neck trying to see into the cargo hold of the Range Rover to see if the contents had been removed. He couldn't see a thing with the falling snow and the tinted windows.

Disgusted with himself and his circum-

stances, Hank carried in the groceries. He
smiled at the childish laughter coming from
the family room.

While Mason unpacked the groceries,
Hank made a fire, then settled himself on the
floor, not close to the twins but just far enough
away so they wouldn't pitch a fit. He watched
them interact with each other as they played
with their toys. From time to time they looked
over at him to see what he was doing. He wiggled his fingers and made funny faces. Then
he rolled across the floor and hid his face. It
was all the boys needed. Suddenly they were all
over him, yanking at his hair, sitting on his
back, then rolling over themselves.

Hank sat up. The boys looked at him as if to
say, is the fun over? "You guys look just like
your daddy. He's one lucky man. You're pretty
lucky, too, to have a dad like Ben. I'm sorry
your mom isn't here. She . . . I know she misses
you, but she has some . . . issues right now. I
think she'll be home for Christmas. God, I
hope she comes home for Christmas."

The boys trundled off when they realized
the giant on the floor was done playing. Hank
rolled over and stared at the fire blazing up
the chimney.

Where are you, Alice? He just knew in his
gut that Alice would be able to explain Mandy's
attitude. Women knew everything about other
women. He sat up and moved over to the gate
to step over it. Time to check the e-mails. He
sniffed; the kitchen smelled just the way a

kitchen was supposed to smell, fragrant and homey. He said so. Mason beamed with pleasure at the compliment.

Hank clicked on the e-mail and saw a note from Alice. Another list! Not a word about her return.

- The boys get a chewable Flintstone vitamin every morning. The bottle is on the kitchen windowsill.
- Trash pickup is tomorrow morning. Both cans are full. Separate the glass bottles from plastic. Containers in the garage. Bundle all paper products and put in separate bin. All bins are labeled in the garage.
- Buy gas for the snowblower. Container is empty. Otherwise, shovel the driveway.
- Wash Churchill's pee pads in Clorox.
- Lightbulbs on front porch are burned out. Replace them.

And that was the end of the list. Hank printed it out.

"I have to take the trash out, Mason. And I need to check the snowblower. I think I'll walk to the gas station for gas. You have things under control here, right?"

"Yes, sir, I do. The pie is coming along nicely. The stew is simmering. I'm going to do some laundry. Do whatever you have to do."

"The boys need their vitamins. They're on the windowsill."

"I took care of that, sir."

"The pee pads need to be washed in Clorox."

"I've taken care of that, sir. The boys' laundry is washing now."

"You're right, Mason, you do have it under control."

Hank grabbed his jacket and entered the garage through the kitchen. He checked the snowblower. He had an identical one at home in New York, so he knew how to work it. Alice was right, though, it was bone dry, as was the gas container. He made fast work of bundling the paper products and separating the glass and plastic bottles. Then he dragged the heavy trash cans through the snow and out to the curb. How the hell did Alice do all this? He was huffing and puffing when he made his seventh trip down the driveway.

Should he start to shovel the driveway, or should he slog his way to the gas station for gas? He looked around for the shovel but didn't see one. He snorted as he grabbed the gas can and started down the driveway. He stopped in his tracks when he heard Churchill bark. He strained to see through the snow. Is that Mandy on the front porch of the Carpenter house? What the hell is she doing now?

"Hey, what are you doing?" he yelled.

"Decorating. Why do you care what I'm doing?" Amy shouted back.

Hank sucked in his breath and got a mouthful of snow. He didn't mean to say the words, they just popped out of his mouth. "Do you need any help?"

Amy strained to see through the swirling

snow. She could use some help. "Yeah," she said before she could change her mind. Maybe she could get to the bottom of whatever it was that was bothering Hank.

He was on the porch a minute later, the orange gas can in his hand. "I was going for gas for the snowblower. I can do your driveway if you like. What are you doing?"

"I'm decorating Mr. Carpenter's front porch. I found all of our old decorations in the garage. Mom bought all of these reindeer one year and the sleigh. Don't you remember?"

"Yeah, yeah, I do remember. Your family won the prize that year for the best-decorated house. Why aren't you putting them up on your own front porch?"

Good question. "I'm not sure why. I just wanted to do something for Mr. Carpenter. He was always so big on Christmas even though he and his wife never had children. Remember how he used to say because he was a teacher all us kids were his children? Maybe it's a send-off of sorts.

"I came back home because I was trying . . . I wanted . . . I guess I was trying to recapture that last Christmas that I never had. You can't go home again, Hank," she said sadly. "I wish so much that I had come back sooner. I wish I had told Mr. Carpenter how much he meant to me growing up. I wish so many things. I guess I'm trying to make up for that. Is it right? Is it wrong? I don't know, and I don't care. I just need to do this. For me and for Mr. Carpenter."

Hank stared at the young woman standing across from him, tears in her eyes. "It makes sense to me," he said. "You're the one who paid for the funeral, aren't you?"

"How did you know?"

"I went to the Mastersons' to leave my donation. She told me an anonymous donor called Mr. Dial and paid for it. Tell me right now, who is Amy Lee? What were you doing with someone else's credit card? I didn't know how to deal with it."

Amy slid down on her haunches, her back against the front door. "Is that what your attitude was all about? Why didn't you just ask me?"

"Well, I didn't . . . All kinds of crazy thoughts were going through my mind. I was devastated when my thoughts . . . We were hitting it off so well. It was like a dream came true, then suddenly there was a glitch. I've been trying to deal with Alice and all that mess. So, who is Amy Lee? The name sounds familiar to me."

"Me. I'm Amy Lee. Flo and the studio wanted me to change my name. Flo wanted to wipe this place, my early years away. And yet she stayed in touch with the people here. She made sure the house was taken care of, cleaned and aired several times a year. It just never made any sense to me."

"Studio? What's that mean?"

"I'm a movie star. I work in Hollywood. I make pictures. Even got nominated for an Academy Award twice, but I didn't win."

"You're a movie star! Well, damn! I guess

that's why the name sounded familiar. I haven't been to the movies in years and years. Are you good?"

Amy laughed. "I get by. I came back here thinking I wasn't going to go back to Hollywood. I had thoughts of retiring after I finish out my contract. I might be able to buy it out, at least that's what my agent said. I never understood how I could be good at something I didn't like doing. I still don't understand it. I've had enough. I'm not sure I want to stay in Apple Valley, though. I was hoping to find some answers here. I know now the answers are inside me. This place is just a memory, but I'm smart enough to know I have to lay it to rest before I can go on. My big regret is it's taken me so long."

Hank inched closer to Amy. "I don't know what to say. I feel stupid for jumping to conclusions. I'm sorry, Mandy. Or should I call you Amy?"

"My name is Mandy. I hated it that they took away my name. First my parents, Apple Valley, then my name. I was just a kid back then, and while I tried to deal with it, I guess I didn't do such a good job of it. What were you saying about your sister-in-law?"

Hank explained the situation. Amy burst out laughing and couldn't stop. "I'm on her side. Boy, did that take guts. She must really trust you, though, to leave her kids with you."

"Well, I didn't do so good. Those kids hated me on sight. Churchill hated me and ran to you. I had to hire a nanny. A guy!" Hank said, his eyes almost bugging out of his head. "He had things under control in ten minutes. He cooks, does laundry. Hey, the guy is *IT*." Then he told her about Ben's e-mail. "So for my Christmas present to the family, I hired Mason for six months to help Alice. Ben will be back home by that time to pick up the slack."

"That's so wonderful, Hank! When are you going to tell Alice?"

"I can't tell her anything because I don't know where she is. She said she was going to a hotel to pamper herself."

"No, no, that's not what she's doing if their financial situation is so precarious. She's probably staying with a friend and talking it all to death. She was overwhelmed, that's the bottom line. I give her another day, and she'll be back. She's a mother, she won't abandon her kids. Trust me."

"You think?"

"I do, Hank. It's not easy being a single mom, and that's what she is with Ben away. It all falls on her. She's just one person, and there are just twenty-four hours in a day. She's frazzled. What you're planning on doing is a wonderful thing. I just wish there was a way to tell her to ease her misery."

Hank nodded. "So we're friends again, right?"

"Of course. If you help me get the sleigh over here, I can finish up while you go for the gas. Are we still going to the wake this evening?"

"Absolutely, but we might have to walk."

"I have boots, so it won't be a problem. Okay, let's go get that sleigh."

Hank reached for her arm and linked his with hers as they trudged across the lawns to Amy's garage. Minutes later, the sleigh was on Albert Carpenter's front porch, and Hank was on his way to the gas station that was only a block and a half away. He started to sing "Jingle Bells" as he trudged along. He looked down when he felt something hit his knee. "Churchill!"

"Woof."

"Hey, big guy, how're you doing? Where's Miss Sadie? Yeah, yeah, she's no fool, I bet she's sitting in that sleigh. It's just me and you, Churchill. You know what, I'm not even mad at you because Mandy's one in a million. You got good taste, I'll say that for you."

"Woof."

"Jingle bells . . ."

Chapter Seven

The caravan of cars leaving the snow-filled cemetery was several miles long. Albert Carpenter had been laid to rest, and the whole town had turned out to show their regard and to honor the man who had done so much for the education system.

It hadn't been a sad affair at all. More like a celebration of Albert's life. The wake that started at six the previous evening had gone on well past midnight to allow all the citizens of Apple Valley to pay their respects. They came in trucks, on sleds, on skis, and the sanitation workers had shown up on the town's snowplow.

During his teaching years, Albert had always conducted the Christmas Pageant, and when the actors took their final bow, the audience and cast alike had stayed to sing Christmas carols. And that's what they did this year before the funeral director closed the doors for the night. Until her passing, Mrs. Carpenter had been in charge of the refreshments. This night, Apple Valley's school principal did the honors.

So many memories had been shared, but the most poignant of all had been the story of Albert's financial problems that so few knew about. All his savings had gone to cover his wife's long illness. He'd been forced to take out a reverse mortgage that allowed him to continue to live in the house until his death. Albert Carpenter had died with just a few dollars in the bank, but he didn't owe anyone a dime. In fact, Charles Leroy from the bank said he'd made his final payment to the hospital just two months ago. Then he said something that brought tears to everyone's eyes. "Albert didn't want to join his wife until all his earthly debts were paid. It wouldn't look right or feel right knowing he was leaving others to pick up his slack."

Hank drove carefully in the long procession, no more than five miles an hour. "I thought the Apple Valley Band did a good job," he said. "You know what else, I'm glad you decided to decorate Albert's porch. I bet the town awards the prize to him this year. Posthumously."

"I liked that we all sang carols, just as we used to in school. It was sad, and yet it wasn't sad. He was so loved. Apple Valley and the people here are so special, Hank. There's so much kindness and goodness here. People actually care about one another. They help out and don't expect anything in return. It's not that way in California. Well, maybe it is, but I've never witnessed it. It's not just the season, is it, Hank?"

"No, Mandy, it's not just the season. This little place is just one of a kind. I used to think I should come back here and live, but then I told myself no, I needed to leave, to move on so someone else could move here and experience this life. For me to stay would have been selfish. Ben now. Ben was different. He said his roots were here, and he wasn't digging them up. This was home to him, and while he and Alice have lived all over, this was the place he always came back to.

"When we were growing up, the population was just a little under four thousand. Today it's almost six thousand. That's not a great increase, but it's something to pay attention to. I do know one thing for certain: I'll come back here to retire."

"Me, too," Amy said happily. "So, are we going to go sledding this afternoon or not?"

"I'm up for it, but first we have to go to the dinner at the church. I offered our services, but Father Mac said if he got any more volunteers, he'd have to move out. In other words, all we have to do is show up and eat. It's all under control. That was a good thing you did, Mandy."

Amy's face turned pink. She just nodded.

Hank pretended he didn't notice her discomfort. "I'm not sure, but I think I saw Alice at the cemetery. She was so bundled up, and the crowd was so dense, I can't swear to it, but I think it was her. She really liked Albert. Ben told me when she cooked she would always take something over. He was partial to peach pie, and she'd make it special for him in the summer when peaches were in season. When in the hell is she going to come home? It's almost Christmas."

Amy shrugged. "My guess would be when she can't stand being away from her sons one minute longer. Which is probably any minute now. Did you finish everything on her lists?"

"Almost. I have to get the tree and put it up. I guess I'm supposed to shop for the boys. I'm clueless in that department. Alice always decorates the house, so I guess I should do that, too, since she'll want to take pictures to send to Ben."

"I have an idea, Hank. Instead of going sledding, let's go get all our trees and set them up. I remember Mom saying you have to put it up in the stand, then let it sit for a day so the branches fall into place. I'd like to put one on Mr. Carpenter's porch, too. I think for sure that will make him a shoo-in for the Christmas prize. After we take care of that, we can go shopping for the boys. What say you?"

Hank reached over to take Amy's hand in his own. "I think that's a great idea."

Amy thought her hand was going to go up in flames. "Something's happening to us, isn't it?" Her voice was little more than a whisper.

Hank's response was husky, almost tortured. "Yeah. Yeah, something is happening. It's a good thing, isn't it?"

Amy laughed. "From where I'm sitting, a very good thing."

Hank squeezed her hand. She squeezed back.

The church parking lot was so full, Hank had to park two blocks away. Once they managed to get inside, they had to get in a line that wrapped all the way around the room and out the side door.

Amy found herself standing next to Karen Powell from OK Florist. They chatted a few moments while Hank met up with a friend of Ben's. "Do you have any extra poinsettias, Karen?"

"A shipment was due this morning. It might have been delayed with the snow, but sometime today for certain. Why?"

"Will you send two dozen plants to the Anders house? Hank and I are going to decorate it today. As a matter of fact, we're going to get the trees this afternoon."

"You might not know this, but I'm selling trees myself. We have them staked up in the nursery. You might not have seen them. And, we deliver!" she added, laughing.

Amy laughed. "Put us down for three trees. We'll stop by when we leave here and tag them."

"Will do."

It was after one o'clock when Amy and Hank climbed back into Alice's SUV to do some Christmas shopping. The crowds in the small village carried gaily colored shopping bags as they walked from store to store. Children bundled in snowsuits and mufflers pulled sleds filled with packages. Gaily dressed Santas stood in doorways handing out candy canes and hot chocolate. Holiday music wafted from loudspeakers mounted on the telephone poles that surrounded the square.

Apple Valley was small-town America at its finest.

"This is nothing like New York." Hank laughed as he accepted a cup of hot chocolate from an elf standing in the doorway of Jones's Pharmacy. Amy opted for a candy cane. They moved on, finally coming to a stop at a small toy store. Inside, they turned into little kids, their selections outrageous until they stopped in their tracks, looked at one another, and reminded themselves the twins were just a year old. Sheepishly, they replaced the Barbie and Ken dolls and the catchers' mitts.

When they finally left the store, the stock boy tagged along behind them, their purchases piled high on a dolly. After they were loaded into the cargo hold and the door shut and locked, Hank turned to Amy, and said, "Do you think we'll have this much fun when we buy toys for our own kids?"

Whoa. She turned around hoping she could be cool. *Cool?* Amy's heart was beating so fast she thought it was going to leap right out of her chest. She struggled for a flip answer of some sort. Nothing came to her. Besides, Hank was looking at her so intently, she needed to respond. "Don't you have to ask me to marry you before the kids come? You haven't even kissed me yet."

"Not true," Hank said lightly. "I kissed you once, and I never forgot the feeling. That kiss lasted twenty-one seconds."

"You counted the seconds?" Amy asked in awe.

"Yeah. I thought I was going to black out. I was in love with you. I realized I was still in love with you the minute I set eyes on you."

Amy was so light-headed with Hank's declaration she reached for the side mirror to hold on to it. Hank had just said he loved her. That's what he said. The words were still ringing in her ears. All her dreams were finally coming true. She was supposed to say something. What?

Hank shuffled his feet in the snow. His voice sounded so anxious when he said, "Your turn."

The words were stuck in her throat. She wanted to say them. Instead, she leaned forward, grabbed his jacket in her mittened hands, and yanked him forward. She planted a lip-lock on him that made her head spin.

"Twenty-*seven* seconds!" she shouted gleefully when she came up for air.

The sound of handclapping brought both of them to their senses as a small laughing crowd moved off.

"Wow!" was all Hank could think of to say.

"That's it, wow!" Amy said. "You up for an encore?"

Hank groaned. He was no fool. He moved closer. All the years of pent-up longing melted away when he brought his lips down on hers. This moment he knew settled his future. When he finally released her he looked into her eyes and saw what he knew was mirrored in his own. In a low, husky voice, he asked, "How many seconds?"

In a voice as shaky as Hank's, Amy said, "Are you kidding, I wasn't counting."

"Oh, who cares? You going to marry me?"

"If that's a proposal, the answer is yes."

Hank backed up a step. He looked to Amy like he was in a daze. She smiled.

He smiled.

"We should go pick out the Christmas trees, Hank."

"Yep. That's what we should do," Hank said.

"But are we going to do that?"

Hank groaned as he opened the passenger-side door for her. "Yes, that's what we're going to do, but later, we are going to do other things."

"Promises, promises." Amy giggled. *My God, when was the last time I giggled? Never, that's when.* She leaned back and closed her eyes. She realized she had never been as happy as she was at this moment.

Hank laughed, a joyous sound. "There's something you need to know about me. I never make a promise I don't intend to keep. I don't know when I've been this happy," he blurted.

Amy laughed again. "Me, too. It's such a wonderful feeling. More so because it's the holiday season. Everything seems to be special during this time." Her voice turned serious a moment later. "But there's Mr. Carpenter and Alice. Are we being . . . ?"

"No. It was Albert's time. Alice . . . well, Alice made her own decisions. While we both understand that, we're doing what we think is right. We're doing what we can for Alice. Albert . . . is beyond our control. Somehow I think he would be very happy for the both of us. No, that's wrong, Mandy. I *know* Albert would be very happy for us. Okay, enough of all this. Are you ready to pick out the biggest, the best, the most-wonderful-smelling tree in the lot?"

"I'm ready, Mr. Anders," Amy said, hopping out of the truck.

An hour later they were covered in pine resin, but they had three trees that Hank said were the best of the best. The young guy working the tree lot shoved the trees through a barrel. They came out the other end covered in white netting. They watched as he loaded them into a pickup truck and hopped into the cab, where he waited for instructions.

While Hank paid for the trees, Amy explained where the trees were to be delivered. The young man nodded and peeled out of the parking lot, snow spiraling backward in his wake.

"Bet you five bucks those trees are home before we get there," Amy said, walking hand in hand with Hank back to the SUV. "Wait! Wait! We have to buy tree stands."

Together they walked back to the tree lot, where Hank picked out three stands capable of holding the big trees. He whipped out his credit card, paid for the stands, then they were on the way home. A light snow started to fall again as they hit the main road.

"Pay up," Amy said when Hank swerved into the driveway. All three trees were exactly where Amy had told the youngster to put them. Hank kissed her instead.

"That'll work." Amy giggled again. She felt like a teenager as she helped Hank cut away the netting to set up the tree in the stand on the Carpenter front porch.

When they were finished, Hank stood back and said, "It's a beauty, perfect in every way. Tomorrow we can decorate it."

"Oh, it smells so good. Growing up, you could smell the tree all over the house. I loved it then as much as I love it now. I guess it's the kid in me. That won't change, will it, Hank?"

Hank for some reason knew this was a very important question, and he had to give just the right answer. "Memories are a wonderful thing, Mandy. Sometimes they fade in time, but if you work at remembering, then I think they'll be with you forever. The special memories. Like this one. Christmas was always the best time of year when we were kids. All the wild anticipation, the frenzy of the shopping, the tree, the snow, the way the house smelled.

Ben and I used to talk about it. For the most part I think he and Alice pretty much duplicated everything. For them it was easier because they're in the house we grew up in. I know it was different for you after . . . but see, you still have those wonderful earlier memories." He looked at her expectantly to see if she was in agreement. She smiled, and his world was right side up.

"Okay, let's set up the tree for the boys. Then we can go back to your house and set yours up and do . . . other things. What say you?"

Amy giggled again. "Won't work, Hank. We have to decorate the house for Alice. I don't know why I say this because it's just a feeling. I think Alice is waiting until that's done before she returns home. Having said that, let's get to it. But before we get started, I think I'd like a cup of coffee. Your house or mine?"

"Well, since we have so much work ahead of us, I guess it should be the Anders house. I imagine the twins will be awake from their nap by now. I can't wait for you to meet them, and Mason as well."

"I have to let the dogs out first. I'll be over in a few minutes." Amy kissed him lightly on the lips before she tripped her way to her own front door.

Inside, she ran to the back door to let the dogs out, then leaned against it. She was shaking from head to toe. She was in love. Hank loved her. She loved him. How wonderful is that? Is this one of those Christmas miracles?

Was this love going to come with a price on

it? Amy closed her eyes and thought about her home in Hollywood, thought about her contract, the few friends she had, and what her agent was going to say when she told him to buy out her contract. What would all those people on her payroll do if she turned her back on Hollywood? She could bonus them out and wish them luck in finding a new job. Was she getting ahead of herself? Probably, but she didn't care.

Hank had asked her to marry him, so that had to mean they would live where his business was. Maybe they could stay at her house and have a home here in Apple Valley. She knew in her heart that Hank would approve. She rather thought Ben and Alice would approve, too. They could watch the twins grow up, and if they had kids of their own, they could play together. Win-win all around. She could hardly wait to tell Hank her idea.

The dogs scratched at the door to come in. She opened the back door to let the dogs in, and they all left together by the front door.

The twins squealed their pleasure when the dogs romped through the family room, Churchill leaping over the gate, Miss Sadie waiting patiently for Hank to lift her over it. Mason stood at the kitchen gate, his jaw dropping at the commotion. He put his fingers to his lips and whistled sharply. The twins stopped in midsqueal. Both dogs turned to look expectantly at the strange new person emitting the high-pitched whistle. "That will be enough of *that.* SIT!" Since both dogs were already sitting, they continued to stare at the person towering over them. "Very good. I am the Alpha. You need to understand that. Having said that, here is your treat for the afternoon." Mason handed out two dog treats, and hard crackers to the boys. Mason turned and was back a second later with a basket of dog toys that had been in the laundry room.

Hank nudged Amy. He hissed in her ear. "I don't know how he does it. He's unreal. Alice is going to be soooo happy. If she ever comes home."

"Mandy, this is Mason. Mason, this is Mandy, she's from California, and she's visiting. Next door."

Mason bowed low, then reached for her hand. "It is a pleasure to meet any friend of Mr. Anders."

"Mandy is a movie star. Her other name is Amy Lee."

"Ah. Am I to assume, sir, that things have progressed, and we are no longer in jeopardy?"

Hank blinked. The guy could talk in code, but he got it. "Yes, it's safe to assume that, Mason. By any chance, do you have any coffee made?"

"No, but I will be more than happy to prepare some. I just baked some brownies."

"I love brownies," Amy said. Mason beamed. The man does love compliments, Hank thought.

"We're going to set the tree up in the living room. Unless you have a better idea, Mason?"

"No, the living room will be fine. I think it

best so the boys won't be tempted to play with the ornaments. And, of course, the animals have to be taken into consideration. I understand via the Internet that male dogs and trees are not compatible. I'll be in the kitchen if you need me for anything."

"That means we're dismissed," Hank whispered in Amy's ear.

The twins toddled over to the gate. Hank bent down and picked them both up. They giggled and laughed as they yanked at his hair and pulled at his nose. "I can't tell them apart," he confessed. "Come on now, give me a big kiss. Ohhh, that was sooo good. Give me another one." The boys obliged, and then they were done with the bonding and wanted down on the floor.

"I can see how they would be a handful," Amy said. "They're sweet as honey, and they both look just like Ben."

They watched for another minute or so as the boys rough-and-tumbled with the dogs, who were happy to play.

"Let's get to it, Mandy. We have a Christmas tree to put up." The doorbell rang and Amy opened it. "Oh, look, our poinsettias are here. I'll set them out while you bring in the tree. By the way, do you know where Alice keeps the decorations? You said she was big on decorating the house. We need to do that, too."

"Probably in the attic. I'll get them down as soon as we set up the tree. Just let me know when the coffee is ready."

* * *

It was four o'clock when Mason and the twins oohed and aahed over the couple's Christmas decorations. The tree was up, and it bathed the house in what Amy called a delicious balsam scent. She said she could smell it on the second floor. Poinsettias lined the stairway and were nestled in all the corners. The foyer held a small artificial tree, decorated with colored lights and tiny gossamer angels dangling from the branches. Amy surmised it had a special memory for Alice because of the care that had been taken when it was packed away. Fat ceramic Santas sat at each side of the door. Thick red candles were placed on each end of the mantel along with branches of live greenery that Hank cut off the bottom of the tree. Amy stuck bright red bows in and among the branches and dangled a few strands of tinsel. "Very festive," Hank said, taking Amy's arm in his. "Just think, next year we can do this in our own house." Amy just smiled. And smiled.

The twins gibbered and giggled as they pointed to the giant-size Santa standing next to the fireplace, his backpack loaded with colored boxes with bright red ribbons. Churchill sniffed it out. His intentions seemed obvious to all of them until Mason cleared his throat in warning. The golden dog lowered his leg and backed away, his tail between his legs.

"Good dog," Mason said as he handed out treats again, then opened the back door. Both dogs ran outside as the twins went back to pushing and shoving each other.

"No, no, no! We do not push, and we do not shove," Mason said as he wagged his finger at the boys. One of the boys, Hank wasn't sure which one, stomped his foot and started to cry.

"Sit down and fold your hands, young man. We do not slap and pinch our brother." The toddler sat down and folded his hands. He sniffed, but he stopped crying. Mason handed out raisins in small cups, and the boys were happy again.

"That guy needs to be cloned," Hank said.

Amy looked around. "I don't think there's anything left to do here. I think I'm going to go home and take a shower. You want to come over for dinner?"

Hank grimaced. "That depends on Mason. I think he might want to go home early. Why don't you come over here? I'm sure we can find something to eat here. In fact, I know we can. He's cooking something that smells pretty darn good, and there are those brownies we bypassed when we had our coffee."

"Okay, if that's an invitation, I accept. We can put my tree up tomorrow. I'll cut the netting off and lean it up against the house. See you later."

Hank kissed her good-bye. He watched from the doorway until she was safely in her own house. *God, I am so happy.*

"It would appear you are in love again. Is that a clear assessment, Mr. Anders?"

"On the money, Mason. I asked her to marry me, and she said yes."

"You do . . . work fast. She's quite lovely. It would appear she returns your feelings. Is there any news on Mrs. Anders?"

"No, I'm afraid not. I'm sure she'll be back soon. God, I hope she comes back soon. The boys seem so happy. It bothers me. Don't they miss her?"

"Of course they miss her. They keep looking around for her. They whimper and suck their thumbs, but they can't talk, so you just have to figure it out for yourself. No one can take a mother's place. No one." This last was said with such vehemence that Hank winced.

What Mason said was true, Hank thought. It also explained Mandy's return and her search for yesterday.

Hank let loose with a long sigh. Thank God he had decided to come back to Apple Valley for the holidays. In doing so he was going to be able to help Alice in both the short and long term, and just by being here, he'd fallen in love all over again. If anyone could help Mandy lay her old ghosts to rest, it was him. He crossed his fingers hoping he was right.

Chapter Eight

Alice Anders paced the narrow confines of her friend's tiny apartment. Tears rolled down her cheeks. Am I out of my mind? No sane person would do what I've done. No sane person would abandon her home, her children, and her husband's dog. Even if Ben was a perfect dad, she'd fallen down on her job and screwed up big-time. That was the bottom line.

She looked down at the tabby cat circling her feet. Chloe was her name. She picked her up and cuddled her against her neck. This little animal didn't mess in the house, she had her own private sanitation boxes in the tiny laundry room and in the bathroom. She didn't make mistakes. And she cleaned herself religiously, unlike Churchill, who messed all over and rolled in mud whenever he felt like it. Giving him a bath always clogged the bathtub drain and then it was eighty-five dollars to get it unclogged. Her budget, stringent as it was, had ceased to exist months and months ago. Her credit cards were maxed out. She lived day to day.

She'd wigged out. How cool was that? More tears flowed. Ben was going to pitch a fit when Hank told him what she'd done. Chloe licked at her tears. God, how she ached to hold her sons.

Coming here to her friend's small apartment had seemed like the answer to all her problems. She'd gotten the idea when her best friend in Apple Valley, a first-grade teacher named Marie, had said she was going home to Seattle for the holidays. She'd given her the key and asked her to check on Chloe from time to time.

Her intention was to veg out, to fall back and regroup. To take bubble baths, to eat when and if she felt like it, to drink wine while she was soaking in a tub, and to sleep peacefully through the night with no interruptions. It hadn't happened that way at all. She was lucky if she slept two hours a night, and what sleep she got was fitful. There was no bathtub to luxuriate in, only a stall shower. She didn't have money for wine, and Marie didn't have cable television. She, too, lived on a budget.

The only thing she'd proved to herself was that she was an unfit mother. A slacker as a wife.

She wasn't Supermom, and she never would be. That title would have to go to someone else, someone a lot more worthy than she.

Did the twins miss her? Probably not. Churchill hated her, so there was no point in even asking herself if the big golden retriever missed her. He probably hoped she never came back. The tears flowed again. She looked like a witch with the dark circles under her eyes. Her hair needed to be cut and styled.

Alice's wild pacing led her to the bathroom and the huge mirror on the back of the door. Well, if nothing else, she'd shed a few pounds.

What did Hank think about what she'd done? How was he coping? She wished she knew what he'd told Ben. Ben was going to be so disappointed in her.

Alice splashed cold water on her face, combed her hair, smoothed down the sweat suit she'd arrived in, and tidied the apartment. She made sure Chloe had bowls of food and water not only in the bathroom but the kitchenette, too. She cleaned the two litter boxes and put in fresh litter. She set the thermostat to seventy and sat down to drink her fifth cup of coffee. She didn't need this fifth cup of coffee. She was killing time, and she knew it. She'd made a mess of things, and now it was time to stand up and take the blame for what she'd done. She started to cry again. Like tears were really going to help her out.

It was totally dark now. Christmas Eve. It had always been the happiest time of the year, at least for her. Ben, too. How often they'd talked about how perfect life was here in Apple Valley. Especially at Christmastime. And she'd ruined it all. Her. No one else. She'd single-handedly ruined everything for everyone with her stupid actions. How in the name of God was she ever going to make this right?

By going home, a voice inside her head whispered, *You go back, you stand tall, you apologize and get your life back.* After . . . after she hugged and kissed her two little boys. She had to apologize to them, too, not that they would understand, but she'd do it anyway.

Still, she didn't move. Because . . . because she was a coward.

Alice stood up, drained her coffee, then washed out the cup and cleaned the coffeepot. She took one last look around the tiny apartment, checked on Chloe one last time by giving her a hug before she settled her in her little bed next to the sofa. She turned out all the lights, put on her heavy down jacket, and left the apartment.

Outside, Alice hunkered into her jacket as she made the long trek back to her house. There was little traffic, the citizenry of Apple Valley were secure in their houses, building fires, having dinner, and getting ready for the big man in the red suit.

It was bitter cold, and the tears escaping her eyes were freezing on her eyelashes. She barely noticed as she trudged along. She had to walk along the roadside because of the piled-up snow. Her sneakers were cold and wet. She'd never been more miserable in her entire life.

When she reached her neighborhood, Alice climbed over the banks of piled-up snow onto the shoveled sidewalk. How pretty it all looked, with the snow on the evergreens and the colored lights on the houses and in the trees.

Christmas in Apple Valley.

Soon the church choir would be out caroling. She and Ben always went caroling since they belonged to the choir. She'd had to give it up when the boys came along. She'd had to give up *everything* when the boys came along. Even Ben. She knew the thought was unfair. She'd known what it meant to marry a military man when she agreed to marry Ben. She had no one to blame for her circumstances except herself.

Alice rounded the corner to her street and stopped short when she noticed the crowds of people at Albert Carpenter's house. Then she smiled when she saw the front porch that was decorated to the nines. For sure the Apple Valley prize would go to this piece of property. How sad that Albert would never know how loved he was.

It looked to Alice like everyone had brought something to add to the decorations someone had been kind enough to set up. The tree was magnificent, with its twinkling lights. The boys would love the reindeer and the sleigh packed with gaily colored packages. Small statues lined the steps. Santas, elves, ceramic Christmas trees. Gossamer angels trailing red ribbons dangled on wires from the beams on the porch.

At first glance it all looked cluttered until

you saw the homemade drawings, the cards tacked to the pillars that held up the porch. And then your second glance said it was the most beautiful sight in the world.

Alice tried to swallow past the lump in her throat. She just knew she was the only person in town who had not left something on that wide, wonderful front porch. Well, she would have to remedy that as soon as she could. Not because Ben would never forgive her if she didn't, but because she wanted to. No, that was wrong, she *needed* to do it.

Alice wondered if there was anyone in the whole world who understood what she had been going through with the exception of Albert Carpenter. She'd poured out her heart to him so many times these past months. For his comfort she'd knocked herself out trying to take care of him—she cooked for him, cleaned his house, shopped for him, and did his laundry. Not that there weren't others who would have helped, but she hadn't asked. She'd wanted to do it because he was like a wise old grandfather, and he dearly loved Ben and Hank and a little girl named Mandy Leigh. No, she was not Supermom or super anything. She was just plain old Alice Avery Anders. Triple A Alice, as Ben called her from time to time.

Alice moved on, and soon enough she was standing at her own front door. She turned the knob, but the door was locked from the inside. How stupid. She'd given Hank her keys. She rang the bell. The door opened. All she could do was stand there with tears in her eyes. Hank stretched out his arms, and she stepped into them. "Oh, Hank, I'm so . . ."

"Shhh. You don't need to apologize for anything. I'm just so damn glad that you're home. God, I can't tell you how glad I am. Come in, come in, it's freezing out there."

Alice stepped back and stared up at her brother-in-law. "I . . . need . . ."

Hank placed his index finger against Alice's lips. "No, you don't need to do anything but love those kids of yours. They're in the family room waiting for you."

Alice shrugged out of her jacket and ran to the family room. Like Hank, she vaulted over the gate and gathered up her twin boys, holding them close. Churchill and Miss Sadie vied for her attention. "Oh, God, I forgot about Miss Sadie. C'mere, you little bundle of love."

Hank backed away and bumped into Mason, who was wiping the corners of his eyes. "It would appear the lady of the house has returned. What would you suggest I do, Mr. Anders?"

"Well, after I introduce you to your new employer, you might want to go home to your own family and enjoy Christmas."

"Unfortunately, Mr. Anders, I don't have a family."

"In that case, Mason, how would you like to spend the holidays with us? As our guest."

"I think I would like that very much, sir. I would imagine Mrs. Anders will . . . ah, want to bathe her sons herself this evening, so I'll tidy up the kitchen. Is there anything else you need me to do?"

"Nope." Hank walked back to the family room and called out to Alice. "There's someone here you need to meet, Alice." Hank drew Mason forward. "Meet your new nanny. Alice, this is Mason. Mason, this is Mrs. Anders. Mason is my Christmas present to you, Ben, and the boys. He's going to be here every day until Ben gets back home. The boys love him, and, if you can believe this, Churchill actually listens and does his business outside. He doesn't jump the fence anymore either."

Tears rolled down Alice's cheeks as she reached out to shake Mason's hand. The boys toddled over to him, begging to be picked up. "It's almost bath time, madam, do you wish to do the honors, or shall I?"

Alice looked like she was in shock. "I . . . really, Hank, I have a nanny until Ben gets home? Oh, God, you dear sweet man. How did you know that was what I wished for? Oh, it doesn't matter." She looked from Hank to Mason and said something Hank found strange. "If you don't mind, Mason, tonight I need you to bathe the boys. I have to go up in the attic to find something. From here on in, I'll do the bathing. I don't want to overwork you."

"Very well, madam."

"Do you need any help, Alice?"

Supermom Alice would have said no, she had it under control. This new Alice said, "Yes, as a matter of fact, I do." She bent over to kiss the boys again before she stepped over the gate. She literally ran up the stairs to the second floor, then up a third set of stairs to the attic. She whirled around at the top, and said, "The house looks so beautiful. Thank you, Hank. Perhaps someday I can make it up to you."

Hank nodded. "What are we looking for, Alice?"

"It's among the Christmas decorations. It's a string of silver bells that Mr. Carpenter gave Ben a lifetime ago. You have no idea what that string of bells meant to him. Each time we moved—and there were so many moves—he always made sure that string of bells went with us. He said you and Mandy got one, too. The sound was so true, so pure. I have to find it, Hank. I didn't leave anything on Albert's porch. There are so many people out there, so many mementos: the cards, the letters, the keepsakes. It just blew me away."

"There are several e-mails from Ben waiting for you," Hank said quietly as he rummaged through neatly labeled boxes.

"Did you read them?" Alice asked.

"Absolutely not!" Hank lied with a straight face. "Now that I know what we're looking for, I can search. Why don't you go and check Ben's e-mails."

Alice whirled around. The expression on her face was so fierce, Hank stepped back. "You know what, Hank, Ben's e-mails can wait. *This is important.*"

Hank didn't know what to say to that, so he didn't say anything. He kept rummaging in the ornament boxes, wondering what he'd done with his own set of bells. He vaguely remembered Albert giving them to him, but from there on it was a blur. Maybe he needed to say something light, or something meaningful. "I'm getting married, Alice. Mandy Leigh came back home for the holidays and we . . . we hooked up again. She helped me decorate the house for you."

"Hmmm. That's nice. Ben always said nice things about her." Alice whirled around and said, "I didn't mean it when I said I wished Ben had left me standing at the altar. Well, I meant it at the time I said it, but . . . you know what I'm saying, right?"

"Absolutely. You were just venting, and I understand that. Look, Alice, I could never do what you do every day, day in day out. I tried and couldn't do it. Ben is a fool for thinking you're some kind of wonder woman. And, I don't blame you a bit. That's why I had to hire Mason. He's the wonder in wonderful, and the boys really like him. So do the dogs."

"Hank."

"Yeah."

"Shut up. I have to take responsibility for my actions. I'm okay with that, and I appreciate all you did and for . . . for Mason. Please don't think I'm ungrateful, but right now I have to find those bells. Oh, God! Here they are. Look! Look! Listen!" Alice shook the bells, and suddenly Hank shivered at the pure melodious sound. The silver bells themselves were tarnished, the red ribbon holding them together was tattered and faded.

"Do you mind telling me what it is with the bells, Alice?" he asked gently.

Alice sat down on an old trunk. "Three or four months ago Albert talked me out of filing for a divorce. I was packed and ready to leave. I had taken him for his chemo treatment that day, and he was so sick, Hank. I mean really sick, but he sat me down and read me the riot act. He told me stories about his own up-and-down marriage. He said you have to work at it to make it worthwhile. He told me other stories about you guys when you were kids. He told me how Mandy was suddenly gone from your lives. He never judged me, never told me not to leave. Somehow or other he convinced me to stay without saying the words. He kept me sane, Hank."

"I see." And he did indeed see what she was talking about.

"I'm going over to that porch at midnight and ring these bells."

"I wish I knew where I put mine."

"They're over there under the window in the box marked 'Hank.' Ben packed up your stuff after your parents . . . He said it was stuff you didn't want anymore."

Hank thought his heart was going to explode right out of his chest. He ran over to the box, popped the lid. He saw all kinds of junk he couldn't ever remember owning. The string of silver bells was wrapped in bubble wrap and tissue. They were just as tarnished, the ribbon just as tattered as the one Alice was holding in her hand. He shook them gently. Tears blurred his vision at the pure tone.

If Mandy had her set, all would be right

with his world now that he understood what
Alice was talking about. If she didn't, two out
of three would be okay, too.

Down on the second floor, Mason was carry-
ing the twins into their bedroom. They smelled
like warm sunshine as Hank bent down to kiss
each one of them. They reached out to Alice,
who took them both into their room. She settled them in their beds, covered them, then sat
down to read a story they didn't even hear;
they were sound asleep. He watched her as she
kept reading till the end of the story. She looked
so motherly, so suddenly at peace he suddenly
felt the same way.

Later on, downstairs, the bells in her hand,
Alice sat down in the kitchen. She looked at
the slice of homemade blueberry pie and the
glass of milk waiting for her. She looked over
at Mason and smiled.

"While you're eating, Mason and I will set
up the gifts under the tree. This way you can
enjoy the quiet evening. I'm going next door
to see Mandy. If you need me, just call my cell
phone."

Alice nodded. "Thanks, Hank, for everything."

Hank pointed to the laptop on the little
desk. She nodded sweetly. "Just so you know,
Hank, I love Ben with all my heart and soul."

"I know that, Alice. I'll see you later."

When Amy opened the door, she was holding a string of bells in her hand. "Oh, Hank, you
aren't going to believe what I found. Look!" She
held up a set of silver bells and shook them.

Hank laughed and pulled his set of bells out of his pocket.

"Alice came home. She wants us to go over to Albert's porch and ring the bells at midnight. You up for it?"

"Oh, yes. I never decorated my tree, and I didn't set out any decorations," Amy said, pointing to the huge evergreen sitting in her living room in the middle of the floor. "I'm not sure what I was trying to . . . to find, to recapture. That time in my life is gone. This is a new beginning for me. I think for all of us. That in itself is a miracle as far as I'm concerned."

"I love you, Mandy Leigh. Always have and always will."

"And I love you, Hank Anders. I always have and always will."

When the clock struck midnight, three people stood on the Carpenter front porch. Silver bells rang, the sound clear, pure, and rich. High above, a kindly old gentleman ruffled his wings.

"Merry Christmas," he whispered above the sound of the bells that seemed to be ringing all about him.

Snow Angels

Chapter One

Friday, December 19, 2008
Eagle, Colorado
Interstate 70

Grace Landry glanced in her rearview mirror to check on Ashley and Amanda, her two "dates" for the evening. She'd been delighted when their mother, Stephanie, had allowed her to take the girls to see their first live performance of *The Nutcracker* at Eagle Valley High School. Both girls were sound asleep in the backseat of her van.

They'd needed some fun and normalcy in their sad and empty lives, especially during the Christmas season. Grace's eyes teared up as she summoned the images of their frightened little faces when the local police delivered them and their mother to Hope House on Monday, four days earlier.

As a practicing psychologist, Grace had witnessed her share of abused women since receiving her doctorate nine years ago. Only five years ago, when her grandmother had left her a sizable estate, she'd started Hope House, a shelter for battered women and their children, and unveiled it to the proper authorities in Denver and the surrounding areas. It had been her hope that they would recommend her safe house to those women in need as a place to recuperate and plan for the future, and more than anything else, a place where they could feel safe. Gypsum was a small town off the beaten path, the perfect location for such a place. She'd been successful and never had any reason to question her decision. Her mother worried because Hope House was in such a remote area, but Grace assured her that was exactly what she'd been looking for when she'd bought the house and the surrounding land.

A light snow began to fall. Grace turned on the wipers, making a mental note to have chains put on her tires. With many treacherous stretches along Colorado's I-70, authorities forbade semis to pass without them. Every winter she had her mechanic install them even though they weren't required for the van. She'd rather be safe than sorry.

In the distance ahead, she noted red-and-blue flashing lights. Praying there wasn't an accident, Grace turned on the radio, locating a traffic report on one of her preprogrammed stations. The broadcaster noted the light snow, but that was nothing unusual for this stretch of highway. Probably a broken-down motorist.

What little traffic there was slowed to a crawl as she drove toward the glaring lights. After a few minutes of creeping along, traffic came to a standstill. Grace glanced at the digital clock on her dashboard. After ten. She'd promised Stephanie she would have the girls back by eleven. At this rate, she'd be lucky to make it before midnight.

When Grace saw police officers knocking on the windows of the vehicles ahead of her, she assumed this was a random license check. Reaching across the seat for her wallet, she removed her license, awaiting her turn to prove she was a legally licensed driver.

The expected tap, and Grace pushed the button to lower the window. A gust of icy air along with wet snowflakes smacked the side of her face. Before the officer asked, she handed him her license.

"Thanks, ma'am, but this isn't a license check. We've established several roadblocks in the area. We're detouring traffic."

"Oh," Grace said, surprised by his words. A roadblock this time of night seemed odd to her. Rather than question the young officer, she listened to him as he pointed ahead.

"I hope there isn't some crazy out terrorizing the roads," she commented.

"No need to worry. We're taking care of it. If you'll take the next exit, 147 to Eby Creek Road, another officer will reroute you around the blockades. We're trying to close this area of I-70 as quickly as possible."

"Of course, officer." Grace rolled up the

window and followed the taillights of the line of slow-moving vehicles in front of her. Glancing at the backseat, she smiled when she saw that Amanda and Ashley were still sleeping. Most children were very resilient. She could only hope these two were also.

Grace closely followed the other vehicles, making it look as if the slow-moving traffic were a train. The snowfall started coming down even more heavily than it had been. She adjusted the defroster to high to clear the fog on the windshield. Traveling downhill, she applied slight pressure to the brakes as she made her way off the exit ramp, stopping when she saw a group of police cars with their lights blazing.

For the second time in what was becoming a frigid night, Grace rolled down her window as another policeman approached the van. Though she was well acquainted with many of Eagle's finest, Grace hadn't recognized the last officer; nor did she recognize this one.

"Where are you heading?" he asked. "We're trying to reroute everyone without creating bedlam." He smiled, but Grace saw that it was just for her benefit because it never reached his eyes. His eyes were watchful, alarmed. Grace knew the look quite well. She'd seen it hundreds of times in her line of work.

"To Gypsum," she said.

"Follow this road for the next seven miles or so. From there you'll turn left on the road leading back to I-70, then that should put you on Trail Gulch Road. The railroad track runs parallel to Trail Gulch if you're not familiar with the area."

After telling the officer she was somewhat familiar with the area, Grace repeated the correct directions before he motioned for her to move on. When she saw there were no other vehicles heading in the same direction, she felt a bit creeped out being alone on such a remote stretch of highway. Hope House *was* out of the way, she reminded herself, which explained why most of the other vehicles were traveling in the opposite direction.

Amanda muttered in her sleep, and Grace checked her rearview mirror again. It wouldn't be a good time for the girls to wake up. Stephanie had told her about their intense fear of the dark. Without streetlights and the usual signs advertising Big Macs and Holiday Inn Express's free breakfast, the two-lane road was totally dark, except for her headlights, which plunged forward into the night like two eerie cat eyes.

After ten minutes of slow driving, Grace checked her mileage. She'd only traveled three miles. Careful to monitor the odometer so as not to miss the upcoming left turn, she reduced her speed to fifteen miles per hour. When the van slid off the road onto the shoulder, Grace turned the wheel to the left, quickly guiding the vehicle back onto the slippery pavement. Her heart fluttered against her rib cage, and her hands were damp as she clutched the steering wheel while continuing to look for the turnoff. She checked her mileage again, surprised when she saw she'd already gone five miles. Taking a deep breath, Grace tried to focus on the road, but with the snow falling faster and heavier, it was becoming almost impossible to see more than a few feet in front of her.

Hoping to soothe her nerves, she adjusted the radio to a station playing cheerful Christmas music. Grace sang along with the familiar tunes, but stopped suddenly, fearing her off-key singing might wake the girls.

Realizing she must have missed the turnoff after she'd traveled another five miles, she stopped in the center of the road, telling herself it didn't matter since she seemed to be the only one crazy enough to get lost on a back road when the weather was getting worse by the minute. Recalling the directions the police officer had given her, Grace did a three-point turn, checked her mileage, then slowly drove back in the direction she'd just come from.

Glancing from side to side as she retraced the miles and careful to watch the odometer, she still didn't see any sign of a road where she could've made a turn, left or right. Continuing to clutch the wheel and occasionally glancing back at the sleeping children, Grace kept the routine up for another fifteen minutes before concluding that there was no turnoff. The police officer must have given her the wrong directions.

Wishing she'd upgraded to a van equipped with a GPS, she remembered that her cell phone had a less sophisticated version of one. She removed it from the side pocket on her purse. Instead of the welcoming green light that usually glowed, the small screen was as black as the night in which she was desperately trying to get home in. She tried to turn the cell off and on again. Nothing happened.

Her cell-phone battery was dead.

Wasn't that one of the first rules she drummed into the women living at Hope House when she distributed the preprogrammed cell phones? *Never* allow your cell-phone battery to die because you never knew when you'd need to dial those three lifesaving numbers: nine-one-one.

But there she was, out in the middle of the night, with two little girls in her care, and no way to contact Hope House.

Deciding that the officer must have miscalculated the miles, Grace proceeded to drive down the two-lane highway, searching for an all-night gas station, anyplace where she could find a phone to call Stephanie to assure her the girls were fine. They'd been through so much, and Grace felt she was putting their safety at risk again.

After driving for what seemed like forever, it was after midnight when she pulled the van off to the side of the road. Fearing what she had to do, yet knowing it must be done, Grace leaned over the front seat and gently shook Amanda and Ashley until they were awake.

"Miss Grace," came the sleepy voice of eight-year-old Ashley. "Where's Mommy?"

Five-year-old Amanda perked up when she heard Ashley asking for their mother. "Is Mommy okay?" Grace heard the fear in their soft little voices.

"Mommy is just fine. She's at Hope House, remember?" Grace knew she was stalling while trying to come up with a plan that would have no adverse effect on the girls.

Both wide-awake, they nodded.

"But we're supposed to be home by now, aren't we?" Ashley asked.

"Yes, sweetie, we are. I seem to have made a wrong turn, and I'm lost. I'm sorry, I don't want to alarm either of you. I just need to make a call to your mother to let her know we're safe, okay?"

Her words seemed to reassure both girls. Grace removed her jacket from the seat next to her. Slipping one arm at a time into the sleeves, she was glad she'd chosen the heavy parka since she was about to venture out into Colorado's ever-dropping frigid temperatures.

"So why aren't you calling?" Amanda asked with a trace of anxiety in her high-pitched voice.

Grace admitted to herself she was not the image of dependability and trustworthiness she'd presented to the girls when she'd convinced them a night away from their mother would be fun. In fact, she was just the opposite.

Reluctantly, Grace said, "I'm afraid my cell phone isn't working."

Over the top of the seat, two pairs of big brown eyes stared at her. Waiting.

"You can't leave us here by ourselves, Miss Grace! Mommy says we're never to be alone. Right, 'Manda?"

The younger girl nodded. "Yeah, Mommy says so."

Saddened at the look of distrust on their small faces, Grace leaned over the seat and brushed her hands over both the girls' heads. "Oh, girls, I would never leave you alone! What I meant to say is you'll both have to come with me. We can pretend it's a . . . treasure hunt. Whoever finds a phone first gets to pick out and decorate the Christmas tree any way she wants to. Deal?" Grace asked as she saw smiles light up their eyes.

"Deal," they said in unison.

"Then let's get your mittens, coats, and hats on. It's much colder now than it was earlier."

Grace bundled the girls up, grabbed a bottle of water and a flashlight from the glove compartment and tucked them inside her coat pocket, then draped her purse over her shoulder so she could take both girls by the hand. It wouldn't do for her to lose contact with them. The snow was so thick, Grace could barely make out the van as they stepped away from its familiar safety.

Gazing up at the sky, Grace tried to determine which direction to head, but unlike the movies, there were no stars to guide her, nothing. She was on her own.

Deciding to walk uphill in the direction she'd been driving, she clasped both girls' mitten-clad hands in her own as they trudged through the deepening snow. Every few minutes they would stop to catch their breath. The high elevation and the effort it took to walk uphill would strain even some of the world's best athletes.

When they'd walked uphill for more than an hour, Ashley yanked her hand away from Grace and pointed to a light up ahead. "Miss Grace, look. *Look!*"

Grace's heart did a somersault. Thank God! At the top of the mountain she saw windows aglow with lights. She grabbed Ashley's hand. "I believe Miss Ashley gets to choose the tree. Come on, girls, let's hurry before—" She started to say before our luck runs out, but given the girls' past, thought better of it, and said "—they go to bed," instead.

As they trudged through the snow, their shallow breathing created swirls of fog in the cool night air. Grace wasn't sure how much longer the girls could stand the bitter cold and wind. Off to the left, Grace spied a road sign telling her they were approaching Blow Out Hill. *Great,* she thought as she pulled the girls along. She'd had a blowout all right. She'd blown the entire evening. Stephanie and the girls would never trust her again.

Heart pounding with every step, Grace rehearsed what she would say to Stephanie. She had to be out of her mind with worry by now. It was after one in the morning. Angry at herself for her stupidity, she calmed down enough to knock loudly on the door of the biggest log home she'd ever laid eyes on.

Chapter Two

Max Jorgenson jerked awake from a sound sleep when Cliff and Ice-D, his two Siberian Huskies, placed four heavy paws on his chest as he lay sprawled out on the leather sofa. When the pair saw that his eyes were open, they started barking and running around in circles.

Glancing around the great room, Max raked a hand through his hair. He'd fallen asleep again, with the lights on and the television blaring. Correcting himself, he mentally changed the words "fallen asleep" to "passed out." Who cared? He sure as hell didn't. Cliff nudged his hand with his furry nose as Max heard a soft pounding at the front door.

"What the heck?" he said as he rambled toward the front of what he referred to as his giant cabin. If there was an emergency at the resort, the management knew not to come to his retreat, knew there would be extreme consequences. He'd have someone's ass in a sling for this unwanted intrusion first thing in the morning. He peeked at the clock above the fireplace. It *was* morning already.

The muffled pounding continued. "Eddie, if that's you, you're fired!" Max yanked the heavy log door aside expecting to see Eddie, his manager at Maximum Glide, the exclusive ski resort he owned in Telluride.

What he saw left him speechless.

Taking several seconds to recover from his surprise, as was his habit when flustered, he raked both hands through his unruly brownish blond hair. "You must have the wrong house." These were the only words he could come up with as two little girls bundled in Pepto-Bismol pink jackets and matching hats and both with huge chocolate-drop eyes and their mother, their *gorgeous, green-eyed* mother, stared at him.

"We need to use your phone," Grace stated in a firm voice, then stepped to the side as both Cliff and Ice-D bumped her free hand with their muzzles.

"Yeah, 'cause our daddy—"

"Not now, Ashley," Grace interrupted.

Realizing the trio must be freezing, Max stepped aside. "Down, guys," he said to the dogs, then to his unexpected guests, "Come inside, you're letting in the cold air."

The woman took both girls by the hand and led them inside. Their faces were just a shade

shy of burgundy when they stood in the bright
light.

"How long have you been out in this . . .
weather?" He wanted to curse but stopped himself when he glanced down at the two girls.

"There are several roadblocks in Eagle along
I-70. We were directed this way, and somehow I
missed the turnoff." Grace touched her purse
strapped around her neck like a bayonet. "My
cell-phone battery died."

"I bet your car broke down, or you ran out
of gas, too," Max accused Grace.

Inching her chin up a notch, just enough
not to appear too haughty, Grace answered in
a firm voice, "Neither."

With a trace of sarcasm Max asked, "So you
decided to take your kids out for a midnight
stroll during a snowstorm?"

He could see by her expression that he'd
made her angry. He hadn't meant the comment to come off as offensive, and didn't care,
but really, what kind of mother dragged her
children out on a night like this?

"Actually, when I couldn't find the turnoff . . .
I just need to use your phone, then we'll be on
our way," Grace explained. "As soon as—"

He gestured with his hands, preventing further conversation. In an impatient tone, Max
said, "Follow me."

"Miss Grace, can we pet the dogs?" Amanda
asked when the pair of Huskies blocked their
path.

Grace looked at the dogs, then their owner.

She'd always been fond of animals but knew some were skittish around strangers. That didn't seem to be a problem in this case, but one never knew. She'd already put the girls at risk once tonight.

"Go ahead," Max replied to Amanda. "They're harmless."

Both girls looked to Grace for permission. "If Mr.—" She stopped, realizing she didn't know his name. "Yes, you both may pet the dogs while I make the phone call."

"Name's Max Jorgenson," he offered.

Grace looked at him oddly, then held out a slim hand. "Grace Landry." He reminded her of someone, but she couldn't place who.

Their host, if you could even call him that, was beyond handsome. With golden brown hair that hung way below his collar and robin's-egg blue eyes rimmed with long black lashes most women would die for, "sexy" didn't begin to describe him. Then there was the body. Grace couldn't help but admire the broad shoulders that tapered down to a slim waist. She'd also noticed that his faded Levis clung to his rear end like a glove.

Max reached for her hand, then stopped. He'd promised himself after Kayla's death he wouldn't touch another woman. At the moment, that promise seemed irrational and stupid. He was thirty-six years old. Did he really think he could live the rest of his life without touching another woman? Without companionship? Without love? Without *sex*? It was just under two years since Kayla had died. He hadn't

given women much thought before tonight.
And then this . . . snow angel appeared on his
doorstep. Literally.

"The phone's in the kitchen. This way,"
Max said gruffly.

Without bothering to see if his guest followed, Max proceeded to the kitchen. He
viewed his home as they made their way to the
kitchen. Thick round pine logs made up most
of the walls throughout the custom-built home.
In the daytime, sunlight filtered through large
floor-to-ceiling windows facing the mountains,
revealing blue skies, puffy white clouds, and
snowcapped mountains. The designer he'd
hired to decorate used deep shades of forest
green, with bright splashes of candy-apple
red. With the custom-made pine cabinets,
splashes of red and green in framed pictures
of bright red apples, and pottery in matching
shades of red and green from local craftsmen,
the desired effect of hominess and cheer
would have been complete had there been any
personal touches added. Like a shopping list
stuck to the bright red refrigerator with a mag-
net or a tea towel draped over the sink. Maybe
a few unwashed dishes in the sink. Instead, the
kitchen looked like it had the day he'd moved
in, something right off the pages of one of
those catalogues he'd seen advertising log
homes. Max couldn't remember ever making a
real meal in the kitchen.

"Phone's over there," he said, pointing to an
area in the kitchen comprised of a small counter,
where a laptop sat upon the black marble, its

screen as blank and impersonal as the rest of the space. A cordless phone was sitting next to the computer.

"Thank you," Grace said. She stared at him, willing him to step out of the kitchen and allowing her a modicum of privacy, but he didn't budge. Taking a deep breath, she quickly punched in the private number to Hope House. When nothing happened, she dialed the number again, this time hearing the requisite *beep beep beep* as she hit each number. Lifting the phone to her ear, expecting to hear a ring, instead she heard nothing. She tried the number a third time. Still nothing.

"The phone lines go down when there's snow," Max offered.

No kidding, she wanted to say but refrained.

"Do you have a cell phone I could use? I really need to make this call. The girls"—Grace nodded toward Ashley and Amanda, who were busy petting the dogs—"they need to . . . I just need to make a call, then we'll be on our way." She was about to explain that the girls' mother needed to know they were alive and *safe* but thought better of it.

Leaning casually against the pine-log wall, Max said, "Nope, never bothered with one. Sorry."

Grace tried the number again, but there was still no dial tone. Realizing it was fruitless to continue trying to make a call on a phone that didn't work, Grace placed it back on the base unit.

Not knowing what else to say, she hurried

past the man with the familiar face to the girls, who were still playing with the lovable Huskies. She rubbed her hands together, trying to warm them. She dreaded what she was about to do, but there wasn't much choice.

"Girls, tell Mr. Jorgenson thank you for his hospitality. We have to leave. Now," she stated firmly, hoping the girls wouldn't question her.

"And just where in the hell do you think you're going?" Max asked.

Galled that he had the audacity to question her, Grace turned around to face him. "Really, Mr. Jorgenson, it's none of your business. Thank you for the use of your phone."

Turning back to the girls, Grace spoke gently to them. "Amanda, Ashley. It's time to go."

"But—"

"No buts, girls. It's time to go."

Grace took each girl by the hand. "Put your mittens on. It's still very cold out."

Thundering footsteps came from behind. "Listen, lady, I don't know what your problem is, but you can't take these kids out now! The snow is getting heavier by the minute." He pointed to the floor-to-ceiling windows that faced the mountains.

Grace realized he was right, but what other choice did she have? "We're going back to the van. I'm sure a patrol officer will find us." She realized she should be staying put. Taking the girls back out into freezing temperatures was stupid, but once they got back to the van, she'd crank up the heat. There was plenty of gas. And who knew? Maybe a patrol officer would find them.

It wasn't the greatest plan, but it was all she could come up with given the circumstances.

In complete frustration, Max combed his hands through his messy hair. "Why don't you spend the night here? I've plenty of room. In the morning, I'll drive you back to your van myself."

"Please, please, Miss Grace? Let's spend the night here. We can play with the dogs. *Puh-leeze?*" Amanda asked.

It would be the smartest choice. Really, it was their *only* choice. She couldn't take the girls out again in this weather. For the girls' sake, she swallowed her pride, making a snap decision. "Thank you, Mr. Jorgenson. We accept—but just for the night."

Grace turned to him. He seemed surprised she'd agreed to his offer. "That's all I'm offering."

She wanted to tell him to forget it, but there was more at stake than her pride. She had two small children to consider. "If you'll show me our room, I'll take it from there," Grace insisted, knowing that the invitation had cost him. Though how much, she didn't realize.

"What about some food?" He stared at the girls. "Maybe something hot to drink?" He shot Grace a questioning look.

Maybe he had a trace of manners after all. Grace turned to him. "I think we're okay, but thanks for the offer."

"I'm hungry!" Ashley said. "And thirsty. And I need to use the bathroom."

"Me too," seconded Amanda. "Really, *really* hungry!"

Grace raised a sculpted brow. "I guess I spoke too soon."

Max didn't know where this sudden urge to be hospitable came from, but when he saw the excitement on the little girls' faces, something inside him melted. What kind of man would allow a woman and her two kids to venture out into the wee hours of the morning knowing it was below freezing outside?

Him, he realized. Had it not been dark and cold, that's exactly what he would've done. What he really wanted to do was snatch the invitation back, find another bottle of whiskey, and go back to sleep.

Seeing the expectant looks on the little girls' faces, he blocked any further thoughts about what he should have done. This was the right thing to do. It's what Kayla would have done had she been alive.

"Bathroom's that way." He pointed to a door beneath the staircase leading upstairs.

"Thanks." Grace continued her grip on the girls, leading them to the bathroom. Once inside, she helped them remove their coats and mittens. When each had had her turn using the toilet, both girls washed their hands, loving the feel of the warm water.

"I want to take a bath, Miss Grace. I'm as cold as a frog," Amanda announced.

Grace laughed. "Just how cold is a frog?" she asked the little girl.

"Real cold. Like a Popsicle."

Ashley looked at her little sister. "Mommy would tell you to mind your manners right about now."

"She would?"

"Yeah," Ashley said. "Miss Grace, you didn't talk to our mom, did you?"

Fearing Ashley would ask this but knowing there was no way around it, she simply told her the truth.

"And first thing in the morning, Mr. Jorgenson will take us to the van," Grace finished explaining.

"I bet Mommy is scared 'cause she always wants to know exactly where we're at," Amanda said.

Grace felt as though she'd been punched in the gut with an extra large fist. "I know she's worried, but right now there isn't any way to let her know we're okay, so let's just concentrate on getting through the night." She sounded lame even to herself.

Both girls watched her with fear in their eyes. "What if Daddy . . ."

"He doesn't know we're here. I think it might be a good idea if we didn't talk about your daddy for the rest of the night. Are you girls okay with that?" Grace didn't want their host asking any more questions than necessary.

Both girls nodded.

"Then let's see if Mr. Jorgenson has something to drink, then we'll rest," Grace said.

With both girls following at her heels, she relaxed. They were safe for the moment and accepted her decision without question.

If she could only remember where she'd seen Mr. Jorgenson before, then maybe *she* would feel safe.

Chapter Three

With the girls trailing behind her, Grace returned to the kitchen, surprised to find their host pouring boiling hot water into four red mugs. "I only have the instant stuff," he pointed out, indicating packages of instant cocoa mix next to the cups. "Milk spoils too fast."

"Thank you, Mr. Jorgenson. I appreciate your hospitality," Grace said. She opened four packs of the instant hot chocolate and added the contents to the cups of hot water. "This is just what the girls need, something to warm them up." Grace stirred the hot drinks, then called the girls to the kitchen. "Sit at the table, okay?" she suggested to the two.

"Can we give the dogs some?" Amanda asked

Grace, as Ashley helped her climb onto the chair.

"Never *ever* give chocolate to dogs! Are you crazy?" Max shouted from his position in front of the sink.

Instantaneously, both girls began to cry, their little faces masks of fear and horror. Grace hurried over to them. "Shhh, it's okay. Mr. Jorgenson didn't mean to yell"—Grace shot him a death look—"did you?" Her green eyes flared like sparkling emeralds.

"Uh, no. I didn't. It's just that anyone knows not to give chocolate to a dog."

"Not everyone, Mr. Jorgenson. Especially a five- and an eight-year old." If not for the worsening weather, Grace would've left the house immediately. The last thing the girls needed was an angry man yelling at them. That was what had brought them and their mother to Hope House in the first place. Of course, there were also the beatings, but Grace truly didn't believe their host would resort to that behavior.

Grudgingly, he said, "I'm sorry, okay?"

"I'm sure you are," Grace said to him, then to the girls, "Finish your drinks."

She wanted to shout at him, tell him exactly what these two innocent children had been through in their short lives, but it wasn't his business, and she never discussed her guests' private affairs with strangers, or anyone else who wasn't a member of her inner circle.

Grace used her sleeve to dry their tears. "It's

okay. Really. Let's go to our room, and I'll tell you a Christmas story." Again she eyed their host with a look that she hoped shamed him.

"What about the tree? Can I still pick out the decorations?" Ashley asked, all traces of fear gone from her big brown eyes.

"Of course. Now come on, let's get some sleep. Before you know it, morning will be here, and I want you both to get some rest. You'll need lots of energy, so you can decorate the tree."

The idea seemed to excite both girls, and for that Grace was extremely grateful. Max Jorgenson hadn't shown them where to sleep, so she took the initiative. "If you'll tell me where to find a room?"

Raking his hands through hair that Grace thought a bit on the long side, he nodded. "This way."

Taking their hands in her own, Grace followed Max up the stairs, looking at everything and anything while trying to avoid Max's rear view, plastered mere inches from her face.

A loft overlooked the downstairs. Shelves were lined with trophies, and covers of magazines were expertly framed and hung on the pine walls. In a built-in area that had special lights shining on its contents was an Olympic Gold Medal. It was then that Grace knew why she recognized Max.

"You're the skier," she stated to his back.

"Yep. That would be me," Max answered with more sarcasm than she thought necessary.

He stopped at the end of the hall to open a

door and turn on the lights. "A king-size bed. That should hold the three of you. There's the bathroom." He pointed to a door at the end of the huge room. Grace canvassed the large bedroom in one sweeping glance. What she saw took her breath away.

The room was the size of the entire downstairs at Hope House. Pine furniture that matched the logs throughout the house appeared to be custom-made since each piece occupied its designated location with absolute precision. Pictures of winter scenes hung on the rounded log walls. Briefly, Grace wondered how that was possible, but the physics of picture-hanging was the least of her concerns. On the large bed in the center of the room, a navy blue, maroon, and cream-colored quilt invited her to hunker down beneath its comfort for warmth. The bath was as large and extravagant as the rest of the house. A deep tub that would hold at least six people, windows that looked out into the blue-black snowy night. Grace could only imagine the view in the daylight. Navy and cream towels hung on warming rods. No expense had been spared when the house was constructed, of that she was sure.

Not wanting to appear impressed, Grace simply said, "This is very nice. Thank you."

Ushering the girls over to the bed, she was about to help them remove their dresses when Max spoke.

"I have some flannel shirts they can wear. They're warm." Without another word, he left, returning minutes later with three red, green, and white plaid flannel shirts. The colors of Christmas. Grace was sure it wasn't intentional as there were no decorations of any kind, or anything that she'd seen to indicate that her host celebrated the holiday season. To each his own. Personally, she couldn't imagine *not* decorating.

However, touched by his suggestion, she was too startled to offer any objection. "That's very kind of you, Mr. Jorgenson."

"Max. Mr. Jorgenson was my father," he said from his position at the doorway.

Surprised once again, Grace glanced at him, then recalled his earlier hostility and wondered what had caused the sudden change of heart. Probably realized he was stuck with them for the remainder of the night and was just trying to make the best of a bad situation. The man was like a faucet. Hot one minute and cold the next.

Staring at him, Grace spoke in low tones, hoping he'd take the bait. She needed some quiet time for her and the girls. They'd had enough excitement for one night. "Okay, then, Max it is."

He lingered in the doorway. Grace wanted him to leave, but something told her he had more to say before calling it a night. She continued to stare at him, while the girls each took a flannel shirt from her. "You can change in the bathroom," Grace said to the expectant girls.

"Why do they call you Miss Grace?"

Ah-ha! She wondered when he'd ask. "For

some reason they took to calling me that, and it stuck. Myself, I think it's just a matter of respect. They're good girls."

Max wrapped one jeans-clad leg in front of the other, hands crossing his massive chest. "Why Miss Grace? Is there something wrong with being called 'Mother'?"

Grace smiled, knowing where he was leading and determined to take him there via the long route.

"No, I don't think there is anything wrong with it at all. I couldn't imagine calling my own mother anything else."

He took two long strides, and suddenly he was in the room. Two feet in front of her. "Yet you won't allow your own children to address you as such?"

Grace took a deep breath, then offered a slight smile of defiance. "They're not my children." There, now he knew.

"I get it. They're your husband's," Max asked, a hint of annoyance overshadowing his handsome features.

Enjoying the verbal duel, Grace said, "I'm not married."

Max shook his head. "Look, lady, I'm tired. Either tell me what I want to know, or first thing in the morning, I'll have no choice but to contact the authorities. A lone woman out on a night like this. Two kids who don't belong to her. You tell me, what would you think if the situation were reversed?"

Grace realized he was right. She'd enjoyed toying with him for some odd reason, but to do so at the girls' expense was totally out of character for her. This man had allowed three complete strangers into his home. No matter how rude or inquisitive, it was wrong to let him think she was anyone other than herself.

Giving her a brutal, and very unfriendly stare, he raised his winged brow in question. "So?"

"I'm sorry. I shouldn't have led you to believe the girls belonged to me. They came to me, rather their mother came to me, for help. I gave them a place to stay. Tonight, I took the girls to see *The Nutcracker* at Eagle Valley High. I thought it would give them a chance to enjoy the Christmas season and offer their mom a much-needed respite. And then I encountered the roadblock on my way home. You know the rest of the story." Satisfied with her answer since she hadn't betrayed Stephanie's confidence, Grace waited for Max to say something. Anything. When several seconds passed, and he still hadn't spoken, she did.

"You look at me as though I've . . . committed a crime or something! What?" Grace asked, beyond flustered, not liking these feelings one little bit.

"I'm trying to decide if you have. Or not."

They stared at each other across the bed. His blue eyes darkened as he held her verdant gaze. Grace held his infuriating stare with an equally wicked one of her own. It was as though they were playing a game. Dueling eyes.

Max's stare wavered for a second. Watching him with a professional eye, Grace detected a glimmer of sadness behind his hard glare. Like a wave slamming against her, Grace surmised this man had known sorrow. A very deep and personal sorrow. Why hadn't she noticed it before? She didn't know. Maybe the fact that her carelessness had caused two little girls and their mother unnecessary worry? Blinded by her own stupidity. Pure and simple. There was no other explanation for her not seeing between the lines where this angry man was concerned.

Tearing her glance away from Max, Grace walked over to the bathroom and knocked on the door. "Are you girls finished in there?"

When she didn't get a reply, she knocked again. "Amanda? Ashley?"

Max was behind her now, concern etched on his face. "I have a key around here somewhere."

"I don't think the door is locked." Grace tried the knob. Sure enough, it turned in her hand. She stepped inside, fearful that something had happened to the pair. When she didn't see them, her heart skipped a beat. Then another.

"They're not in here!" she shouted to Max. "Is there a door . . . ?"

"This is the only way in or out."

"Ashley! Amanda!" Grace called. "This isn't funny."

A noise, something that sounded like a "shhh" came from the direction of the over-sized tub. Grace looked at Max, who'd come up behind her. She placed a finger to her lips.

He nodded. She walked over to the tub, where both girls were huddled, their arms wrapped tightly around each other.

"Amanda, Ashley," Grace stated softly as she stared down into twin sets of brown eyes.

"We got scared, Miss Grace," Ashley explained.

"It's okay, there's nothing to be afraid of," Grace coaxed.

"We're afraid of him," Amanda said, pointing a small finger at Max, who stood behind Grace.

Momentarily at a loss for words, Grace didn't know what to say. Both girls had been through so much. Max wasn't a friendly man at all; no wonder they were terrified of him.

With an air of exasperation, Max said, "Hey, I promise not to bite, okay?"

Grace thought he could've chosen his words better, could've softened his tone somewhat, but at least this was a start.

"See? Mr. Jorgenson isn't angry," Grace said, as both girls began their climb from the tub.

As innocent children often do, Amanda said the first thing that came to mind, "Then why doesn't he have a Christmas tree? You said all happy families have Christmas trees. Isn't Mr. Jorgenson happy? Does he have a family?" Amanda asked Grace.

Good questions, she thought, eyeing their host. "I'm afraid that's Mr. Jorgenson's personal business, sweetie. It's one of those questions that your mother wouldn't want you to ask."

"It is?" Amanda looked to her older sister for confirmation.

"I think so," Ashley said, sounding as unsure as Grace felt.

"Let's not worry about Mr. Jorgenson right now, girls. It's really, really late. At this rate we won't have much time to sleep before it'll be time to get up and go back to the van. Now, let's get you all snuggled up in this big comfy bed, and I'll tell you a Christmas story."

Both girls jumped on the bed and slid beneath the covers, eyeing Grace expectantly.

"Once upon a time . . ."

Chapter Four

Max stormed out of the room before the kid could pose any more nosy questions. He hadn't missed the questioning look from the woman. *Grace.* He'd be damned before he revealed his personal life to a total stranger. It was one thing to invite them into his home; he really hadn't had a choice. It didn't mean he had to get chummy with them. Though he admitted to himself, the girls were cute and seemed well behaved. But not his problem.

Downstairs in the den, Max aimed the remote at the giant plasma television. Nothing happened. He tried again, then concluded the satellite was out. That was nothing new, especially during a snowstorm.

When he'd purchased the land at the height of his career several years ago, he'd assumed that by the time he built a vacation home, not having cable TV, satellite TV, not to mention Internet service, would be something he'd never have to worry about. Of course, he'd built his so-called vacation home a lot sooner than he'd originally planned. Blow Out Hill was still as undeveloped as it had been two years ago, when he'd moved into the giant log home.

This was supposed to be his and Kayla's, and any children they'd had, home away from home, from the mansion in Denver that he'd practically given away after Kayla's death. When he had purchased the land, he'd envisioned teaching his kids to ski on Powder Rise, the mountain, albeit a small one, behind the house. Those were dreams, and nothing more.

All his hope for the future died when Kayla, a police officer, was shot and killed in the line of duty two years earlier on Christmas Eve. No more holiday celebrations for him; it was too painful. Memories gouged him like a sharp knife, each twisting deeper, the hurt lingering like a bad odor. Friends told him his grief would lessen, the hard, brittle edges softening with time. So far they'd been wrong. There wasn't a day that he didn't think of his and Kayla's life together, what could have been. Putting his memories aside for the moment, Max hurried into the kitchen.

Searching for the transistor radio and batteries he always kept for such an occasion, he found them in the kitchen drawer next to the Viking stove. Top-of-the-line. He'd bought the best appliances money could buy in memory of all the times he and Kayla had spent together on Sunday mornings making breakfast and whatever else Kayla decided. Now they just sat there like a silent reminder of all he'd lost.

Putting fresh batteries in the radio, Max tuned to a local station, searching for an updated weather report. When he found the station he usually listened to, he turned the volume up. The meteorologist's static-laced report filled the kitchen, then Max heard something about road-blocks, but the rest was bleeped out. No doubt the storm at work. He made a few adjustments to the dial again, and this time the reporter's voice was loud and clear:

"And it appears as though residents of Eagle, Colorado, and the surrounding areas will have a white Christmas after all. We're expecting more than three feet of snow before morning. A travel advisory is in effect until further notice . . ."

Max put the four empty mugs in the dishwasher, not liking the direction his thoughts were headed. If the report was accurate, and he had no reason to believe otherwise, his "house guests" could be there for a while.

"Damn!" he cursed out loud. Max wasn't prepared for a snowstorm. Hell, he'd be lucky if there was enough food in the house for *him* to get by on for a few days, let alone two children and another adult. He could kick himself for not planning ahead. He'd been taking care of himself for a very long time now without giving a thought to another human being. The way he figured it, his lack of preparation was justified as far as he was concerned. Then he remembered the freezer in the shed. Maybe someone had remembered to fill it.

Soft footsteps startled him from his thoughts. He wasn't used to anyone in his house other than himself and the two Huskies, who were curled up on the leather sofa he'd vacated earlier.

"I just wanted to thank you again for putting us up. It was stupid of me to take the girls out on a night like this," Grace said.

Max wanted to agree, but in all fairness he couldn't. If she were telling the truth, and he had a gut feeling she was, there was nothing wrong with her taking two children to see a Christmas ballet. Rotten luck had placed her in the wrong place at the wrong time.

He looked at Grace, *really* looked at her. She was tall for a woman, a bit on the thin side. Milky white skin made him think of the clichéd term "peaches-and-cream complexion." Long black hair reached the middle of her back. Her eyes were an unusual shade of green, reminding him of the wild grass that grew alongside the mountain in the summer, their color so bold. He wondered if they were contacts, but something told him everything about this woman was real, even though she'd been evasive with information about herself. Really, he didn't blame her. She didn't know him any better than he knew her. Add to the equation she had two little girls with her, alone on a mountain with a strange man. He wouldn't be quick to offer information either if he were in her shoes.

Max waved his hand in the air. "Not a problem." It was, but he wouldn't tell her that. He figured he'd been rude enough already. Resigned to the loss of privacy for the next few days, Max decided he'd better inform Grace just how unprepared he was.

"The weather report doesn't look good." He nodded toward the radio on the countertop. "They're saying three feet of snow before daybreak."

Grace stepped into the kitchen. "I have to get out of here at first light. Stephanie will be sick with worry!" Grace eyed the phone. "It's still not working?"

He took the phone off its stand, punched a button. "Nothing. Phone's always the first to go and the last to be repaired. People around here are more concerned with the roads."

"If they clear the roads so quickly, then my getting back to the van shouldn't be a problem," Grace stated flatly. The thought of staying under the same roof with their host for more than a night sent a shiver of alarm down her spine.

"The roads will be cleared as soon as it's safe. Eagle County is well prepared for winter storms. They'll start with the main roads first. Blow Out Hill is always last on their list."

"I take it there's no other way off the mountain?"

"Some of the local pilots keep their planes

in the hangar over at Eagle County Regional Airport. They won't come out unless it's a true emergency. Life or death. Especially in this weather. So to answer your question, there is no way off the mountain other than by foot. I don't think you want to risk taking those two kids outdoors in three feet of snow. Even if this were a true emergency, I wouldn't be able to contact the airport."

Contemplating her circumstances, Grace took a deep breath. As much as she hated the idea of being stuck here with a man she didn't particularly care for, she realized she had to stay put. With any luck, a police officer would run across her van and remember they'd stopped her. *Maybe*, and it was a big *maybe,* one of the officers would run her plates and remember her. Someone had to figure out who she was and contact Hope House.

She said a silent prayer that her mother had decided to spend Christmas with her this year instead of staying home in Denver. She knew she would offer comfort to Stephanie until they discovered Grace's whereabouts.

Bryce, her younger brother, was due to arrive Christmas Eve. This year would be the first time her entire family would spend Christmas together at Hope House. Since its opening, Grace had always stayed at Hope House during the holidays if there were guests. She missed her mother and brother, but they both understood her need to make the women and their children feel as comfortable as possible. In some cases, a few of the women-only Christmas celebrations had been at Hope House. She prayed Stephanie would stay put until she could get word to her that the girls were fine and not in danger. Or at least not in any danger from the man that they'd been running from when they'd been brought to her doorstep by a police officer. Husband and father. It made her cringe just thinking of what the women at Hope House had gone through before they arrived. She was committed to doing whatever was humanly possible to assist them in turning their lives around. Being stuck on a mountain was simply a bump in the road compared to what they'd been through.

Lost in thought, Grace was about to sneak a quick glance at her host when everything went black.

"It never fails," Max said in the darkness. "I've got flashlights and candles somewhere in here."

Grace heard him opening and closing drawers. Rummaging through a few, he found what he was looking for when a thin beam of light illuminated the small space between them. "I've got a generator in the shed out back."

"That'll help," Grace said as she inched her way to the kitchen table.

"Yeah. I've never used it. Never had a reason to."

Grace wanted to ask what he normally did when the power went out, but she heard his heavy footsteps bounding up the stairs before she could get the words out of her mouth. Instead, she ran a hand along the countertop

until she found a small box of matches beside
a box of candles. She lit one, then another,
placing both candles bottom side down on the
counter while she searched for something to
use as a holder. Searching the cabinets, she
found a rock glass that would serve her purpose.
Putting the candles in the glass, she headed toward the stairs to check on the girls when a gust
of icy air blew in from an open door, extin-
guishing her light.

She heard a door slam. Grace called out
into the darkness, "Max?"

When she didn't receive a response, she
called again. She heard the apprehension in her
voice when she spoke. "Max, is that you? I . . .
never mind." Wishing she'd brought the box of
matches along for such an emergency, Grace
inched her way back to the kitchen. *Maybe Max
hadn't heard her*, she thought as she skimmed
the surface of the countertop searching for
the matches. When her fingers brushed
against the small box, she grabbed it like a life-
line. Striking two matches at once, she relit the
candles, and was relieved when the room flick-
ered with their soft golden light. Tucking the
matches in her pocket, Grace went back in the
direction of the stairs when she heard a noise.
Something creaked, like hinges on a door.

"Max? I don't think this is funny."

She stopped in the center of the den, waiting for a sarcastic comeback. Getting no reply,
she yelled, "Max" so loud she was sure she'd
wake the girls. Feet rooted to the floor, heart
rate accelerating, Grace felt perspiration dot

her forehead even though the room was chilled from the burst of cold air.

Becoming increasingly uneasy as the seconds ticked away, Grace tried another strategy. Using a stern voice usually reserved for the fearful women she dealt with, she called out, "Mr. Jorgenson? Max? If this is some kind of game, I don't want to play."

Standing still, she heard the floorboards above her creaking. No doubt her shouting had awakened the girls. Putting her anxiety aside, she carefully made her way up the unfamiliar staircase. When she reached the top, she raced to the master suite to check on Amanda and Ashley.

She remembered leaving the door open when she'd left the room earlier. Now it was closed. Maybe the gust of air from the door's opening downstairs had somehow caused it to close. Telling herself this must be what happened, she turned the knob, careful not to make too much noise in case the girls were still sleeping. Pushing the heavy log door aside, she stepped into the large bedroom.

Holding the candles in front of her as she tiptoed over to the king-size bed, Grace leaned across the wide expanse to make sure the girls were covered. When her hands continued to feel nothing but cool, smooth sheets, she knew something had gone terribly awry.

Because both girls were missing.

Chapter Five

"Amanda? Ashley?" Grace called out into the darkened room. Remembering their fear of the dark, she tried another tactic, hoping to calm their fears. "The power went out. Max is fixing it now." She hoped. He didn't seem to know his way around his own home.

When she received no response, she tried again. "Girls, this is one of those times that your mother would want you to show yourselves. There's nothing to be afraid of."

Slowly, so as not to startle the girls, Grace entered the bathroom. Just as she'd expected, both girls were huddled in the tub. She lowered the candle so they could see that it was her. The damage their father's cruelty had inflicted upon them infuriated her.

"We got scared when the lights went off.

Then we heard pounding on the steps. Mommy always told us to hide and cover our ears when Daddy got mad," Ashley said in her defense.

"Oh, sweetie, your daddy isn't here. The noise you heard was Max. He had to race upstairs for his warm clothes before he went outside to the shed. There's nothing to be frightened of." Grace held a hand out to assist the little girls as they climbed out of the bathtub.

"Miss Grace, could you tell us another Christmas story?" Amanda asked.

After leading them back to the bed and making sure both were warm and snug beneath the quilt, Grace eased in next to them. "Absolutely."

Ten minutes later, and a condensed version of *A Christmas Carol* minus the ghosts of Christmases past, present, and future, both girls were sound asleep. Grace quietly slid off the bed and went downstairs. Surely Max had had enough time to find the generator.

With the flame of the candle as her guide, Grace went from room to room in search of him. "Max?" she whispered loudly, but not so loud that she would wake the kids.

She searched downstairs and was about to give up when she felt a burst of cold air enter the room. "Max? Is that you?" she called.

"Yeah. I couldn't find the darned generator. I was sure Eddie put it in the shed," Max said.

When Grace heard him, relief flooded through her. "I have to admit I was getting a bit concerned."

"Why?" Max asked as he dropped a large bag on the floor.

She could've kicked herself for telling him that, but it was too late now. "You were gone a long time." Grace approached him as he entered the den.

Max slung off his worn leather jacket, tossing it on the back of the sofa, where both dogs slept peacefully. "There's a freezer out there. Loss of power won't affect it since the temp's below freezing. I figured I'd better scope out its contents since we're going to be stuck here for a while. It's stocked with everything we'll need though I haven't a clue who took the time to bother with it." Probably Eddie. The man thought of everything. He was due for a raise this month. And a paid vacation, too.

Grace eyed the large bag on the floor. "If you'll bring that to the kitchen, I'll put everything away."

"Sure," said Max gruffly, hoisting the heavy bag over his shoulder.

Grace laughed.

"You find this amusing?"

"No, not at all. You just reminded me of Santa Claus."

Max stopped in his tracks, dropped the bag and turned around to stare at her. Though the only light came from the candle, Grace saw the anger in his eyes. Cold and stark, like the harsh winter storm outside.

Between gritted teeth, he said, "Don't ever say that to me again!"

Grace had had enough. She didn't know what had happened to turn this man into such . . . a Scrooge, and she really didn't care. She was simply trying to make a joke.

"Look, Max. Whatever issues you have, they're not with me. If you can't take a little joke, you've got big problems. Might want to see someone, a professional. It could help," Grace said, then dragged the heavy bag the rest of the way to the kitchen.

"Wait! You can't talk to me like that! Who in the heck do you think you are? This is my house. You're the guest," Max ranted as he followed her to the kitchen.

"Yes I am, and you're the rudest host I've had the misfortune to encounter. If it's any consolation, I don't want to be here any more than you want me here. I'm an adult, I will make the best of it." She wanted to add, "Unlike you," but that would have lowered her to his level.

He raked a hand through his hair. On another man it might've been just an ordinary action. On him it was just . . . well, she wouldn't admit it to anyone, but it was rather sexy.

"Look, I don't like the holidays. Can we just leave it at that?" Max yanked the heavy bag off the floor and placed it on the counter.

Grace was right. He *was* a Scrooge! Biting her lip to keep from smiling, she announced, "What you like or don't like is no concern of mine. At daybreak, I just want to get to my van. I'm not really concerned with anything else at the moment." Of course, she was, but her concerns were none of his business. Unlike him,

Grace wasn't about to voice her likes and dislikes. Certainly she wasn't going to tell Max how Christmas was her favorite time of the year and how she detested those who spoiled it for others.

She wouldn't tell him that she'd already spent days in the kitchen baking cookies, cakes, and pies for several of the soup kitchens in Denver. And she wouldn't tell him how much money she had spent on gifts for Stephanie and her girls. What kind of person didn't like Christmas? Maybe he'd had a rough time as a child. Those incidents had a way of haunting one, even as an adult. As a professional she knew that. As a woman, she couldn't imagine being with a man who didn't celebrate and enjoy the Christmas season as much as she did. Christmas was the highlight of the year for her family.

Max peered out the kitchen window. "I don't think you're going anywhere come morning. Look." He gestured at the window.

Reluctantly, Grace went over to the window and stood beside him. She couldn't help but notice the smell of winter and pine emanating from his skin. She breathed deeply, closing her eyes for a moment, wondering, then jerked her eyes open. The cold was getting to her. She glanced outside. Snowdrifts were at least three feet high. Big fluffy flakes of snow swirled through the inky night sky like miniature fairies with wings as light as a spider's web.

"I suppose a snowplow would be too much to hope for," Grace observed as she turned away from the window. Another time this might amuse her. However, with two girls whose mother was probably frantic with worry, she was anything but.

"Yep, it would be. Like I said, I'm not very prepared for this. I came here to . . ." He paused. Grace waited for him to finish, but he didn't.

"Whatever your reason, I, for one, am glad I found you," Grace added, hoping a compliment of sorts might draw him out of the black mood that seemed to hover over him.

Max removed the contents of the bag, placing them on the counter. "I'm not much of a cook other than bacon and eggs. You might want to see if there's something here you and the girls would like."

Grace was about to tell him bacon and eggs were fine with her, then thought better of it when she realized that, without power, they wouldn't be able to cook anything.

"I'm going to get the fireplaces going. There's more wood in the shed," Max said, before wandering outside again. At least he'd had the foresight to see to the wood supply. Or someone had.

She wondered if Max was incapable of taking care of his own needs. She knew his reputation on the slopes. Ski or die. She remembered Bryce telling her this during the Winter Olympics years ago. Why would she remember that now? Bryce was in high school then. Grace calculated it'd been at least twelve or fifteen years ago.

She could cook using an open fire. Searching through the food supply, she found several packages of meat. Bacon, a whole chicken, a roast, and a package of hot dogs. The latter might come in handy for a weenie-roast for the girls she thought as she proceeded to check the food supply. There were bags of frozen vegetables. Carrots, potatoes, peas, and there was even a container of frozen chicken stock. Loaves of French bread, white bread, and wheat bread. Peanut butter. Someone had known what they were doing when they'd stocked Max's freezer. In the cupboard she saw at least a dozen cans of soup, two boxes of saltines, and jars of strawberry jam and grape jelly. Max *was* prepared for a storm whether he realized it or not. Grace made fast work of storing the breads and peanut butter in a cabinet. Since it was below freezing outside, she repacked the meats and vegetables, placing them back in the bag before taking them to the front porch. She hoped there weren't any coyotes or bears in search of their next meal. If so, they were all in trouble.

Hurrying back inside, she observed Max as he placed more logs on the fire. Bright yellow flames shot up the flue, sending tiny red sparks shimmering everywhere. The woodsy smell reminded her of her father. He'd always kept a fire burning in the winter. They'd popped corn and made what her father referred to as hobo packs. Aluminum foil filled with ground meat, potatoes, and whatever vegetable they wanted. They'd toss them in the fire, then they'd finish off their campfire meal with either s'mores or toasted marshmallows. *One of Dad's burnt marshmallows would taste good,* she thought as she watched Max from a distance. She hoped he knew what he was doing. According to Bryce and those trophies and medals she'd seen upstairs, his expertise seemed strictly limited to the slopes. Briefly, she wondered what skills he brought into the bedroom.

What is wrong with me? she thought as she watched Max. It hadn't been that long since she'd had a date!

"Like what you see?" Max asked.

Grace was sure he referred to the roaring fire. "Yes, it's perfect. And I think it's time we went to bed. I'm beyond tired. I doubt the girls will sleep late. Kids their age never do."

"You seem to have a lot of experience with kids for a woman who doesn't have any of her own," Max observed.

Grace wasn't sure if this was an invitation to reveal more about herself or just his way of making polite conversation. Something told her she could trust him even though he'd been rude and had frightened the girls. She recalled the look of pain etched on his face. He had suffered in his life. And not just physical injuries from his profession. He'd walked through the fires of hell. Grace wasn't sure if he'd completely returned.

"Why are you looking at me like that?" Max asked.

"I'm sorry. Professional habit I guess."

"So you stare at people for a living? You an

artist or what?" he inquired with a trace of humor.

Grace took a deep breath, unsure of how much she should reveal to him. While her gut told her she could trust him, she had to consider the safety of the girls and their mother before she revealed too much about herself. Not wanting to lie or reveal any details about Stephanie and the girls, Grace opted for a simple version of the truth. "I'm a counselor."

"I see. So"—he took the fire poker from its stand and pushed several logs aside before adding more—"in your professional opinion, exactly what did you see when you were staring at me?" He waved a hand in the air. "Never mind. Don't answer that. I'm sure you see what everyone else sees. A burnout who's screwed up his life and doesn't care."

Grace couldn't have been more shocked by his words. "Actually, I saw nothing like that at all." She could tell him the truth, there was no reason not to. "I see someone who's been hurt by . . . a tragedy." She paused catching his eye. "You've suffered a personal loss so . . . consuming that it's taken over the person you used to be." Grace waited for a response, a reply, anything. He perched on the hearth, shaking his head.

"Well, you're wrong, lady. I'm the man I've always been. Nothing will ever change that. Trust me. I like to drink and sleep. Nothing more." Max hesitated for a moment as though he was testing her reaction. "A real prize, huh?"

Taking a chance Grace replied, "I think you were a real prize, Max Jorgenson, at one time. Whatever happened to strip away your self-confidence, it's still there. You have to want it back."

He looked at her for several minutes, a tense silence filling the space between them.

"Yeah? Well, you're wrong. I don't ever want to be the man I was. Never." He looked down at the pine floors. "Never," he added in a low, husky voice.

Grace wanted to say, "Never say never," but it wasn't the right time. With this man, she wasn't so sure there would ever be a *right* time.

Putting concerns about her host's mental status on the back burner for the remainder of the night, she told him good night and went upstairs. As soon as her head hit the soft down pillow, she fell into a deep, dreamless sleep.

Chapter Six

Blinding sunlight filled the bedroom, casting a burnished glow across the pine furniture. Grace sat up quickly when she realized she wasn't in her room at Hope House. Then it all came back. The roadblocks and the loss of communication with the world.

She looked at the girls next to her. They slept like babies. Careful not to wake them, she pushed her hands down on the mattress in order to ease off the bed without either child feeling the movement.

Grace used the bathroom, splashed cold water on her face, and rinsed her mouth, using mouthwash she found in the medicine cabinet. Taking a comb from her purse, she ran it through her long hair and secured it with an elastic band. Checking to make sure both Ash-

ley and Amanda still slept, she quietly made
her way downstairs to the kitchen.

She stopped at the foot of the stairs, surprised when she saw Max in the kitchen. Grace
felt a tingle trail up her spine as she observed
him. He wore a fresh pair of faded jeans with a
tight black T-shirt. Chest muscles pulled the
fabric so taut that Grace laughingly thought
how lucky his T-shirt was. She took a deep
breath. He was certainly something to look at,
but most skiers were. She remembered going
to the slopes as a teen, then later during college breaks. All the cool guys, the ones that
really knew their way around the mountains,
were hot and handsome. She'd never bothered with the type simply because those she'd
met were either so conceited it was pathetic, or
they didn't have an intelligent thought in their
heads. She figured Max Jorgenson must be a
combination of both because most men living
on a mountain in the middle of nowhere planned
ahead. The thought hit her then; maybe Max
really *didn't* care about his future.

The aromatic scent of coffee pulled her
away from her musing and into the kitchen.
Max poured boiling water from a pot into a
European coffee press. "That smells divine,"
Grace said upon entering the kitchen. Surprised that he owned such a simple yet sophisticated coffee press, she waited as he pushed
the press, slowly sending the dark brown liquid
to the bottom of the clear carafe.

"Almost finished," Max said with a look of

satisfaction on his face. He removed a small cup from the cabinet, filled it, then placed it on the counter. "I have sugar but . . . wait. Here's powdered cream," he said as he rummaged through the cabinets. "I didn't know I had this stuff."

Max dumped the powder and several spoons of sugar in his coffee. Grace smiled. She'd thought for sure he would take his java straight up.

"Thanks," she said, sipping her coffee. "Black is fine. This is good stuff."

"What? You didn't think me capable of making a decent pot of coffee?" Max said in a teasing tone. Both Huskies ran into the kitchen, barking.

"Down, boys," Max managed to say. Ice-D and Cliff hunkered beneath the kitchen table, apparently waiting for their breakfast.

"Truly, I hadn't given it much thought." She eyed the telephone. "Are the phones working yet?"

"Nope. Just checked. I did hear snowplows about an hour ago. That's a good sign."

"How so?" Grace asked, suddenly hopeful.

"Usually that means they'll head this way. I'm thinking about taking one of the snowmobiles down the mountain to check. While I'm there, I'll try to locate your van."

Grace was filled with an overwhelming desire to wrap her arms around her rude host but stopped herself just in time. "Miracles do happen!"

"You think this is a miracle?" he asked, shaking his head, his damp blond curls reaching just below the collar of his shirt.

"You said yourself it could be days before the plows head up the mountain, so I guess this is a miracle. Of sorts. I do know Stephanie, that's the girls' mother, is probably insane with worry. I wish . . . if you can't get the van here, do you think you or possibly a member of the road crew could call her just to let her know the girls are safe and that we'll be home soon."

"I'll see what I can do," Max replied.

Grace took another sip of her coffee. "I can make breakfast before you leave. I'm sure the girls will want something when they wake up. I can't believe they're still sleeping. Poor things. No doubt last night's hike tuckered them out."

Max seemed to hesitate. "Breakfast would be good. I haven't had a home-cooked meal since . . ." He paused as though he'd lost his train of thought. "Forever. Breakfast sounds good. Thank you."

Miracles of all miracles! The man said thank you. "Better wait 'till you're finished before you thank me. It's been a while since I've cooked over an open fire. As a kid I used to love it. My dad would often cook in the fireplace during the winter. He called it 'campfire night.' Which basically meant Mom needed a break from the kitchen." The memory brought a wry, twisted smile to her face.

Max grinned. Grace realized it was the first real smile she'd seen since arriving on his doorstep. His teeth were as bright as the snowcapped mountains. "Campfire night? Never heard of that."

She explained, "Dad would take ground meat, potatoes, and whatever vegetable Mom had too much of, then he'd wrap the food in aluminum foil and toss it in the fireplace. Sometimes we'd do s'mores or popcorn for dessert. It became a family tradition of sorts. Dad built the fire, and we helped prepare the hobo packs. Maybe for lunch . . . if we're still here," Grace suggested. "Breakfast first though," she finished.

Max looked at her as though he were contemplating a private memory, his face sobering with whatever thought swirled through his head. "I'd better get out of here before the road crew decides to leave. Breakfast is highly overrated anyway. Come on, guys, let's go outside." Both dogs leapt to their feet and raced to the door.

"But I thought . . ." Grace floundered.

"Yeah, I'm sorry. Take care of your girls. I'll be back as soon as I check the roads. I'll need that phone number."

For a second Grace almost forgot she was stuck in the middle of nowhere with a man she wasn't sure she even *liked*, plus two little girls whose mother must be frantic with worry. Mentally shaking herself, she focused on the here and now.

Flustered, she looked around for something to write on. "Is there a pen and paper?"

Max retrieved a pad and pencil from the kitchen drawer and gave it to her. She scribbled out the number with Stephanie's name. As an afterthought she also added her mother's cell-phone number. Who knew? They could be out looking for her right that very minute. Grace didn't want to miss her one chance to let them know they weren't in any danger. Well, the girls weren't in any immediate danger, but she could be if she didn't stop thinking about Max Jorgenson's personal life and how it might mesh with her own.

"Miss Grace! Miss Grace!" both girls called in unison as they ran down the stairs. "Can we build a snowman? Look at all the snow outside!"

Grace glanced at Max, giving him an, *Oh boy, this is where I could get into trouble* look.

"I don't know. We don't have the proper clothes, remember how cold it is. I was about to make breakfast in the fireplace. How about you two give me a hand? I bet I can find some Christmas music for us to listen to while we're cooking. How does that sound?" Grace asked, adding an extra dollop of cheer to her voice.

"Okay," Amanda said. "But I would really, *really* rather build a snowman than cook. Just so you know."

Grace burst out laughing. She was shocked when she heard Max's slight laugh. She didn't think he had it in him. Wrong again.

"I'll try to remember that, kiddo. Now why don't the pair of you run upstairs and get dressed. I'll need your help in a few minutes."

The girls raced upstairs, shrieking and laughing. Grace was thrilled to hear their childish

gibberish because she knew it was a sign that
they would eventually be fine despite the trau-
matic home life they'd only recently escaped.
Kids bounced back quickly after tragedy struck.
Too bad some of their lightheartedness couldn't
rub off on Max. Permanently.

Out of the corner of her eye, she saw him
grab her keys where she'd left them, turn, and
head for the front door, allowing the dogs to
come inside after a quick but brisk run.

"Be careful," she called out to his silhou-
ette, framed in the sunlight. She watched him
walk down the steps she'd used just hours ago.

Max Jorgenson was a loner, a wounded man
who obviously wanted nothing more than to
live his life here on this mountain in the middle of nowhere, undisturbed. So why did she
feel the urge to count the minutes until he returned? Why did she feel as if a humming-
bird's wings fluttered against her rib cage when
she looked at him? Telling herself it was nothing more than middle-aged lust, she stepped
outside and removed a slab of bacon from the
bag she'd placed there earlier that morning.

Grace couldn't have predicted the last twelve
hours if her life had depended on it. Reliable,
steady, sure of herself, she remained cool-
headed and in control of almost any situation
she found herself in. Now she found her
thoughts wandering and was having trouble fo-
cusing. The past few hours had been almost
surreal. She'd never been in a situation where
she'd felt so totally out of control. Until now.
Saying a silent prayer that Max or someone

would contact Stephanie, Grace returned to the kitchen to make breakfast.

Locating a radio station playing Christmas carols, she searched through the cupboards until she found a well-used iron skillet, which surprised her. Must be what he used for his bacon and eggs. Using a fork to pry the frozen bacon apart, she lined the frying pan with several slices. She found a cookie sheet and brought it over to the fireplace. Having placed the baking sheet on the logs, she waited until she could see that it was steady, then set the skillet on top. Within minutes the scent of bacon frying permeated the room. Grace realized she was hungry. "Girls," she called up the stairs, "I need your help." She didn't really, but wanted to include them hoping it would take their minds off venturing outside in the freezing cold.

"Here we are! We don't have a toothbrush, Miss Grace. Mommy tells us to brush our teeth first thing in the morning. And nighttime, too. But we can't without a toothbrush. Do you think our teeth will fall out?" Amanda asked in one giant breath.

"No, I think you'll be just fine. When we finish breakfast, we'll clean our teeth with a washcloth and baking soda if we can't find any toothpaste. That should do until we get you two home."

"No! We can't go home, Miss Grace! Mommy said Daddy might really hurt her bad next time," Ashley explained, as tears filled her brown eyes.

"Oh, honey, I meant back to Hope House."

Grace steadied the skillet before standing up and taking the two girls in her arms. "Listen up. As long as you're with me, I promise you'll both be safe. Max is going to try to call your mother and tell her you're okay. As soon as I'm able to get to the van, we'll leave. Deal?" she asked.

"And we can still decorate the Christmas tree, right? Ashley says it's only five more days till Christmas. Is that true?" Amanda asked, changing the subject so fast Grace had to pause to count the number of days in her head.

"Yes, that's right. Five more days, and Santa will be here." Grace still had gifts to buy, plus a tree to decorate. She hoped to be off the mountain in time to get everything ready before Bryce arrived Christmas Eve.

Amanda started to cry hard. Giant tears spattered on her dress. She hiccoughed a few times before she could talk. "But . . . we . . . won't . . . be . . . home. How . . . will . . . Santa . . . know . . . where . . . to . . . find . . . us?"

"He'll find us, won't he, Miss Grace? Mommy says he always finds little children. Right?" Ashley asked.

Some parents didn't believe that instilling a false image of Santa was healthy. She'd seen it more than once when she was in practice. Grace was all about honesty, but in this case she couldn't come up with one reason, professional or personal, why a child shouldn't be indulged in such a fantasy. She'd believed in Santa Claus until she was twelve and remembered the disappointment when she'd learned the truth. But as her mother and father always told her, *Santa Claus is alive and well. He just moves to your heart when you're older.*

"Absolutely! He'll find you both I'm sure. Now, if I don't get some help, I'm going to burn breakfast."

She removed the skillet from the fire and took it to the kitchen. In minutes, she and the girls were seated at the table, munching on crispy bacon and soft white bread slathered with strawberry jam. With both dogs acting as guards around the table, Grace laughed, watching as Ice-D and Cliff inhaled every morsel that fell to the floor.

Grace couldn't remember the last time she'd enjoyed breakfast as much.

Chapter Seven

Max blasted down the mountain like a stick of dynamite. Slivers of ice zoomed past his head as he plowed through a snowbank. He couldn't put sufficient distance between himself and Grace fast enough. He wanted her out of his house. And the kids, too.

Emotions he'd put on ice long ago were starting to thaw. He knew what that meant but didn't want to acknowledge it, telling himself it was too soon. He'd felt guilty the moment he laid eyes on her. All thoughts of bachelorhood, the promises he'd made to himself would be null and void if she remained in the picture. Good thing she was just passing through.

He was halfway down Blow Out Hill when he spied Eddie's shiny black Hummer parked next to a county snowplow. Thinking there could've been an accident at Maximum Glide, he twisted the throttle to wide open and the snowmobile skyrocketed recklessly to the bottom of the hill. He braked quickly, sending a shower of freshly packed snow shooting through the air like a blaze of fireworks.

He shut the engine off, leaving the keys in the ignition. He saw Eddie talking to a group of men gathered around the Hummer. Max shook his head. The man adored his ride, never missing an opportunity to pay tribute to the vehicle's superiority over other four-wheel-drive transport.

Eddie saw him and waved. "What brings Muhammad down from the mountain in this kind of weather?"

Max gave a short laugh. "You wouldn't believe me if I told you. Everything okay at Maximum Glide?" He wanted to tell Eddie three snow angels on a mission appeared on his doorstep last night, but thought that a bit too drastic even for Eddie. "A woman broke down somewhere around here late last night. Has a couple of kids with her and needs to get word to her family that they're okay. You see any gray vans on the side of the road?"

"Place runs smooth as silk, thanks to me. Funny you should ask about the van. We"—he nodded to the group of men gathered behind him—"were just discussing whose turn it was for the next tow."

"Don't bother. I'm here for the van. Think it'll make it up the mountain?" Max asked, assured Eddie would know.

"It's front-wheel drive. It should. Want me to follow you in the Hummer, just in case?" he asked.

Max thought about it for a minute. "No, I think I can make it. You got your cell phone? I need to make a call."

Eddie whipped his iPhone out of his jacket pocket. "Never leave home without it."

Max took the scrap of paper from his pocket, eyeing the small, neat numbers. He could've sworn he smelled night-blooming jasmine wafting off the slip of paper. Shaking his head to clear it, he touched the numbers on the phone's silent pad. Max would never get used to technology. This reminded him of something right out of *Star Wars*.

The phone rang twice before someone answered. "Hope House. This is Juanita."

Hope House? Juanita?

"I'm calling for someone named Grace," he said.

"Do you want to speak to her?"

"No, no. She wanted me to call and let someone know that she and the . . . girls were okay. She got lost last night on her way home from a play. The snowstorm, she couldn't see to drive."

"Thank God!" the woman said. "Where is she now? I'll send Bryce after her. He arrived early this morning. He was so anxious to spend Christmas with her this year, he couldn't wait until Christmas Eve."

Max heard Juanita whispering to someone else. Most likely it was the girls' mother. "Hello?

Who is this? Where are my children?" Another woman. The mother. Right on the money.

"I . . . Grace wanted me to call you and let you know they're safe." Why did he say that? Of course they were safe. Why wouldn't they be? "I'm on my way to get her van now. Your girls are at my house with her. They were making breakfast when I left."

"Oh, I can't thank you enough! I was sure Glenn had escaped somehow. When will you be bringing them back to Hope House?" the woman he now knew was Stephanie asked.

"She'll be there as soon as the weather permits. She just wanted me to call. My phone lines are down. She said her cell-phone battery died."

Max heard an intake of breath.

"Miss Grace would never allow her battery to die! That's one of the first things she tells us when she issues our phones. Are you sure she's all right? What did you say your name was?"

Issues our phones? Hope House? Why did that name sound familiar to him?

"My name is Max, and I assure you, *Miss Grace* was fine when I left her. As soon as she's able to travel, she'll be home. Tell Bryce not to be in such a hurry next time." Max hung up the phone.

"Catch." He tossed the cell phone back to Eddie.

"Easy, buddy, those things aren't cheap. What got you so riled up? You look like you've just swallowed a spoon of vinegar. No, make that a glass. What gives?"

Bryce. What kind of name is that?

"Nothing, just point me in the right direction so I can get the woman's van to her before *Bryce* has a . . . hissy fit."

"Well, well. I'll be a monkey's uncle! It's about time, don't you think? I do believe Mr. Jorgenson is jealous!" Eddie roared with laughter.

"Look, Eddie, cut the crap. This woman is stranded at my place with two kids. I want her out of there as soon as possible. Just tell me where her van is, and I'll be on my way."

"Don't get all whiney on me, man. Look, I'll drive you to her van. I was about to leave anyway. We've got a group of ten-year-olds on the black diamonds today. I want to stay close by, just in case."

"Thanks, Eddie." And when had ten-year-olds started skiing on black-diamond slopes? He'd been at least thirteen before he even dared to ski on such challenging terrain, but when he did, as they say, the rest is history. Three years later he was on the U.S. Ski Team preparing for Olympic tryouts. He didn't make it that year, but four years later he made Olympic history in Albertville, France, in 1992, when he won all the events in the Alpine competitions. He had five Olympic Gold Medals for his performance on the slopes. After the Olympics, he'd made millions off endorsements. He'd invested most of his earnings, so when he was ready to settle down, money hadn't been an issue.

He'd met Kayla while sitting next to her on

the ski lift at Maximum Glide. She was there with a group of female police officers from all across the state. She wasn't like all the other women he'd dated, who wanted nothing more than to be seen with him in hopes their names would wind up on the front page of whatever rag made it their mission to catch "Colorado's most eligible bachelor" doing something he shouldn't. That lifestyle got old after a while. When he met Kayla, he was older, wiser, and ready to settle down. Their marriage was nice, easygoing. Max had begged her to quit her job, but she'd refused, telling him that her father and his father were police officers. She said it was in her blood. Feeling the same way about his skiing career, even though his father hadn't expressed an interest in skiing, Max never asked her to give up her job again. If only he'd been more persistent, Kayla might still be alive. And they would've had a son or a daughter, as Kayla had just learned she was three months' pregnant the week before she was killed.

If only. There were so many ifs.

"That's it," Eddie said, pointing to a gray Dodge van. "I assume she gave you the keys?"

"No, she didn't. I took them this morning. Smart thinking, huh?" Max asked.

"Smart-*ass* if you ask me," Eddie said dryly.

"I didn't," Max commented.

"Want me to hang around to make sure she starts?"

"That might be a good idea," Max said, then

went over to the nondescript van, inserted the key in the lock, and opened the driver's side door. He put the key in the ignition, and the van started up on the first try. "It's running," he shouted to Eddie. "Thanks, man. I owe you."

Eddie stuck his hand in the air and waved before pulling back onto the road. Max saluted him as he passed.

Thankful for the front-wheel drive, Max drove the van up the mountain in record time as the roads were all clear. More snow was expected later, but if he were lucky, Grace would be long gone before it hit.

Something about his conversation with the girls' mother struck him just then. Just exactly who was Glenn and where had he *escaped* from? Max was positive the woman had used that word.

"Escape."

Could it be possible this Glenn had *escaped* from jail or prison? And was it possible his *escape* was the reason for the roadblocks? The more Max thought about it, the more he knew he was right. He'd lived in the area most of his life. The only time he'd witnessed a roadblock was on I-70 when there was a possible avalanche threat, or bad weather closed the pass.

Stepping on the accelerator, Max wasted no time plowing up the long drive to his cabin. If he were right, and this man Glenn had escaped, Grace and those two kids could be in grave danger. How or why he knew this, he didn't know. He did know that if it was in his power to prevent another woman from dying at the hands of another human being, he would do so, no questions asked.

Racing up the steps to the cabin, Max yanked the door aside, unprepared for what greeted him.

Grace and the two girls were in the den, with Ice-D and Cliff flanking a small bearded man wearing the typical orange jail uniform. Both dogs were in attack mode, waiting for his command.

"Are you all right?" he asked Grace as he scanned the room.

She nodded, and that was when Max realized her hands were tied behind her back. Both girls were sitting next to her. Their hands weren't tied, but Max saw thick tears streaming down both of their faces. His heartbeat quadrupled at the pitiful sight.

Not allowing another second to pass, Max walked over to the man, who he assumed was Glenn and who had his back to him, and snapped his fingers. Instantly, both dogs backed off but remained alert, low, threatening growls deep in their throats.

"Don't move!" Max wrapped his hand around the intruder's neck and shoved him against the wall toward the door. Knowing the girls were watching prevented him from smashing his fist square in the guy's face, so he opted for the next best thing.

Dragging him out the door to Grace's van,

he shoved him into the passenger side. "Move a muscle, and I promise you I won't be as nice as I was in there." He nodded toward the cabin.

Glenn, a stick of a man with a receding hairline, tattoo-covered arms, and several missing teeth, held a bony arm in front of him as Max crammed his fist in his face. Blood spewed from his mouth seconds later. "Bastard," he spat out. "Those are my girls you got in that cabin! I came to get 'em! No woman's gonna take what's rightfully mine! You hear that?"

Max didn't know the story behind Glenn's claim and didn't really care. "I hear you loud and clear, you worthless piece of shit." Max ripped his belt off and used it to tie Glenn's hands behind his back. The skinny man yanked and pulled, but Max was too strong for him. He shoved him against the seat, then used the seat belt to hold him in position. "Move a muscle, and I promise it will be your last twitch." He jammed his fist into the man's nose and heard the cartilage snap.

Glenn dropped his head to his chest, wincing in pain. Before the bound man could recover from the effects of the punch, Max raced back inside the cabin, knowing he had only a few minutes before Glenn wiggled out of the seat belt.

Without saying a word, he removed the piece of extension cord with which Glenn had tied up Grace. "Stay here and don't do anything until I return."

Grace nodded, rubbing her hands. "Hurry!"

She wrapped her arms around both girls, who continued to whimper and cry.

The last thing Max heard before he raced out of the cabin was Grace telling the girls that everything was going to be just fine.

She'd promised.

Chapter Eight

Three hours later, Max drove back to the cabin with good news for Grace and her charges.

Max entered the cabin and found Grace, along with the two girls and dogs, curled up on the sofa in the den sound asleep. And he'd thought they'd be waiting on pins and needles for his return. So much for that.

Ice-D and Cliff bolted off the sofa when they saw him. He rubbed both between the ears, then allowed them their usual licks to his face. "Okay, boys, that's enough." Max went to the kitchen. He saw that both dog bowls were full of water, and the food bowls were empty. He was about to load them up with dog food when Grace entered the kitchen.

"They both had three hot dogs apiece, plus

a bowl of dog food. I don't think they're hungry."

Max stopped and shook his finger at the pair. "You know I ought to turn you two out, make you work for your grub." Both dogs whined, and Max fluffed the space between their ears. "Go on, you two." The dogs complied, their muzzles lifted high in the air as they made their way back to the den.

"They've convinced themselves they're kings today," Grace said as she watched the dogs jump back onto the sofa, one on either side of the girls.

"They okay?" He motioned to the sleeping girls.

"As okay as they can be under the circumstances." Grace eyed the poor things to make sure they still slept. "What happened? I was sure Glenn was gone for good. Stephanie had him arrested. He was in jail the last I heard."

Max motioned for her to follow him upstairs.

"We can talk up here without waking them. Apparently, Glenn was being transported to Denver. The deputies driving him stopped in Grand Junction for a bite to eat. Thinking Glenn was as innocent and harmless as he claimed, they let him come inside to have his meal with them. He went to the men's room, and that's the last they saw of him."

"This makes no sense! How did he know where to find Amanda and Ashley? I didn't plan on any of this happening." Perplexed, Grace dropped down on a small wooden chair.

"Those roadblocks last night, they were searching for him. He had no idea he'd find his girls here. As luck or whatever you want to call it would have it, I just happen to have the only house around here for miles. He must've walked all night and wound up here, the same as you. It's a heck of a coincidence, don't you think?"

Grace wasn't sure what to think and told him so.

"I called the number you gave me and talked to a woman by the name of Juanita. Told her you were fine and that you'd be back as soon as possible."

"Thanks so much, really. Juanita is my mother. I'm sure she and Stephanie were beside themselves with worry. Did you tell her the girls were with me and that they were okay?"

"I did."

Grace was about to ask Max if they'd said anything else, but he piped up. "Your mother said Bryce was there. Said he couldn't wait until Christmas Eve to see you."

Her eyes lit up like a Christmas tree. "Fantastic, I can't wait to see him. It's tough to schedule visits now that we live so far apart. I can't wait to see him. It's been almost a year. I can't believe I let so much time pass. It's just that—"

"You'd better leave before it starts snowing again. We're supposed to get another two feet by nightfall. I promised your family you'd be home today," Max said, staring intently into her verdant eyes.

Grace felt a little piece of her heart break at the thought of leaving Max behind. She barely knew the man, and what she did know she wasn't sure she liked. Still, there was something about him.

She nodded. "You're right. I know the girls are excited; they want to decorate the Christmas tree. I promised them they could."

"I gathered as much," Max said.

Before he could stop himself, before he had a chance to second-guess himself, Max pulled Grace into his arms kissing her softly on the mouth. Her intake of breath, shock or desire, surprised him because instead of pulling away, she kissed him back.

"Grace." The sound of her name filled him with emotions that had been dormant for so long, their intense return stunned him.

Before either could react Max pushed her away. For a moment neither spoke. When the silence between them became too uncomfortable, Max looked at her with more than just a casual interest.

Grace looked away, then something pulled her attention back to him. She gazed into his deep blue eyes, seeing more than just the man who'd offered her a place to stay.

Hesitantly, Max smoothed the hair away from her face. "I want to say I'm sorry, but I'm not."

Grace smiled. "It's okay, really."

Max nodded. "You'd better go. The snow and all."

Neither made an attempt to move their

gazes as they locked on to one another, both amazed at the sudden attraction between them.

Max spoke up, breaking the connection. "What about Bryce?"

She squinted her eyes as though he were suddenly out of focus. "What about him?"

"Never mind," Max said softly.

"Wait. Why are you asking me about Bryce? Do you know him?"

"No, and I don't want to either. Look, Grace, it was just a kiss, okay? Heat of the moment, nothing more. I've been without a woman too long. You're very attractive. I just lost control, okay?" Visions of Kayla danced before him while his heart hammered to the tune of *guilty, guilty, guilty!*

"Why you . . . jerk! What kind of . . . never mind. Give me my keys. I can't believe I even kissed you! What an idiot I am!" Grace raced down the steps as fast as her feet would move.

"Amanda, Ashley! It's time to go," she called to the pair, who were now wide-awake.

Quickly, both girls put on their jackets, shoes, and mittens.

"Can we kiss the dogs good-bye, Miss Grace?" Amanda asked.

Grace glanced at Max.

"Of course you can. They like pretty girls."

"Just like their owner," Grace muttered between gritted teeth.

Beseechingly, Max asked, "Tell me one thing before you leave."

Taking a deep breath and promising to see

her own counselor as soon as she could, she rolled her eyes upward. "What?"

"Why do you keep calling your home 'Hope House'? Where is this . . . place?"

Deciding there was no point in lying or dragging this exit out any longer than was necessary, Grace turned to face him.

"Remember I told you I was a counselor?" She waited for him to reply. He nodded.

"Actually, I'm a psychologist. Women who've been battered and abused come to Hope House. It's a safe haven. They're brought to me by local law enforcement when they need a place to stay, somewhere they can feel safe until they either face their attacker in court, divorce him, or, in some cases, leave only to go right back to the man who sent them running in the first place. This year, Stephanie and the girls, plus my own family, will be celebrating Christmas at Hope House." Grace wanted to invite him to spend Christmas Day with her even after he'd humiliated her when he made an excuse for kissing her. There was just something lonely about him. Thoughts of his spending the holiday alone dampened her holiday spirit.

"Its location is a secret," she added.

Grace watched the numerous expressions roll across his handsome face as she spoke. Curiosity, then she was sure she saw anger. Why would this make him angry? Obviously, she didn't know the man well. It didn't matter because she had a Christmas gathering waiting for her.

"Come on, girls. Let's go decorate that tree I promised you."

Excited they shouted, "Yeah! Yeah! Let's hurry, Miss Grace, please!"

Grace gave Max one last glance before speaking. "I appreciate your hospitality, Max. Thanks again."

The girls gave kisses to the dogs, who willingly returned them with big, sloppy kisses of their own.

"Bye, Ice-D. Bye, Cliff!" they chorused, before racing out the door.

"Be safe," Max called out to Grace, then closed the door.

Suddenly the cabin seemed too big for him and the dogs. "Let's go for a run, you two. I can't remember the last time I exercised you guys. Better yet, let's go to Powder Rise, and we'll ski down the mountain."

He made quick work of gathering the dogs' boots and coats. His skis were in the shed along with everything else from his former life. Dressing the dogs wasn't easy, but necessary. They ran alongside him while he skied, and their paws had to be protected as well as possible to avoid frostbite.

Thirty minutes later, Max drove his spare snowmobile up to the top of Powder Rise. His mountain. And what would have been Kayla's mountain, their child's mountain.

Standing on top, he felt small in comparison. He stared at the miles of white and green surrounding him. Kayla hadn't enjoyed the snow that much. She probably would've been content to stay in Denver for the rest of her life. Why was he remembering that? What did it matter if Kayla hadn't liked the snow, or skiing, or anything else about it? He hadn't been all that thrilled with her chosen profession either. Couldn't understand why she wanted to put herself at risk every time she walked out the door. And he would never know, he realized.

At the top of Powder Rise, which was at best a decent blue run, Max shoved off the top, Ice-D and Cliff running on each side.

The snow made a soft swishing sound as his skis cut through it. The mountain trail narrowed to a catwalk. Large pines towered above him, an occasional gust of wind brought snow from the branches dropping in his path as he maneuvered his way side to side down the hill. Traveling at a slow and steady pace so that both dogs could keep up without becoming tired, Max realized for the first time in many long months just how lonely he was.

Yes, he had friends, but they'd stopped coming around a long time ago. They stopped coming around because he'd turned into another person after Kayla's death. Max had crawled into a cocoon of grief. He remembered the guilt he felt just for being alive. Day by day, he'd cursed Kayla for the choice she'd made. And day by day his grief had changed him, turning him into the hard, bitter man he was today. For the first time since Kayla's death, he didn't want to be that bitter, hateful man.

He wanted to be the man he used to be in spite of what he'd said to Grace.

He remembered all too well the minutes that led up to the exact moment when his entire universe tilted. Max didn't like reliving the memory, but today he would. Because today he was going to put the past behind him and move forward.

It was Christmas Eve, and Max was looking forward to spending the next week pampering his wife. Excited didn't describe what he felt when he learned they were pregnant. A child of his own. Being an only child, Max wanted at least three, if not more. Kayla said two would be her limit. He didn't care if they had just the one or a dozen. Max couldn't wait to give Kayla her Christmas gift, a brand-new fire-engine red Jeep. She'd been driving a Datsun pickup given to her by her father ever since he'd known her. He wanted her to have a vehicle that was a little more reliable, something that wouldn't break down on her all the time. She'd be angry that he'd spent so much money, but he knew she would get over it. Heck, he had enough money to live like a king for the rest of his life.

Glancing at his watch, he noticed it was after midnight. Kayla was working the three-to-eleven shift, so he expected her anytime. For the next week she belonged to him and no one else. No work, no calls in the middle of the night to come to a crime scene. In fact, he thought they might take a trip to Denver to look at a crib, something for the baby. How he loved thinking about his child!

Damn, he was getting sappy-eyed! It was the holidays. They always did that to him. He loved the bright cheerful red and green lights that twinkled on their Colorado blue spruce, the smell of pine, clean and sharp. He'd finished his Christmas shopping. There were dozens of brightly wrapped packages beneath the tree that hadn't been there when Kayla left for work. Yes, she would be surprised. He laughed. That was an understatement.

Looking at his watch seeing that it was a quarter to one, Max jumped when the phone rang.

Most likely it was Kayla calling to let him know she was going out for breakfast with a few friends from the department. She did that about once a month, and it was fine with him. She needed the time to unwind.

Max answered the phone on the third ring.

"Max Jorgenson?" a male voice inquired.

"Yes, this is Max."

"We're sending a cruiser to pick you up. Officer Jorgenson has been involved in a shooting. . ."

Both she and the baby died before they made it to the hospital.

Chapter Nine

Sunday, December 21, 2008
The First Day of Winter

Grace tied the bright red ribbon around the last package, then added a matching bow. She surveyed the mountain of gifts she'd spent the morning wrapping. This was truly going to be the best Christmas Stephanie and her girls had ever had.

She'd bought both girls the latest *American Girl* books along with a special doll of their own: a *Julie Albright* for Ashley and an *Ivy Ling* for Amanda. Both American Girl dolls were going through big changes in their home lives, too. Grace thought the girls would identify with the dolls and the stories that accompanied them. She'd purchased all the extra clothes, shoes, and ribbons that she could find for the dolls. The girls would love changing their clothes and fixing their hair.

She bought Stephanie a new ski suit and jacket because she'd never owned a new one, saying all that she'd ever owned were second-hand castoffs. There were skis, poles, boots, hats, and gloves that promised warmth in sub-zero temperatures. Briefly, Grace thought of Max. Stephanie had been an avid skier before marrying Glenn. Maybe now that she was putting her life in order, she would find time to take up the sport. Max would've been an excellent instructor for her.

She barely knew the man, yet she couldn't seem to shake the image of him standing at the door when she'd left. It had been barely twenty-four hours, and here she was pining away like a lovesick teenager. Maybe a *lust*-sick teenager. It'd been a while since she'd had a real relationship. Actually, she hadn't had a real relationship since Matt, her college sweetheart, who turned out to be anything but. Oh, she'd gone on tons of dates. There was always a friend of a friend who had a cousin in town, or someone's newly divorced brother who needed a date for his annual company picnic. She liked dating but had never thought too much about marriage. She was thirty-five years old. Marriage might not be in the cards for her. That was okay because Grace was reasonably happy, loved her profession, enjoyed the life she'd made for herself. More than anything, she felt like a proud parent, helping the many women who passed through Hope House. If she didn't accomplish anything else in her life, she knew she was okay with that. Opening

Hope House had been her biggest dream. She'd fulfilled it, and anything extra was simply a bonus.

"Are you about to finish in there?" Juanita called out to Grace. "I have a few things I'd like to wrap."

Grace watched her mother standing in the doorway. Hope House had six available bedrooms. With Stephanie and the girls as her only "guests," just two of the other bedrooms were in use. Grace had turned the smallest bedroom into a temporary wrapping station, where she could wrap presents without being caught. She loved surprises and couldn't wait to see the look on the girls' faces Christmas morning.

"It's all yours, Mother dear," Grace said. "Promise not to peek, okay? Some of those silver-and-gold packages are yours."

"Why don't you put them under the tree?" her mother suggested.

"I am. I just wanted to wait so Amanda and Ashley could help. They're having their hair washed right now."

"That's a grand idea, darling. You certainly know how to treat those girls. Too bad you don't have any of your own."

Oh no, Grace thought, *the marriage talk.* Surely, her mother wasn't going to do this to her again. Not at Christmas.

"Mom, we've talked about this before. I'm not getting any younger. If a child and marriage aren't in my future, then please allow me to spoil and love those I can."

Juanita looked at her daughter, tears filling her matching green eyes. "I don't know how I raised such a wonderful and wise woman, but I did. Come here," her mother said. Grace stepped into Juanita's loving embrace.

"I just followed your lead, Mom."

"Oh, I don't know about that. I don't think I was ever brave enough to do some of the things you do, dear. Have I ever told you how proud I am of you? All the women and children you've helped throughout the years. Your father would be so proud of you."

"Stop it, or I'll get all teary-eyed and ruin my mascara," Grace said with a grin. "You know how clumsy I am when it comes to putting on makeup."

"Oh, go on. Let me get these packages wrapped before Bryce discovers what I'm doing. You know what a sneak he can be."

"I'll keep him occupied downstairs while you're wrapping. Hide them under the bed when you're finished."

"Good thinking."

Downstairs, Grace found Bryce where else but snooping into the fridge. "Is that all you do?"

"What?" He shot her his all-American smile. Bryce was as handsome as their father had been, with his coal black hair and dark eyes. He'd just completed the requirements for his Ph.D. in history, same subject as their father, who'd been a professor at the University of Colorado. Starting in January, he would tackle his first real teaching job at the same college.

Seeing Bryce all grown-up would have made her father proud. He'd died of a massive heart attack when Bryce was sixteen.

"Every time I look at you, you're eating," Grace teased.

"Hey, I'm a growing boy. I haven't had real food in ages. I wish I could cook."

"Then I'll make sure to get you a cookbook for Christmas."

"Thanks, Sis. I can always count on you to be practical," Bryce said between bites of banana nut bread.

"You better save some of that for the girls. And what's that supposed to mean?"

Bryce poured a large glass of milk, downed it, then answered, "Just that you've always been the more practical one. That's not a bad thing to be, Gracie."

Suddenly, Grace wanted to cry. Good old practical Grace. Tears shimmered in her eyes. "Think that's why no one ever . . . well, you know, fell head over heels in love with me?" Grace could ask Bryce anything, and she could count on him to tell her the truth.

"Probably. Or they never thought they were good enough. My money's on the latter." Bryce winked at her.

"You're a good brother, you know that?" Grace wrapped him in a hug. Though she was older by six years, he was twice her size, a rock of solid muscle. Years on the ski slopes had guaranteed that.

Which made her think of Max. "Remember that guy you used to go all gaga over? The

Olympic skier?" Grace wasn't sure if he would remember, but she wanted to see if it was possible if Bryce knew anything about Max, other than what had been in the news during his career.

"Max Jorgenson? Darn straight I remember him. As a matter of fact, some of the guys and I are going to Maximum Glide next week. Jorgenson owns the resort. Why? You thinking of taking up skiing?"

"I might. I was just curious. I don't know if Mom mentioned it or not, but I . . . uh, spent the night at his house." Grace grinned when she saw how big Bryce's eyes got. They looked like two giant black holes.

"What do you mean, you 'spent the night at his house'?"

Grace swatted him with a kitchen towel. "Not spent the night like the way you're thinking. When I was coming home from Eagle Valley Friday night, I was detoured by the local cops. The snow was so bad I couldn't see, my cell phone wasn't charged, long story short, I wound up knocking on his door at one in the morning. Amanda and Ashley were with me."

"Maybe I was wrong when I used the word 'practical.' 'Sneaky' might be better."

"Stop it! I knew you were a big fan when you were in junior high, just thought you might want to know."

"So that's it? Did you two do . . . anything?" Bryce asked, his eyes downcast, a grin the size of Texas spreading across his face.

"Why you little shit!" Grace laughed so hard

she lost her breath. Of course, that was when her mother chose to make her grand entrance.

"Grace, I haven't seen you laugh that hard since you wrote 'I love you' on all of your brother's Valentine cards."

"Oh my gosh, I did do that, didn't I?" She folded over laughing as she remembered when Bryce was in the fourth grade. He came home from school swearing he wouldn't ever return because all the girls thought he liked them. It'd been a rotten thing to do, but Grace and her mother both had told Bryce a dozen times to write out his Valentine cards for his classmates. When Grace offered to do them for him, she decided to play a joke by writing "I love you" on all the cards for the girls in his class. He'd never let her live it down.

"Yes, and to this day Ramona Clark still has the hots for me."

"What's wrong with that?" Grace asked.

"She weighs about four hundred pounds, that's all. Nice girl, but not my type."

"What is your type, Bryce? Mother and I would love to know. Wouldn't we, Mom?" Grace asked teasingly.

"Well, I suppose this is one of those times when I need to leave the room. So I can eavesdrop."

They were all laughing when Stephanie brought the girls to the kitchen. "They're hungry again, Miss Grace. I don't know how I'll ever repay you. The food bill alone will take me years. They just might eat you out of house and home."

"Nonsense! They're growing girls. I was just telling Bryce what a pig . . . how nice it is to see someone eat all these baked goods." She winked at Stephanie.

"How about peanut butter with strawberry jam on a slice of banana nut bread?" Grace suggested.

"Yummy, Miss Grace," Amanda said.

"Yeah," Ashley added with less enthusiasm.

Grace made sandwiches for the girls while Stephanie fixed each a glass of chocolate milk. Grace would never allow anyone who came to Hope House to go hungry. Many of the women and children who passed through Hope House came to her not only helpless and beaten down. Often they were hungry as well. In many of the so-called homes, food hadn't been a priority. Grace was sure the girls hadn't had enough to eat because when they had first arrived, they were skin and bones. Though they were still on the thin side, Grace was glad to see some pink in their cheeks, and their eyes were much brighter. It still amazed her how a loving, caring touch could change one's life.

Which brought her back to her conversation with Bryce. Practical? Is that what had turned Max off after that kiss? The kiss that took her breath away. The kiss that was unlike any she'd ever experienced. The kiss that almost knocked her whole world askew. Was she a practical kisser doomed to be denied all the passion and romance she'd secretly read about in all the romance novels she hid in her room?

She laughed. Love and romance of that nature was pure fiction.

"When will it be time to decorate the tree, Miss Grace?" Amanda asked when she finished her sandwich.

"As soon as your sister is finished, we'll get started." Grace smiled at the girls. When they had returned yesterday afternoon from their adventure, she'd taken them to Jingle Bells and More, one of her favorite Christmas shops in Gypsum, where she'd purchased several Dora the Explorer ornaments for Amanda and *High School Musical* ornaments that all her friends back home would love for Ashley. She'd enjoyed seeing the looks on their faces each time she said yes to their, "Can we buy this one?" The trip had cost her a bit more than she'd budgeted for, but the delight she'd seen in their eyes was worth every penny.

"I'm finished," Ashley called out loudly.

All the adults laughed.

"Then let's get started," Grace encouraged them.

Three hours later, the twelve-foot spruce sparkled with red, green, and white lights, the ornaments she'd bought for the girls, plus dozens and dozens of her own personal ornaments that she'd collected over the years. She still had the hot pink star she'd made for her mother in sixth grade.

"I think there's something missing under the tree. What do you think, Amanda? Ashley?"

The girls looked to their mother for an answer, but Stephanie just shrugged. Bryce and her mother shook their heads.

"Are you sure you don't know?" Grace inquired.

"Nope, Miss Grace we don't. We never had a tree this big before. We just had one Mommy had from when she was a little girl, but it wasn't real. It didn't smell good either," Ashley continued. "It was glass."

Grace's eyes welled with tears when she realized this was the first *real* Christmas tree the girls had ever had.

"Well, since you can't guess, I'm going to tell you." Grace smiled, wrapping one arm around each of their shoulders.

"I believe we are missing some . . . presents!" Grace emphasized the last word as loud as she could without scaring them.

"Presents? Real presents with sparkly wrapping paper and shiny bows?"

"Yep," Grace said.

With a questioning look, Ashley said, "But we already have our presents, Miss Grace. You bought us all these pretty ornaments."

"Oh, sweetie, those aren't your Christmas presents. Those are presents for the . . . tree. Yes, trees get presents, too," Grace improvised. Bryce gave her a high five. She *was* practical, wasn't she?

"They do? Mommy never got presents for our tree," Amanda said.

"Well, only real trees get presents because

when they're cut down they leave all their . . . tree friends and family behind."

"You're pushing it, Sis," Bryce interjected.

"Yes, I suppose so. But it doesn't matter. Either way, I'm going to need the help of two little . . . elves. Ashley, Amanda, do you want to be my elves for a while?"

"Do we have to wear those shoes that curl up in the toes like the elves at the mall wear?"

Again they laughed. "All you have to do is follow me," Grace instructed, then headed toward the steps.

As the two little girls trailed behind her, she heard Amanda whisper to her older sister, "See. I told you there really was a Santa Claus."

Chapter Ten

The road leading off the mountain was completely cleared of the afternoon snowfall. The forecasters had been wrong. They'd barely gotten a foot of snow. Max was glad because he didn't want to wait any longer to do what he'd decided to do as he'd skied down Powder Rise yesterday afternoon.

With both dogs securely buckled in the backseat of the fire-engine red Jeep, Max carefully drove down the mountain to his destination: Denver. He couldn't remember the last time he'd been to the city, but now was as good a time as any.

The traffic on I-70 was heavy since it was Sunday morning. Hundreds of residents of Denver and the surrounding area drove to the resorts on the weekend. With Christmas just four days away, the traffic was horrendous.

Three hours later he'd made it to the city. First on his list was the Hummer dealership, where he traded in the Jeep he'd bought for Kayla for a bright yellow Hummer. Eddie would love this.

Next, he drove downtown to the police station. He had already dropped the dogs off at a doggie spa for grooming, figuring by the time they were finished, he would be, too.

He was taking a chance, hoping to take advantage of his acquaintance with Kayla's former partner, Paul McCormick, who, he remembered, was a decent guy.

Luck was with him. According to the girl manning the front desk, Paul's shift had just ended. She paged him and told Max to have a seat.

"Max Jorgenson, good to see you," Paul said when he saw him. "I couldn't imagine who it was when Kathy paged me. How are you?"

"Actually, I'm doing okay. Listen, I need a favor. I hate to ask you, but it's important, and I don't know who else I can trust."

"Sure. Let's go to the break room. I can't guarantee the coffee, but it's private."

"Great," Max said.

Once they were seated, Paul poured them each a cup of coffee. Max sipped his, trying hard not to gag.

Paul got straight to the point. "So what can I do for you?"

"Have you ever heard of a woman's shelter called Hope House?"

Paul raised his eyebrows. "Everyone in law enforcement knows about it. It's one of the best-kept secrets in Gypsum. Why? Do you know someone who needs protection?"

"No, no, nothing like that. You see . . ." This wasn't as easy as Max thought it would be. It felt like a betrayal of Kayla. "The woman who runs the place, Grace Landry. What can you tell me about her?"

"Now wait a minute, Max, Grace Landry is as good as it gets. Just ask around. Whatever beef you have with her, I'll warn you, there's a thousand guys that'll come to her defense."

"Look, Paul, I owe the woman a favor. She broke down on Blow Out Hill the other night. She had two little girls with her. I just need to find a way to contact her."

"In my day, when a lady wanted any contact from a man, she usually gave him her phone number."

"I have her number. Here." Max removed the crumpled slip of paper that Grace had written her number on from his pocket. "I want to surprise her. I don't want to call her. Can you help me or not?" Max didn't like begging, but if he had to, in this instance he would.

"Remember the old Sutton Mansion in Gypsum? It was in the paper a few years ago, something about it being on the historical register." Paul looked him squarely in the eye. "No one knows about this, Max. If word got out that it

was a shelter, the women Grace works so hard
to protect wouldn't stand a chance. There are
a lot of angry husbands and boyfriends out
there who would like nothing more than to see
her shut down."

"You have my word I won't tell a soul. Thanks,
Paul. I really appreciate your going out on a
limb for me."

"Anytime." Paul stood, and Max clasped his
outstretched hand.

"Whenever you want to go skiing, take a ride
up to Maximum Glide. Ask for Eddie and tell
him I said to give you and your family anything
you want."

"Thanks, Max, I might just do that. Skiing is
getting a bit pricey these days."

Max laughed. "Don't I know it. Be careful
out there."

Max left the police station, picked up Ice-D
and Cliff, who now smelled like strawberries
and cream. There was one more stop Max
needed to make on his way home.

He was going to buy a Christmas tree. He
was sure the decorations were stored in the
shed, along with everything else he'd packed
away when he moved. Better yet, he'd buy all
new decorations. He'd kept the ones Kayla
had purchased packed away, but if he was
going to make a fresh start, he might as well go
all the way.

Three hours later, with two dogs that smelled like dessert, a fifteen-foot blue spruce
strapped to the top of the Hummer, and six

hundred dollars' worth of decorations, Max drove his new vehicle up the winding road heading for home.

Home. How strange it sounded to refer to his log cabin as *home.* He'd been living there for two years and never once thought of the place as anything other than a place to sleep, eat, shower, and drink. Funny, he hadn't even thought of taking a drink since Grace landed on his doorstep.

"That's a good thing, right, guys?" Max asked the two dogs.

"Woof, woof."

Max let the dogs out and unloaded the Hummer. Once inside, he put the stand together, wrestled with the tree until he got it in the stand, then filled the stand with water and the package of stuff they'd given him to help the tree stay fresh longer. Both dogs barked at the front door.

"I'm having so much fun I forgot all about you guys." Max stood aside as the two leapt through the door. Both cocked their heads to the side when they saw the giant tree in the center of the den. To prove they were still in control, both Huskies trotted over to the tree, where they lifted their hind legs and proceeded to piss all over it.

Max stared at the pair, shocked by their actions, then he started to laugh. He laughed so hard his sides hurt, and his eyes filled with tears.

"I take it you guys don't like the tree. Too bad 'cause it's staying. If you want to pee on it, be my guest, but you'd better not mess with the decorations. Or else."

"Woof! Woof!"

Max strung the multicolored lights on the tree, then one by one he carefully placed the ornaments on the branches. Ice-D and Cliff were mesmerized when he turned all the room lights off and plugged in the tree lights. The giant log cabin instantly became a home. To honor the woman who'd been his wife, he'd bought a silver star and placed it on the front of the tree where he could see it. To honor the woman who'd given him his life back, he carefully placed a crystal snow angel next to the star.

Max stepped back to admire his handiwork. He gave a long whistle as he stared at his tree. This was a time for new beginnings, a time to start fresh. Kayla would want this for him, but more important, now he wanted it for himself.

It was about time he gave old *Bryce* a run for his money.

Chapter Eleven

Christmas Eve, 2008
Ten Minutes before Midnight

Grace had just turned off her bedroom light when she heard the doorbell ring. She dressed quickly in jeans and a T-shirt before quietly making her way downstairs. Thankful she had purchased two turkeys and a ham at the butcher shop that afternoon, she wondered how many more would join her for Christmas dinner.

Grace carefully punched in the numbers on the alarm panel before peering through a small hole at the top of the door. When she didn't see anyone, she opened her front door to see who was out there. Sometimes the women were afraid when they arrived. Grace understood this as she stepped out onto the porch in the frigid night air.

"Hello," she called. "It's okay. There's nothing to be afraid of." She waited a minute or so to see if anyone materialized from either side of the long porch that wrapped around the perimeter of the old house.

Wrapping her arms around her for warmth, she waited another minute before calling out again. "Is anyone there?" She didn't like this. Something wasn't right. Grace was about to step inside and call her contact at the police station when she heard someone call her name.

"Who's there?"

A large figure stepped out from behind the shadows of tall pine trees grouped in a corner on the side of the house. Fearing this was an angry husband or boyfriend Grace stood next to the front door with her completely charged cell phone in her hand. "I'm going to count to three. If you don't show yourself, I'm calling the police. One. Two—"

"It's me. Please don't call the police."

Grace wasn't sure what was worse; being surprised by an angry man looking to beat his wife or an idiot who didn't have any social graces.

"Max Jorgenson, what are you doing here? Furthermore, how on earth did you find me?" Grace's hands shook, and her heart beat so fast she feared it would wear out before she had a chance to calm herself.

He stepped away from the shadows. The light coming from inside the house outlined his large frame. "Can I come inside? It's cold out here, plus I'm lost."

Grace smiled, glad for the darkness. "I suppose I owe you this. Tell me you're not running from some crazed girlfriend before I let you inside," Grace joked.

He stepped onto the porch, then followed her to the kitchen.

Grace turned the kitchen lights on, pointed to a chair. "Sit."

Max obeyed.

"I'm going to make a pot of tea. I hope by the time it's ready you have a good explanation for coming all the way out here just to scare me half to death." Grace was as good as her word. She filled two mugs with tap water, nuked them for three minutes, dunked a tea bag in each one, grabbed sugar and cream from the fridge.

"Okay, tell me why you're here." She glanced at the clock on the microwave. "Do you realize it's officially Christmas? I can't wait to see . . . never mind. Just tell me why you're here. And it better be good."

Max smiled at her—a smile that actually reached his eyes. "This is probably the most outrageous thing I've ever done in my life."

"It's not, trust me. I've seen your Alpine, downhill skiing."

Max grinned. "Pretty wild, huh?"

"Bryce appreciates it much more than I do."

Max clammed up. "Maybe coming here was a mistake. This . . . *Bryce*, I know it's none of my business, and you can tell me that, but before you do, there's something I need to say. Then if you still want me to leave, I will. No questions asked."

"That's fair enough. Say what you came to say." Grace took a deep breath trying to calm the erratic beating of her heart.

"Two years ago my wife was killed in the line of duty. She was a police officer, and she truly loved her work. She and her partner were called to the scene of a domestic dispute. The man had just beaten his wife and two-year-old daughter. When Kayla and her partner arrived at the house, the guy threatened to kill the child if they didn't back off. Kayla's partner Paul radioed in asking for a hostage negotiator. Knowing it would take time before they could get to the scene, Kayla spoke with the man, asking him to let the child go. She offered to exchange herself for the child. Apparently the deranged guy liked the idea of holding a female cop hostage. But when Kayla approached him, he must've changed his mind, something happened to scare him, I don't know, and her partner didn't either. Whatever the reason, he changed his mind. He shot Kayla twice in the chest, then put the gun in his mouth and shot himself. But at least the wife and child were safe. Paramedics got Kayla to the hospital, they even sent a patrol car to bring me to the hospital. By the time I got there, it was too late. She died, and when she died, everything in me died, too. I stopped eating, stopped socializing, I stopped everything. Then I started to drink. It never got out of hand, but it could have." Max watched her to see her reaction.

"I remember now when that was on the

news. I am so sorry, Max. I don't know what to say, or what it has to do with me."

"You'll think I'm crazy when I tell you."

Grace laughed. "No more so than I do right now. Go on." She was used to listening to people. It's what she did.

"When you and the girls showed up on my doorstep the other night, I was angry. Not at you, but angry at myself. I was . . . hell, I was instantly attracted to you. I even thought of you as a snow angel." He took a sip of the tea. "I felt incredibly guilty, too. There hasn't been anyone since Kayla. I'd buried myself in my grief for so long, I think I became comfortable with it. You and those two little girls reminded me that life is worth living. I even bought a Christmas tree with all the trimmings. Looks pretty good, too. Though the dogs didn't like it. Before I had even started with the decorating, they both pissed all over it." Max laughed loudly.

Grace smiled. "Shame on them. I remember you telling me you didn't like the holidays. Is this why?"

Max nodded. "Kayla died on Christmas Eve, two years ago. She'd just found out she was pregnant."

"Oh Max, how terrible for you! I'm so sorry."

"Yes, I was too. More than I ever imagined. That first year was hard. Then it got a little easier, and when it did, I felt so guilty that I'd plunge myself right back into that dark place just to ease the feelings of guilt that I had for being alive."

"It's called survivor's guilt and is quite common. Mother went through a period like that when my father died. She'd always been the one to catch everything from the flu to ear infections. My father never had a sick day in his life. He dropped dead of a massive heart attack while he was teaching a history class."

"I guess you never get over it, you just learn to live with it."

"That's true. We all have our own ways of dealing with grief. There's no right or wrong way, Max. Guilt is a terrible thing for those who are left behind."

"Which brings me to the reason why I came here in the first place. Or one of them."

"I'm listening," Grace said.

"You're good at this stuff, but I suppose you already know that."

"I've done it a time or two."

"First tell me about Bryce."

Grace's eyes lit up like the tree back at the cabin. *Home*, he corrected himself, *it's home now*.

"He's absolutely wonderful. I can't imagine my life without him. We don't get to see one another as much as we used to, but we're okay with it. We talk on the phone whenever we can. Bryce isn't too good at answering his e-mail, but I'm sure once he gets settled into his new routine, he will. From what I understand, most colleges use their e-mail systems to communicate with their students. Bryce is going to teach history at the University of Colorado after the first of the year. He's very excited about his career."

"I guess I don't stand a chance. A ski bum versus a college professor."

"Max, Bryce is my *brother.*"

His eyes brightened like two blue moons. "Why didn't you tell me?"

"I guess I just assumed you knew. When Bryce was in junior high school, he was one of your biggest fans. He followed your career, watched you win all those Olympic medals. For a while, Mom and I feared he might take to the slopes instead of going to college, but he's too much of a history buff, just like my father."

"So does this mean I have a chance? A slight chance of asking you out on a date?"

Grace was so thrilled, everything around her blurred. "You can ask all you want, Max."

"But you don't have to say yes. Am I right?"

"No, you're not. Listen, there's something I want to ask you. It's a bit . . . personal, but since you drove all the way here and on Christmas Day, there's no reason not to. When you kissed me, did you really mean what you said? That it was just a kiss?"

"That's the biggest lie I've ever told in my life. I wanted to wrap you in my arms, drag you upstairs, but I couldn't. It took a lot of soul-searching for me to realize that it's okay to be happy. That's why I'm here."

"There's just one more thing," Grace asked. "Do you think I'm practical?"

"You? Practical? No way. Not in the least. Though I have to admit I don't know you very well, but I intend to."

"You're sure," Grace teased.

"One hundred percent, cross my heart. Why do you ask?"

"Bryce told me I was practical, said it could be one of the reasons I've never settled down to raise a family."

"Well, I'm going to have to tell your brother a thing or two. If you were practical, you'd be married with a houseful of kids. Where is he?"

"Actually, he's upstairs sleeping," Grace said. "Follow me. No, never mind. Wait here. I'll be right back."

Grace didn't bother knocking when she saw the light shining beneath his door. Shoving the door aside, Grace stepped into the room. Bryce was sitting up in bed, reading. "You ever heard of knocking?"

"Yes, but this is my house, remember?"

"So?"

"I have your Christmas present. It's in the kitchen."

"And it's something that can't wait until everyone else is up?"

"No, actually it can't. If you don't want it, I can give him, I mean it, to someone who'll appreciate it."

"All right, you're not going to give me a minute's peace until I see what you've cooked up. Oh crap, Gracie, is this about that cookbook you said you were giving me? Because if it is, I'll see it soon enough."

"Bryce, march your ass downstairs to the kitchen right now. Don't ask me another question. Now go."

"Okay, okay. Women," he muttered as he slipped a T-shirt over his head.

Grace felt like a kid at Christmas. Max wanted to get to know her better. Bryce was about to get the surprise of his life. And it was going to be the best Christmas she'd ever had.

Max sat at the table sipping his tea when Bryce entered the kitchen. "Hey, Bryce, what's up?" he asked casually.

Bryce looked at Grace, then Max. "Tell me I'm not dreaming. Please."

"See?" Grace said to Max. "I told you he was your biggest fan."

Epilogue

Christmas Day, 2009

Grace paced back and forth inside her suite. She looked at her Rolex, a gift from Max. It was almost time. She couldn't believe she'd agreed to this, but wanting to prove to everyone that she, Grace Landry, was anything but practical, when Max asked her to marry him, she agreed to his request about the location of the ceremony. And so, her wedding ceremony was about to take place on a ski slope at Maximum Glide. She smiled. She was anything but practical.

So there she was, thirty-six years old, decked out in a five-thousand-dollar *white* ski suit, waiting for Stephanie, who was now her dearest friend and also her maid of honor. Ashley, nine going on twenty, would act as lead flower girl, and, of course, Amanda would do whatever her sister told her to do.

A loud knock startled her. It was time.

"Don't you look gorgeous, all decked out in white," Stephanie remarked as she perused the white ski suit she'd chosen for Grace. Stephanie had become the manager of the sporting goods' shop at Maximum Glide. When she wasn't selling ski equipment, she acted as an instructor. Both her girls were now expert on the slopes. Max had high hopes for Ashley in the 2018 Olympics and her sister four years later.

Max had high hopes about everything. Grace couldn't be happier. Though it had only been a year since she met Max, she'd fallen in love with him the very first time he kissed her. She wouldn't have admitted it then, but now she would.

Bryce was beside himself when she told him she was marrying Max. He said it was a dream come true for him. Grace told him she was happy her dream made his dream come true, but if he thought for one minute that he was going to mooch off Max for free lessons, he'd better think again. He'd have to enroll in the classes just like everyone else.

Max was spending his time as a ski instructor at Maximum Glide. Eddie was still the manager. He and Stephanie were dating hot and heavy. Grace was sure there would be another wedding in the near future.

Glenn had been sentenced to eight years in prison, not for hurting Stephanie alone, but for escaping also. Their divorce had been final for almost eight months.

"It's time, Grace. I think this is the most exciting thing that's ever happened, don't you?"

"It is, it really is. I thought I'd never get married, and look at me now." She hugged her dear friend.

"We better go before all the lifts are taken," Stephanie teased, knowing Max had reserved a lift for the wedding party and the guests.

"Let's go." Grace grabbed her twenty-pound ski boots, her poles, and her hat and gloves. Her new "Maxie skis" were stored at the lift.

Outside, the sun shone brightly. There wasn't a cloud in the sky. The temperature was in the low twenties, but Grace didn't mind the cold. She was about to marry the sexiest man alive.

He waited for her at the top of Gracie's Way, a new trail named in her honor.

Max, Bryce, and her mother were all gathered at the top of the mountain when Grace and Stephanie jumped off the lift. She adjusted her sunglasses and skied across a small patch of ice to get to Max.

They'd opted for a simple ceremony, or as simple as one got considering they were going to take their vows at the top of the mountain, then ski to the bottom for the pronouncement that would unite them as husband and wife. A friend of Eddie's, who was also a justice of the peace, had agreed to marry them.

"Are you sure you want to do this?" Max asked as he bent down to kiss her.

"Get married? Are you kidding? I can't wait," Grace assured him.

"I meant are you sure you want to get married on the slopes?"

"I'm not a practical person, Max. You should know that by now. Frankly, I wouldn't have it any other way. Now, let's get this show on the slopes."

"Grace, I love you," Max whispered in her ear.

"I know you do, darling. The feeling is mutual." Grace slid around to face the justice of the peace. Stephanie stood to her right, and Eddie, the best man, stood to Max's left. Bryce and her mother stayed with Amanda and Ashley. Max had arranged for the lift to take Juanita back down the mountain.

Everything was perfect, Grace thought as she cleared her throat. Nothing in her life had ever been as perfect as this moment on top of a cold, snowy mountain with the sun shining down on her.

"Dearly beloved, we are gathered here on this mountain to unite Max Jorgenson and Grace Landry in holy matrimony."

After reciting the traditional wedding vows, with Grace and Max saying their "I do"s, the justice of the peace stepped aside and tucked his small black book inside his ski jacket before spinning around and directing his ski tips downhill toward the bottom of the mountain. "As planned, I will unite the couple in holy matrimony at the bottom of the mountain." Max used his poles to position himself by Grace,

and once there was a reasonable distance between them, he looked at her. "Are you ready?"

Her grin was so broad it hurt. "I don't think
I can wait another minute," Grace said, before
shoving off. "I'll meet you at the bottom."

Bryce, Stephanie, and her girls followed behind.

With the wind at their backs, they curved
and zigzagged down the mountain in near-
record time. When they reached the bottom,
there was a crowd gathering. "Do you know
these people?" Grace whispered to Max.

"No, but apparently they know us. Look."
Max pointed to several in the group who were
holding signs that read CONGRATULATIONS MAX
AND GRACE!!!

The justice of the peace cleared his throat.
"By the powder, uh, I mean power vested in me
by the good state of Colorado and by the fans
cheering behind us, I now pronounce you
man and wife. You can kiss her now, Max."

Max dropped his poles and turned to his
wife, who had dropped her poles, too. Together, they slid to the ground, embracing one
another. When his lips touched hers, Grace
was sure the world actually tilted. His kiss was
deep and passionate. Her senses were alive
and tingling.

"Max?" she mumbled while they were kissing.

"Hmm?"

"The snow is going to melt if we don't stop!"

"I'm that hot?"

"Yes, Mr. Jorgenson, you are that hot. Now

help your wife up, or I might break something. And if I break something, that means we'll have to cancel our honeymoon, and I really don't want to because I've never been to Hawaii, or Ireland, or Spain."

"If you put it that way, I don't have a choice, now do I, Mrs. Jorgenson?"

"Say it again, Max."

"What?"

"Call me Mrs. Jorgenson."

"Mrs. Jorgenson, you're going to be so sick of hearing me call you that for the next two months, you just might resort to using your maiden name."

"Never, Max. Never in a million years," Grace said, as he lifted her into his arms.

"Mrs. Jorgenson?"

"Yes, Mr. Jorgenson?"

"There's something I've been wanting to say to you all day, and now seems as good a time as any."

"What would that be?"

"Merry Christmas, Grace. Merry Christmas."

"Merry Christmas, Max. I think I'm about the happiest woman alive right now."

"I love you, Grace. Always and forever."

"Oh Max, I love you, too!"

"Hey, did we order a wedding cake?"

Grace looked at Max, the love of her life and now her husband. Her life was so very rich at that moment, she wanted to burn it into her memory.

Forever and always.

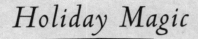

Holiday Magic

*I'd like to dedicate this novella
to all the "snow bunnies" in my life.*

Chapter One

Telluride, Colorado
November 26, 2010
Black Friday

Stephanie glanced at her watch again, making
sure she wasn't running behind her self-imposed
schedule: 5:50 A.M. They were opening the
doors at seven o'clock sharp as today would be
the busiest day of the year at Maximum Glide's
ski shop, Snow Zone, where Stephanie had been
working as manager for almost two years.

With an hour to go before the doors opened,
she adjusted the volume on the hidden stereo
filling the ski shop with the soulful sounds of
Michael Bolton singing "Have Yourself a Merry
Little Christmas." She took four large cinnamon-
scented candles from beneath the counter,
grabbed a pack of matches, then lit and placed
each candle in a secure place where it couldn't
be knocked over by a customer reaching for

something or an accidental bump from a ski. Though there were signs posted at the main entrance and throughout the shop stating NO SKIS ALLOWED INSIDE, that didn't mean that customers always paid attention to the posted rules. She'd brewed coffee and heated water for hot chocolate and bought several dozen donuts for the early risers. Judging by the amount of sugar consumed, shopping must be hard work.

Stephanie smiled, thinking about the upcoming Christmas season. For the next four weeks, Maximum Glide would be packed with vacationers from every part of the world, and, of course, the locals, who came in droves on the weekends. Scanning the shelves one last time, she refolded three bright red sweaters with matching scarves and toboggan caps. The many styles of ski boots on sale were stamped with bright orange stickers. Last season's waterproof gloves were placed next to this season's newest designs. People could decide for themselves if the price difference was worth purchasing the latest style. Personally, Stephanie thought they were pretty much the same except that the current style had a zippered pocket for an extra set of hand warmers.

She adjusted the Spyder jackets and the North Face ski pants, making sure they were evenly spaced on the racks. These were the biggest-selling items in the shop. She'd ordered more than she had last year, not wanting to risk running out before the holidays were over. Last year, the general manager of Maximum Glide, Edward Patrick Joseph O'Brien, who preferred to be called Patrick though privately she always thought of him as Eddie, like that cute kid on *Leave It to Beaver,* insisted that she place the order on her own. After checking her inventory, Stephanie had decided they had enough ski pants and jackets in stock for two seasons. What she didn't know then was that the famous ski shop, part of a resort owned by an Olympic gold medalist, attracted skiers with bushels and barrels of money to spend. She'd ended up placing another order, then had to spend hundreds of the ski shop's dollars for an overnight delivery. A lesson learned. More secure in her position this year, she'd placed her order with confidence, knowing she'd be lucky to have anything left after the holidays. For the moment, Stephanie was sure she'd ordered enough to get them through the busy holiday season. She wouldn't get a day off until after New Year's, but she didn't mind. She needed the extra money this year. With all of the overtime pay, plus her Christmas bonus, she would finally be able to afford the down payment on her very own home, a first for her and her two daughters, Ashley, ten going on twenty, and Amanda, an adorable seven-year-old. She'd been searching the paper for months and had finally found a perfect three-bedroom, two-bath ranch-style house that she adored and could afford.

Last week she'd made a special trip into town to Rollins Realty, who'd listed the property. Jessica Rollins, a smartly dressed woman in her mid-fifties, took her to the house, and Stephanie was immediately smitten. She'd practically salivated when she saw the deep garden tub in the master bath, a luxury she hadn't counted on. When Jessica saw her reaction, she explained that the former owners were avid skiers. Stephanie figured that covered about three-quarters of Colorado's population but knew a good soak in a tub of hot water was considered a necessity after a day on the slopes. After she viewed the house of her dreams, one she could actually afford, she had made a silent promise to herself and her girls: They would have a home of their very own, and unbeknownst to the girls, she planned to surprise them with a new puppy sired by Ice-D, Max's Siberian husky. She intended to keep both promises no matter how hard she had to work.

Placerville was her home now. She'd hated leaving Gypsum, but she was only a twenty-minute drive from Telluride. Grace and Max often made the four-hour drive to visit the resort. They always stopped at the shop to see her, and, of course, Grace wouldn't dream of missing a chance to see the girls. Grace was like the sister and best friend Stephanie had never had.

For nearly two years, Stephanie and the girls had been living in a one-bedroom garage apartment that Grace had found for her when they left Hope House, a shelter for battered and abused women. Grace, along with her new husband, Olympic skier Max Jorgenson, who just happened to own the ski resort where

Stephanie worked, had announced yesterday during the Thanksgiving dinner they'd shared that they were expecting their first child. Grace had made jokes about her age, and Max had insisted she didn't look a day over twenty-one. Almost forty, and finally Grace's dream of having a child was about to come true. Funny, how it had all come together. If anyone had told Stephanie two years ago she and the girls would be on their own, *happily* on their own, she would have told that person he was out of his mind. Women like her couldn't support two young girls on their own, certainly not without financial help or a husband.

Well think again, buster!

So far she'd proved herself wrong, and she intended to keep doing so. She'd escaped from her abusive husband, high school-sweetheart Glenn Marshall, who was now serving eight years at the State Penitentiary in Canon City, Colorado, a maximum-security prison, for escaping the minimum-security prison he had been sent to when he'd originally been jailed for abuse. Stephanie cringed as she remembered how he'd managed to escape while being transported to another minimum-security facility.

It had been her first week at Hope House, just a few days before Christmas. She'd allowed Grace to take the girls to see *The Nutcracker* at Eagle Valley High School. On her way back to Hope House, Grace had to take another route because roadblocks had been set up along I-70 in an attempt to catch the escaped convict.

She'd gotten lost with the girls, wound up searching for help at the first house she'd located, which just happened to be the home of Max Jorgenson, the famous gold medalist Olympic skier. Stephanie recalled the horror-filled night she'd spent when Grace did not return to Hope House with her girls. Fortunately, Grace and the girls had found Max's log cabin on Blow Out Hill and remained there until the roads could be cleared, but not before Glenn, lost and on the run, also found Max's cabin and the girls. When Max found Grace tied up and the girls frightened to death, he'd made quick work of returning Glenn to the deputies who'd lost him in the first place, but not before delivering a few choice knocks that shattered Glenn's nose. Stephanie detested violence, but secretly she'd been delighted when she heard that Glenn had received what he'd dished out to her on a daily basis. And as they say, the rest is history. Almost two years later, Max and Grace were married and expecting their first child. Stephanie couldn't think of a better gift for the couple. They were made for one another.

Unlike her and Glenn.

Two years ago had found her beaten down and afraid to do anything to change her life. With no immediate family, and no close friends to speak of, Stephanie had resigned herself to a life of misery until she'd read an article on battered women. She remembered the part that convinced her she had to make a change, and she'd best make it fast.

It wasn't uncommon for the abuser to turn his anger on his children. . . .

Stephanie knew then she had to get away from Glenn no matter how difficult it proved to be. Two police officers had escorted her and the girls to Hope House immediately after Glenn's arrest. Since they'd been living with Glenn's best friend and drinking buddy, Stephanie had nowhere to go. Shamed, hopeless, and frightened for her children, she'd swallowed what little pride she had and allowed the officers to whisk them away in the middle of the night. Grace had greeted her and the girls like old friends, made them feel welcome, made Stephanie feel as though she was more than just another woman who'd remained in a bad marriage for the sake of the kids. Grace had set Stephanie on a path that had changed her life, and the girls' lives, too.

No longer did she feel worthless and afraid. The girls were resilient, just as Grace had predicted. Though Stephanie knew they were well aware of Glenn's violent behavior, she didn't allow them to dwell on it. Instead, with Grace's effective therapy, they'd acknowledged that some men hit women, and those that did needed to be punished by the proper authorities. Though Glenn wasn't eligible for early parole, Stephanie knew the day would come when he would be released. Until that day arrived, she would continue to work hard to provide a safe and happy home for Ashley and Amanda.

Melanie McLaughlin, her landlord's daughter, had just finished her last year of college when she answered Stephanie's ad for a sitter, explaining that she wanted to take a break before she headed out into the business world. Stephanie was delighted, and the girls adored her. Two mornings a week, Stephanie had to open the shop early for deliveries, so she'd needed someone to see the girls to the bus stop and be there when they returned. Melanie had been a godsend the past two years. She'd started a computer graphics business from her new apartment, which allowed her to continue caring for the girls. This week, they were out of school for Thanksgiving break. Melanie, ever the trouper, was bringing the girls to Maximum Glide later in the day to spend the afternoon on the slopes.

That night was the official lighting of the resort's main Christmas tree. Stephanie had promised the girls they could attend. It would be a long day for all of them, but fun. And she would see Patrick. He'd asked her out several times when she first started working at the shop, but she'd always told him no, saying she wasn't going to date until her divorce from Glenn was final. He'd said he respected that and would ask again. The day her divorce was final, she called to tell Grace, who informed Max, who then let Patrick know. That evening, he'd arrived on her doorstep with flowers for her, two Disney movies for the girls, and a piping-hot cheese pizza for all. She hadn't the heart to turn him away. They'd been out three times since then.

On their last date, they'd gone to the movies. She remembered the movie was a romantic comedy about a couple who each had six kids and married in spite of the antics the kids pulled hoping to keep the couple apart. As expected, the movie ended happily. Stephanie had enjoyed the movie immensely and remarked to Patrick how wonderful it was that the children finally accepted their new step-parents in spite of their earlier misgivings. He hadn't called since. Something was up with him, though she hadn't known what it could be and didn't ask. He was her boss, and she wasn't going to jeopardize her job by asking him why he hadn't called again. If she were completely honest with herself, she would admit it'd hurt her feelings when he hadn't bothered to call or offer an explanation for his sudden lack of interest in her. Even worse, Amanda and Ashley continued to ask when Patrick was coming over again. She'd put them off, telling them it was the busy season at the resort. They'd accepted her answer, but Stephanie knew it was more than that.

Putting all thoughts of her personal life aside, she inspected the store one last time. Everything seemed to be in place. Last but not least, Stephanie plugged the extension cord into the outlet, filling the small shop with bright twinkling lights on the eight-foot blue spruce. Candy Lee Primrose, a bright and witty high school senior and part-time employee, had spent the day before Thanksgiving decorating the tree. Tiny sets of skis, tiny snowboards, miniature sets of ski poles, scarves, brightly colored mittens, and hats hung from its branches. Fresh pine perfumed the air, reminding Stephanie of the giant pines that flanked her favorite blue run, Gracie's Way.

Glancing at her watch for the umpteenth time, Stephanie booted up the computer, clicked a few keys to record the time, then counted out the cash drawer. The credit card machine was up and running for a change. She replaced the white spool of paper with a brand-new one, then went to the alarm panel and punched in the security code to turn off the alarm.

Twenty minutes later, Candy Lee raced through the back door. "Smells wonderful in here," she said as she removed her snow boots and replaced them with a pair of tan Uggs.

"It does, doesn't it?" Stephanie said as she took in the shop, decorated in all its Christmas finery.

She took a deep, cleansing breath.

Here we go, she thought, *let the season begin.*

Chapter Two

Edward Patrick Joseph O'Brien, Patrick to his friends and family, placed a gloved hand on the dash of his most beloved possession, his bright shiny black Hummer. The love of his life. His passion, his reason for getting up in the morning.

Shit!

He was losing it. Too much cold weather had warped his brain, he figured, as he cranked the engine over. He'd become obsessed with Hummers ever since he purchased this baby two years ago. Couldn't get enough of them. He knew just about everything there was to know about the vehicle. If asked, he could tell you there were six different styles; they were originally designed for the military; some were equipped with caterpillar tracks for use in heavy snow and were nicknamed the Snow-Vee. He could go on and on, and did when asked, but mostly he appreciated their performance in the often harsh Colorado winters.

He adjusted the rear-window defroster, then clicked on the fog lights as he maneuvered the Hummer out of the narrow drive at the base of the mountain where he lived in a newly constructed log home. Today was usually one of the busiest days of the season at Maximum Glide, where he was the general manager. He wanted to get an early start before he was bombarded with lost skiers, missing skis, snowboarders monopolizing the slopes, and the broken bones that were sure to happen to some poor unlucky souls. Glancing in his rearview mirror, he caught a glimpse of himself. His coal black hair was in need of a trim, big-time. His dark blue eyes were shadowed with gray half-moons. He'd spent too many late nights carousing with the guys. But what the hell? He was a single guy. What else was there to do after-hours? Currently, there was no special female in his life, no woman for whom he really cared. Not really, or at least no one that he would admit to. He'd been out with Stephanie Casolino-Marshall, the manager of Snow Zone, a few times, but he'd put a stop to that going anywhere real quick-like. Not that he would admit this either, but that woman had touched a part of him that had remained *untouched* for all of his thirty-nine years. He wasn't about to involve himself with a woman whose past was as dark as his black Hummer. No way. Women like her did nothing but cause pain and heartache. At least that was what he believed. He'd seen too many of his best buds go down that path. A woman with kids and an ex was pure trouble with a capital *T*.

That last evening he'd spent with Stephanie had sent him running. That damned movie with all those kids and that *Brady Bunch* happily-ever-after stuff was definitely *not* for him. He'd never asked her out again, and she'd never questioned it. She probably knew she wasn't prime meat on the for-sale market, but hey, that was her problem. She'd been sweet, and in spite of all that she'd been through, there seemed to be a hint of innocence about her. That part had touched him. Before he allowed himself to explore exactly what that meant, he'd boogied his way right back to his old tried-and-true rule. If he hadn't slept with the woman by the third date, she was history. He'd been on four dates with Stephanie and hadn't even kissed her. Definitely time to move on. A vision of dark eyes and long brown hair caused him to veer off the road. And those two girls of hers, well they were absolutely adorable, but kids were totally off-limits for him. No way. His sisters' three boys and one girl were enough kids for an overprotective uncle. Besides, he'd seen what had happened to his sister Colleen. Kids were not on his life list.

"See! This female/kid crap is for the birds," he said. "I'll wreck the Hum if I keep thinking along those lines." He shifted into low gear before turning onto the winding road that led to

Maximum Glide. It was still early; the lifts didn't start running until nine. As it was one of the busiest days of the year at the ski shop, he wanted to check in early, make sure Stephanie and Candy Lee had things under control. He didn't want another episode like last year. He'd thought Stephanie had been ready to take over all the duties at the ski shop. Patrick had insisted she order all the stock for the upcoming season. She'd been doubtful, but said she would do her best. And dammit, her best had cost the resort big bucks. Her order was modest, not near enough to cover them for the month of December. He hadn't been too hard on her because she was so damned . . . well, she was so kind and apologetic. He hadn't the heart to scream and yell at her as he was known to do when things didn't run smoothly. Patrick simply wanted to do the best job possible. As general manager, it was his responsibility to make sure his employees knew exactly what their jobs entailed; otherwise, it was his ass on the line. Max Jorgenson and Patrick, or "Eddie" as Max still insisted on calling him, had been friends since they were in their early twenties. While Max was busy making Olympic history, Patrick had immersed himself in college at the University of Colorado, where he'd also received his master's degree in political science, thinking someday he would change the world. Like all young men, he'd had an idealistic view of the world's potential for change, and felt it was up to him to contribute to that change. So after he'd graduated, he went to work for the state senate. Eight years of dirty politics destroyed his idealistic vision of making a difference. He'd had his fill of self-interested liars, cheaters, and backstabbers who had anything but the interests of their constituents at heart. Leaving a successful career, Patrick spent that first winter out of politics doing absolutely nothing except hitting the slopes. He reconnected with Max. They'd bummed around for a while, then Max married Kayla and hired him to run the resort. For two years after Kayla's tragic death, his good friend had sat on the sidelines, but now he was happily married to Grace, who Patrick thought was the best of the best. A good egg.

Coming from a large Irish family, with four older brothers and three younger sisters, had made him extra protective of women but guarded, too. He knew what little sneaks they were most of the time. Growing up, he'd been the best big brother he knew how to be. Which in his family meant he'd been to six proms, three of them with his youngest sister, Claire, who'd explained she simply needed him to act as her date because the guys in high school were just "totally immature." Which was a crock of crap. Claire had been trying to hook him up with her best friend Lisa Grimes since the first time Claire brought her home to meet the family her freshman year of high school. Patrick was flattered, but she was too young, and she was like a kid sister to him.

Then there was Megan, a year older than Claire. Megan was the family dreamer. She sailed

through school without any problems but did-
n't have much of a social life. Patrick worried
about her and told her so. Shocked that he'd
felt that way, she revealed that she'd been dating a college man since her sophomore year.
When he'd asked why she hadn't brought him
home, Megan had clammed up. After much
screaming and many threats, Megan had finally told Patrick why she hadn't brought her
boyfriend home to meet the rest of the brood.
He was married. Patrick wanted to find the son
of a bitch and kick his butt, but Megan refused
to reveal his name. She'd made Patrick swear
he wouldn't tell their parents. He'd reluctantly
agreed. Megan reminded him that she didn't
pry into his love life, and he should grant her
the same respect. She'd had him on that one,
but he'd always kept an extra close eye on her.

Three years after Megan graduated from
high school, her married lover divorced his
wife and made an honest woman out of her.
Patrick didn't care much for the guy, now a
high school math teacher. He treated his sister
and their three boys, Joseph, eight, Ryan, six,
and Eric, who'd just celebrated his fourth
birthday, extremely well. As long as Nathan
continued to do so, Patrick would accept him
as his brother-in-law, though not without reser-
vations. Patrick took Megan aside once and
told her if Nathan cheated on his first wife, the
odds were good he'd cheat on her. They'd
been married for twelve years. As far as Patrick
knew, Nathan hadn't strayed.

Finally, there was Colleen, only a year younger

than Patrick. Married to her high school sweetheart as soon as she'd graduated high school,
she didn't bother with college. She'd always
made it very clear to the entire family that becoming a mother was her life's desire. And she
had. Almost one year to the day after she'd
married Mark Cunningham, she delivered a
healthy baby girl, Shannon Margaret. Eighteen months later, Abigail Caitlin came along.
Colleen couldn't have been happier. Mark had
accepted a job with Apple, and they had
moved to Seattle. Their life together had been
almost perfect until Shannon Margaret became ill. At seventeen, Shannon was in her senior year of high school doing all the exciting
things seniors do. Mark and Colleen planned
to surprise her with a bright red Hummer as a
graduation gift. Shannon had been as much in
love with Hummers as he was. A week before
graduation, Shannon had complained about
being extremely tired and short of breath.
Colleen had laughed, telling Shannon her
endless pre-graduation activities would wear
out a triathlete. Shannon continued to com-
plain over the next few days, but no one really
paid much attention. Three nights before
Shannon was due to graduate, Colleen found
her in a heap on the bathroom floor, almost
comatose. She'd called 911, and they'd rushed
her to the hospital, where doctors were mysti-
fied until the results of her blood work came
back from the lab. Shannon suffered from a
rare and oftentimes deadly blood disorder,
Thrombotic thrombocytopenic purpura. The

doctors shortened it to TTP. Her platelet count had dropped to eight thousand, and her red blood count was so low, they'd had to give her red blood cells intravenously. A hematologist was called in. He'd explained to Colleen and Mark exactly what was happening inside Shannon's body. Something had gone wrong with her blood's ability to clot. Patrick was so shocked when he heard she was in the ICU, he didn't really remember the details. Suffice it to say, Shannon died on the very day she should have graduated from high school.

Patrick went through hell for several months, but it was nothing compared to what Colleen, Mark, and Abigail were still going through. No way could he ever withstand that kind of personal loss, hence his desire to stay single and kid-free. He knuckled away an unshed tear and parked the Hummer in his assigned parking place. He slid out of the driver's seat into the bitter early-morning air and jammed his hands in his pockets. His heavy boots crunched against the slush and ice as he walked across the parking lot to the employee entrance of Snow Zone. *Damn it's cold!*

Heavy snow was in the forecast for the weekend. He smiled. Fresh white powder would have skiers waiting in the lift lines for hours. The resort would be especially jam-packed that night as well. It was the night for the Christmas tree-lighting extravaganza. Patrick usually got a big kick out of it, but this year his heart wasn't really into the holiday spirit. His thoughts always returned to Colleen and Shannon. This would be the second year without her.

His parents had retired to Florida after Shannon's death. Claire remained in California, unmarried, a workaholic. She had a successful law firm that took up her every waking moment. She'd flown in for Shannon's memorial service and left immediately after. The rest of the family living in Colorado had gathered at the oldest sibling's house. Last Christmas, his four brothers, Connor, Aidan, Ronan, and Michael, all of whom had married only within the last ten years, and their wives and kids had made a halfhearted attempt at a celebration, for the sake of the kids, but none of their hearts were into the holidays either. Since they were an extremely close-knit Irish family, Shannon's loss had devastated them all. Shannon had been the first grandchild, the first niece. Nothing would ever be the same again.

Patrick pushed all thoughts of sadness aside. There would be time for those memories later. Before opening the employee door, he scraped the ice and brown slush from his boots on the boot scraper beside the door. He could have gone in through the store's public entrance; he had the keys and knew the security code, but he wanted to make a surprise visit. It was his way of checking up on his employees. They never knew when to expect him, kept them on their toes. Max didn't approve of this tactic but allowed it since Patrick ran the entire operation. He'd already spied dozens of early birds waiting patiently in their heated vehicles in the parking lot. Patrick hoped Candy Lee and Stephanie were prepared for the rush.

Entering through the back door, he was greeted by the pleasing scent of coffee and a hint of cinnamon. Before Stephanie or Candy Lee saw him, he made his way up and down the aisles, inspecting the shelves piled high with sweaters, hats, scarves, and a dozen other varieties of clothing that promised to keep their wearers warm. Personally, he never hit the slopes without wearing his Hot Chillys, long johns that truly stood up to the test. He saw that the Hot Chillys display was stocked in all colors and sizes for men, women, and children. Satisfied that there was enough stock to keep the shoppers shopping, Patrick weaved his way through the narrow aisles to the front of the shop. Stephanie and Candy Lee were both sipping from forest green mugs and munching on donuts. Damn, what did they think this was? Snack time? They should be . . . working, not smiling and eating.

C'mon, Patrick, they have to eat!

He shook his head, hoping to clear his thoughts of any negativity. Today called for a positive attitude. Optimism, his mother always advised, when faced with negativity. Growing up, she'd taught him and his brothers and sisters that they were the masters of their lives, and always had the power to choose between optimism or pessimism. Since Shannon's death, more often than not, he'd chosen pessimism. Maybe it was time to turn over a new leaf? Wasn't

Christmastime considered to be a time of goodwill and charity? With his mood suddenly shifting to buoyant while he watched Stephanie laugh as she conversed with Candy Lee, he decided he would choose to be optimistic that day. And it had nothing to do with the image in front of him either. At least that's what he wanted to believe. But deep down, he couldn't deny the simple joy just being in her presence gave him. He felt warm all over as he continued to watch and, yes, admire her. Any man would admire those long legs encased in tight black ski pants that accentuated every curve of her body. A moss-colored Hot Chillys thermal turtleneck clung attractively to her petite frame. She definitely had curves in all the right places. Add the warm brown eyes and hair the color of nutmeg, and Patrick couldn't find a single thing he didn't like about her physical appearance. Hell, he couldn't think of anything he didn't like about her period except for the fact that she was the mother of two young daughters. Amanda and Ashley were as sweet as sugarplums, too. They'd pounced all over him when Stephanie had introduced them. They were very much in need of a father, but he was *not* willing to play that role.

Before he had a chance to make his presence known, Stephanie spied him lingering in the center aisle opposite the front registers.

"Patrick, I had no idea you were coming in this early. Come and have some coffee and donuts before they're all gone. Candy Lee and I have concluded that shopping makes you extremely hungry." She smiled at him as though he were the greatest thing since sliced bread. His heart flip-flopped, then did a backward somersault.

"No thanks. I'm only here for a minute. Just wanted to make sure you were prepared for the onslaught." Patrick crammed his hands in his pockets for fear he'd reach out to smooth the unruly curl that clung to Stephanie's peach-colored cheek.

Stephanie placed her mug on the counter and wiped her mouth with a paper napkin covered with snowmen and reindeer. "I think we're more than ready. Between the two of us, we should be able to handle the rush. If we get too swamped, Melanie said she would help out. She's bringing the girls over to ski today."

Patrick wasn't sure how to reply, so he just nodded. Damn this woman. She made him feel like an inexperienced teenager. All clumsy and unsure of himself. He hated the loss of control.

Stephanie stared at him, the smile leaving her face. "Is that all right? If not, I can tell her to forget it. She said she would stop in before they hit the slopes."

Patrick heard the words, but couldn't have repeated what they were if his life depended on it.

"Patrick! Are you listening to anything she's saying?" Candy Lee asked, her voice several octaves higher than normal.

He blinked his eyes, then shook his head. "Uh, yes, I was thinking."

Candy Lee, never one to mince words with Patrick and always getting away with it because she was not much younger than the age Shannon would've been had she lived, came out from behind the counter to stand beside him. She cupped his elbow in her small hand, guiding him to a stool behind the counter. She put a small finger to his lips. She poured coffee, a large portion of Half and Half, and three scoops of sugar into a white mug decorated with Santas. She plated three donuts from the box beneath the counter. A chocolate-covered glazed, a cream-filled, and a French cruller. "Get some sugar and caffeine into your system. You sound really stupid, Patrick. And I don't believe you were thinking either," she added, squinting her bright blue eyes into slits.

Patrick took a sip of the hot coffee, then took a huge bite of the chocolate-covered confection. Damn, maybe Candy Lee was onto something. This was decadent, almost pure bliss. "Stupid, huh?" he said, then finished off the rest of the donut.

"Well, yes. You have that *off* look on your face, you know, like you're *off* in another world or something," Candy Lee explained.

Patrick took a sip of coffee, then bit into the French cruller. He finished it off in three bites before attacking the cream-filled donut. He would have to spend hours on the slopes burning off all the sugary carbs he'd just consumed. When he finished, he wiped his mouth with one of the snowmen-and-reindeer napkins placed next to the pot of coffee. "Thanks for the compliment and the calories, kid. Stephanie, if you get in a bind, call my cell number. I'll send a Maximum Glide employee from the ski school to help out. I can't risk Melanie's getting hurt or injuring someone else."

Stephanie started to speak, but before she could utter a single word, Patrick spoke up. "It's company policy. Sorry."

"Of course, I understand, it's just that Melanie offered. I told her to stop by just in case." Stephanie swatted at the hair clinging to her cheek. "I doubt we'll need the extra help, but of course I will call you if we do." She swallowed, lifted her chin a notch higher, and met his gaze.

Avoiding her direct stare, Patrick glanced at the display of flavored lip balm on the counter for fear he'd give his feelings away.

Feelings? He wasn't going there. No how, no way!

Absorbed in a sudden rush of unwanted emotions, new and *unwanted* emotions, Patrick gave her a disparaging look. After all, she was nothing more than an employee. "I'll expect nothing less. Maximum Glide can't afford another costly mistake."

Much to his surprise, she showed no reaction to his comment. She simply turned her back to him as though he'd said nothing.

He hurried toward the door without another word said. Feeling like the idiot that he was, he started to return and offer an apology, then decided against it. He didn't want her to think he was sorry for his comment. He truly meant it. Maximum Glide was in the red. If he didn't pull off a financial miracle this year, they would all be out of jobs.

Chapter Three

Expert at hiding her emotions, Stephanie was too stunned to reply to Patrick's hateful comment. She'd spent years deflecting Glenn's insults. One would've thought she would be used to such verbal abuse. Too stunned to cry, not to mention how humiliated she was to have Candy Lee witness her being reprimanded, she swallowed back any thought of an outburst.

She tossed her Christmas napkin in the garbage can and downed the last of her now-cold coffee before turning to Candy Lee. It was all she could do to keep from commenting on what a jerk Patrick had acted like, but she knew it was best just to forget about it. And him. He was right. Sort of. She *had* cost the shop loads of money last year. There was no way she would repeat that mistake again this season. With a new sense of determination, Stephanie set out to prove just how wrong he was about her. She was quite capable of working as many hours as needed to see that Snow Zone turned a profit. She didn't care if she had to peddle their wares on the slopes.

As soon as the back door closed, alerting them to Patrick's departure, Candy Lee voiced her opinion. "He can be such a nitwit. I don't know why you let him talk to you like that. You need to speak up for yourself." She sprayed window cleaner on the glass-top counters. "If he doesn't think we're capable of doing the work, he should tell us straight up."

Stephanie thought he just had, but didn't bother saying so to Candy Lee. They had a busy day ahead of them. Whining and arguing would only put them both in a negative frame of mind. She was sure this was the last thing the Christmas shoppers wanted to encounter on the busiest day of the year. They wanted *holly-jolly-ho-ho-ho,* and she would give them *holly-jolly-ho-ho-ho* no matter what.

Wanting to discourage further talk of Patrick's behavior, Stephanie cleared her throat. "He's just doing his job. Forget about it because I intend to this very second."

Candy Lee shook her head. "Well, then you're a nicer person than I am. I don't even know why I work here; well, I need the extra cash but still . . . I was in the storage room the other day and overheard two guys that work the lifts talking about him. I guess Mr. O'Brien chewed them out after four people fell when

they were getting off the lift at their check-
points, which we all know isn't really anyone's
fault," Candy Lee stated as she vigorously polished the glass-topped counters. "I'm pretty good
on a pair of skis myself, and I still suck ice
every now and then."

"Suck ice?" Stephanie inquired.

"Fall down, you know, suck ice," Candy Lee
informed her.

Stephanie laughed. "No, I hadn't heard that
term, but do me a favor and try not to use it in
front of the girls." They'd seen enough in their
short lives. Stephanie was trying her best to
make up for what they'd witnessed. She
wanted to keep them innocent as long as possible.

"Sure," Candy Lee said. "Though they'll hear
it soon enough on the slopes. Especially from
the snowboarders. They always cuss and spit.
It's so gross."

Stephanie gave a small laugh. "I've heard
them more than once myself. I just want to
keep the girls away from anything . . . off-color,
at least for a while. Now"—Stephanie glanced
at her watch—"let's lower the drawbridge and
prepare for battle."

At precisely seven o'clock, Stephanie unlocked the main door, where a line of shoppers
anxiously waited to spend their money. Stephanie said hello to those she knew, greeted others she didn't, then headed to the register,
where she spent the next four hours ringing
up ski jackets, ski pants, mittens, hats, and ski

boots. It was almost lunchtime before they had a chance to take a break. Tallying up the morning sales in her head, Stephanie figured if this was any indication of how busy the season would be, not only would she be working overtime, she'd prove just how wrong Patrick was about her ability to manage the shop and turn a profit. Plus, she'd have a bit of extra cash, even after putting the down payment on her dream house in Placerville. She would use the extra money to purchase a new bedroom set for the girls.

They'd been without the basic comforts for most of their lives, and for this reason they were appreciative of any gift they received, no matter how large or small. They were good girls, and Stephanie found herself visualizing tucking them into a brand-spanking-new white-canopied bed in their new home. Plus she couldn't wait to see the look on their faces when she announced they would be adopting one of the pups sired by Ice-D. They'd begged for a pet for the past two years, but Stephanie knew it wouldn't be fair to the girls or an animal if she were to bring a pet home to the small garage apartment. There was barely enough room for the three of them as it was. As the girls grew older, she knew they would want and need their privacy. A new home with three bedrooms, not to mention two bathrooms, would be pure heaven for the three of them and a pet. Angry that she'd wasted so much valuable time with Glenn, Stephanie fig-

ured she had to make it up to the girls, and a
home of their own would be a good place for
new beginnings.

Cheered by her thoughts, Stephanie felt a
renewed sense of purpose. She could manage
her life at last, but this time around it would be
on her own terms. She didn't need a man to
take care of her. Look at where that had gotten
her. Actually, Glenn's jailbreak was the catalyst
that had sent her in search of a better life.
Stephanie had learned at an early age that life
wasn't always easy, but at thirty-two, she felt as
though she'd learned enough about life not to
repeat the mistake of allowing a man to have
complete and total control of her life. After
her mother flew the coop to parts unknown,
when Stephanie was three, she'd been sent to
live with her mother's older sister, Aunt Evelyn, who'd loved her like her own daughter.
While they hadn't had much in the way of ma-
terial things, Stephanie knew she was loved.
Sadly, her aunt had passed away the year she
graduated from high school. While grieving
for the only mother figure she'd ever known,
Stephanie had allowed Glenn to step in and
control her every move. At first she'd enjoyed
her newfound lack of responsibility as she'd
spent most of her life caring for Aunt Evelyn,
who'd been severely crippled with rheumatoid
arthritis. However, her independence was
short-lived. She and Glenn married right after
graduation; he started drinking, and within a
year turned into an angry, bitter, controlling
man. Having no outlet for his anger, he made

Stephanie into his punching bag. And as they say, the rest is history. Though this time around, Stephanie was writing her own story.

Stephanie had a job to do in the here and now, so she pushed all negative thoughts of her past to that little dark corner of her mind, where they remained dormant most of the time.

"Why don't you take your lunch break now. We're staying open until seven tonight. This might be the only chance you'll have. Once the lifts are closed, I expect we'll be swamped."

Candy Lee looked at the Minnie Mouse watch on her wrist. "Okay. You want me to bring you something back? You have to eat, too," Candy Lee informed her in that all-knowing teenage way.

"Yes, that's why I brought my lunch with me. I knew I wouldn't have time to go to The Lodge for lunch today. Now, go on and get back here," Stephanie said, using her mothering tone.

Candy Lee grabbed her purse from beneath the counter, gave a quick salute, and raced out the back door. Stephanie watched her as she tore through the icy parking lot. Had she ever been that young and carefree? If she had, she couldn't pull up the memory. She had new memories to make, and this time around they'd be the kind she'd always dreamed of.

Wouldn't they?

Chapter Four

Melanie held a mitten-clad hand in each of hers. The slopes were always dangerously crowded the first day after Thanksgiving. If she let go of Ashley or Amanda, it would be very easy to lose sight of them. Stephanie had made sure to tell the girls to dress in their neon yellow ski suits; that way they would be easy to spot. Melanie glanced around her, seeing at least a dozen other young children dressed in the same neon yellow suits that her charges wore. *So much for sticking out like a sore thumb,* she thought. Melanie wouldn't let the girls get too far from her sight no matter what.

"Auntie M," Ashley said. Melanie laughed when Ashley called her by the new nickname they'd christened her with after she'd allowed them to watch *The Wizard of Oz* four times last week. "Can we ski on the blue trails today? *Please?* Uncle Max says we're as good as most of the older kids, and their parents let them ski the blue runs."

"Puhleeze," Amanda echoed.

"I guess so, but not by yourselves. I'll go with you," Melanie stated firmly. "There are a lot of skiers out today, so we have to be extra careful."

"Yeah, or we'll get hurt, right? And then Mommy will have to take us to the hospital, and we'll have to stay there cause she won't have enough money to pay the hospital bill, *right,* Auntie M?" Amanda crooned in a squeaky voice.

At five-foot-nine, Melanie had to stoop in order to be at eye level with both girls. She wanted to wrap them both in her arms and tell them she would never allow that to happen. And she had the resources to keep that pledge, having inherited millions from her grandparents. Nor would her wealthy parents allow it. But Melanie knew how badly Stephanie wanted to make her way in the world on her own, so Melanie had carefully refrained from even hinting at her own financial situation.

Stephanie had told her more than once about her life with Glenn. Determined to provide for her children, Stephanie had rules she'd explained to Melanie when she'd first taken the job, and one of those rules was no financial help, no loans, no expensive gifts. Two years ago, Melanie's parents, longtime supporters of Grace's work with battered women at Hope House, had reduced the rent to something that Stephanie could afford. And to the best of Melanie's knowledge, no one, including Grace, had ever breathed a word of this to Stephanie.

Melanie smiled at both girls. "Well, we won't have to worry about that because you're both such good little skiers, I can't even imagine either of you falling down, let alone getting hurt so badly that you would have to go to the hospital. So let's not even think about that. How about the three of us take the lift up to Sugar Hill, ski to Snow Zone where we'll stop in and see your mom, then maybe grab a cup of hot chocolate at The Lodge?"

Both girls nodded in agreement.

They were both worrywarts, something Melanie wished she could change, but time more than anything else would help to ease the fear and anxiety both girls tended to feel. Again, given their start in life, it was a miracle they hadn't suffered anything more than becoming overly cautious where their mother was concerned. Melanie wasn't sure she would've been able to cope at such a young age had her life been as tragic as theirs had been.

"Are you taking us to the Christmas tree lighting tonight, too?" Amanda asked. "Mommy says it's the highlight of the start of the holiday season. What's that mean?"

Ashley looked at Melanie with a knowing smile. "You want me to tell her?"

"Absolutely," Melanie said, bending over to tighten the hooks on her ski boots.

Ashley pursed her lips, moved them from side to side as though she were contemplating the best answer. "Well, it's kinda like the first day of school when the teacher tells the class what she wants us to learn that year, only the Christmas season is short and a lot more fun." She looked at Melanie for confirmation.

Grinning at the complete and total simplicity of Ashley's explanation, Melanie stated, "I couldn't have said it better myself."

"It's sorta like a new beginning, right, Auntie M?" Ashley said.

She continued to be amazed by the girls' perception. They were both exceptionally intelligent for their ages. Melanie knew Stephanie took great pride in her children's education. Many times Melanie had stopped by their apartment only to find the three of them gathered at the kitchen table with a pile of books in front of them studying anything and everything, ranging from science to geography.

"That's exactly what it is," Melanie agreed.

"Then let's go. I wanna ride the lift now. Can I sit in the middle?" Amanda asked.

Melanie stood up to her full height, gazed to her left, where she saw that the lift lines were getting longer by the minute. If they were lucky, they'd have just enough time for one run before stopping in to see Stephanie. "Let's do our safety check first." Melanie had spent most of her life on the slopes but never took her skill or that of the girls for granted. A loose boot buckle or a stray article of clothing could cause a lifetime disability. Melanie wasn't going to allow the girls to get hurt on her watch. No way. They went through their usual routine.

First, they checked to make sure they had all the basics covered. Skis and boots were fastened properly. Pole straps were checked. Helmets and goggles were secure. Gloves were on properly. Since the season was predicted to be one of the coldest on record, Melanie had given the girls foot and hand warmers to place inside their gloves and boots, plus she now put an extra set of each in the inside zippered pocket of their ski jackets. Each of them had a tube of cherry-flavored lip balm in her pocket, along with a granola bar. As an added precaution, Melanie always made sure Ashley kept a pack of waterproof matches inside her jacket. One never knew. At ten, Ashley had been taught a few basic survival skills. Melanie was sure Ashley would never need them as long as she was around, but that was part of being prepared. One must always prepare for the unexpected.

"Sunscreen on our faces, and we're good to go," Melanie said, removing a small tube of sunscreen from her pocket. She made quick work of slathering their faces with the cream before readjusting their helmets and goggles. "Now remember, I'm in the rear, and you two always stay in front of me. If you need to stop and rest, just stop at the side of the run that faces away from the mountain, okay?"

"Okay," the girls parroted.

Melanie followed close behind the girls as they skied to the long lift lines. Dozens of skiers dressed in every color of the rainbow swished in and out of the lanes, racing to get to the front of the lift line. Melanie kept her eyes on the girls as they carefully maneuvered toward the chairlifts. They were moving surprisingly fast today considering it was the first official day of the Christmas season. Throngs of skiers dotted the mountainside, like the lofty evergreens that flanked the trails.

Above, the skies were heavy with slate gray clouds. The wind was frigid, the conditions perfect for a snowstorm. Melanie wanted to take the girls up for at least one run since the weather might not cooperate later in the day. The forecast called for snow, a necessity for all skiers and snowboarders, but Melanie didn't like the looks of the clouds looming above the mountaintops. Since the snowfall wasn't predicted until later in the afternoon, she reasoned they should have time for at least one decent run.

When it was their turn at the chairlift, the trio slid into position directly behind the bold red line, and gripped their ski poles in their left hands as they'd been taught while looking behind them to see the chairlift as it slowed to allow them to take a seat. Once seated with the safety bar down, Melanie commented, "You two are really getting to be pros at this. It took me forever to learn how to load up without falling."

Since they were going on the blue runs, their ride was longer than normal. It took almost seven minutes for the ski lift to arrive at their designated stop. During the ride up, both girls chatted nonstop, telling her what they hoped Santa would bring them for Christmas. They'd told her about the wall plaques they had made for their mom in art class, and last but not least, they said that their "Aunt Grace" wanted to introduce Melanie to her brother, Bryce.

She couldn't help but blush. She'd seen Bryce at Maximum Glide on more than one occasion. He was the epitome of a true hunk. Melanie thought he fit the image of a ski bum more so than that of a college professor. Lucky for her, they arrived at their stop in time to provide her with an excuse not to answer. But she knew these little mischief makers, and this wouldn't be the last of that conversation. They were relentless when it came to questioning why she wasn't married and didn't have children of her own.

Both girls exited the lift chair with ease, skiing away as fast as possible so as not to block the next group of skiers preparing to exit the lift.

The particular area on the mountain where Melanie was taking them had an elevation closer to thirteen thousand than twelve thousand feet. The air was thin at that altitude, making one almost gasp for oxygen. The temperature was several degrees lower than at the base of the mountain. Wind gusts at this height caused the majestic towering evergreen tops to sway from side to side, their movements producing a soft whisper, a slow dance, with the bone-chilling winds supplying a soft whistle as their music.

Melanie skied to where the girls were waiting. "Are you both ready?" she asked.

Again, they nodded their helmet-covered heads.

Melanie motioned with her gloved hand for them to begin their descent. They pushed off like two little thoroughbreds, traversing downward without getting too close to the edge of the mountainside. Melanie trailed behind them for several minutes before the run led to a bowl of intersections leading to three different areas on the mountain. One ski lift would take them to the very top of the mountain, where they would find the double black diamond runs. The second lift would take them to the opposite side of the mountain, where the terrain park allowed freestylers and snowboarders to hone their acrobatic skills on half-pipes, rails, ramps, and tables. The third lift led to the mogul runs, for those hardy souls brave enough to tackle the minimounds of packed snow that dipped to the bottom of the mountain at a ninety-degree angle. The girls knew that they were supposed to wait for her at the big blue sign directing them back to lift number one at the base of the mountain.

She weaved in and out of the groups of skiers, passed a friend who was on the ski patrol. When she reached the intersection, she searched for the two neon yellow ski suits. Seeing a small group gathered at their appointed sign, Melanie made quick work of poling over

to get the girls. When she arrived, she was a bit
surprised to find that neither of the two kids
wearing yellow neon ski suits was Ashley or
Amanda. She pushed off and circled the bowl.
Seeing that there were no pint-sized girls wearing yellow suits, she stopped once again and
scanned the area around her. Then she skied
slowly around the perimeter of the bowl once
again, and she thoroughly searched the sides
of the run, where a grove of evergreens flanked
the trail. Maybe they'd fallen, hit a small snowdrift, or something, she thought.

Melanie jammed her poles into the snow behind her, trying to pick up speed on the flat
terrain. She went from side to side, looking in
every possible direction, every gully, and even
went off trail, thinking one of the girls might
have gone to the woods looking for a bit of privacy in order to use the restroom. They'd done
this before, and while Melanie didn't approve
of it, sometimes Mother Nature's call had to be
answered no matter what. After searching for
fifteen minutes, Melanie had a sneaky feeling
the girls had decided to go off on their own.
This was not good. Not at all. If she didn't locate the girls at the end of the run, she'd have
to contact the ski patrol and explain the situation.

What was even worse, she'd have to explain
to Stephanie that she'd lost her children.

Chapter Five

Candy Lee returned from lunch in the nick of time. Stephanie had managed to eat a few bites of her turkey sandwich between customers. She'd thought the lunch hour would be quiet, but she'd been wrong again. She'd been so bombarded with customers, she hadn't had time to think. Good thing Patrick wasn't there to witness her poor planning. She took a deep breath, exhaled, and smiled at a young mother waiting in line with two small children clinging to her legs. Amanda still did that at times. Stephanie didn't mind, as she wanted to keep the girls sheltered for as long as she could given that the first years of their lives had been plagued by violence and fear.

She looked at her watch. It was almost one o'clock. Melanie had promised to bring the girls by. Stephanie felt a shiver of alarm run up her spine but remembered this was Black Friday. The lift lines were probably as busy as she was. If they weren't here in half an hour or so, she'd call Melanie's cell to check on them. Both girls were natural-born skiers, and Stephanie knew from experience that once they were out on the slopes, it was quite a task to get them to stop for anything. Poor Melanie. She'd take her to dinner and a movie when the holidays were over. Just the two of them. They needed a girls' night out anyway. Maybe she'd invite Grace to join them.

So caught up was she with the customers coming in and out purchasing everything from lip balm to ski boots that when Stephanie glanced at her watch again she was shocked to see that it was already after two o'clock. Worry caused her brow to furrow, but if there was a problem, Melanie knew to call her at the shop. Stephanie continued to ring up sales while Candy Lee restocked and refolded the pile of sweaters on the half-price table. If sales kept up like this, Stephanie might have to call Patrick and take advantage of his offer to send another Maximum Glide employee to her rescue. It was the last thing she wanted to do, but she and Candy Lee could only stretch themselves so thin. Dreading the thought, she looked up as Melanie entered the shop and hurried to the back of the store. Her cheeks were reddened from the wind, her long blond braid hung haphazardly down her back, and her normal cheerful smile was nowhere to be seen. *Emergency potty break,* Stephanie thought as she walked to the back of the store.

"I wondered what happened to you girls. I was about to worry," Stephanie said. "Where are the girls? I bet they're freezing." As Stephanie was about to turn around and head for the entrance to tell her daughters to come inside and warm up, Melanie grabbed her arm and prevented her from taking another step.

"Melanie!" Stephanie shrieked. "What's wrong? Where are the girls?"

Melanie looked down at the floor, where puddles of water had pooled around her ski boots. She shook her head from side to side, then looked Stephanie squarely in the face. "I was hoping they would be here with you. I've spent the past two hours looking for them."

Stephanie felt her heart plummet to her feet and back, then lodge in the back of her throat. She tried to speak but was unable to utter a single word. She shook her head, hoping she'd just imagined what Melanie had said, but the look on her babysitter's face told her she'd heard correctly.

Glenn? It couldn't be!

Melanie must have read her mind. "They're on this mountain somewhere skiing, I'm sure of it; no way did their dad bust out of jail. They were so excited about going on the blue run, I think they simply forgot to wait for me at the appointed area. I saw them ski all the way down, then I lost sight of them for what couldn't

have been more than two or three minutes. By
the time I got to the meeting point, they were
nowhere to be found."

Stephanie felt as though she would simply
die. Just die and be done with it. But she wasn't
a quitter, especially where her children were
concerned. She'd been this route before and
would do whatever she had to do to protect
her daughters. She wanted to strangle Melanie, but her anger would have to wait. She
had to find her children before it was too late.
Just minutes ago, she'd heard a snow report,
and it didn't sound good. She'd heard a few
customers saying they'd heard the lifts were
going to close early if the snow report held
true.

Springing into action, Stephanie raced to
the office, where she grabbed her old skis,
poles, and boots. She knew this mountain like
the back of her hand. If her girls were lost, she
wasn't going to wait around. She was going to
find them no matter how long it took. She
raced out of the office, shouting to Candy Lee
over her shoulder. "There's an emergency.
Call Patrick and tell him to send someone over
to help you. The girls are lost on the mountain!"

Melanie raced after her. "Stephanie, you
can't go out in this weather. The storm is moving in faster than the forecasters anticipated.
I've contacted the ski patrol, and they're all
out searching for them. They'll need their
mother once they're found."

As Stephanie raced out the back door to the snowy parking area, she stopped to lay her skis down on the crusted snow on the path that would lead her to the lifts. She shot a quick glance at Melanie and saw thick tears streaming down her face and knew she was as concerned for the girls' safety as she was. She leaned in to give her a quick hug. "I can't *not* search for them, Melanie. They're all I have," Stephanie said as she buckled her ski boots and slid her boots into the skis' binding. After she heard the required click letting her know her boots were fitted securely into her skis, she pushed away from Melanie, heading to the lift. She poled as fast as she could through the clumps of ice and brown slush. An injury was the last thing she needed.

Arriving at lift number one, Stephanie practically soared to the chair, where she was met by a young boy of no more than eighteen. She'd seen him around but couldn't recall his name.

"We're closing the lifts. Sorry," he said as he stood in front of the chair Stephanie was preparing to get on.

She shook her head. "No, I have to get up there. My girls are lost. The ski patrol is looking for them now." Stephanie saw the look of indecision on the boy's face. "Look, I won't tell anyone you let me ride up to the mountain in these conditions. I have to get up there, please!" Stephanie shouted. Giant flakes of snow scattered across her cheeks as she stared at the boy. Apparently he decided her request was worth the risk because he went inside his mini-booth, and the chair began to move slowly.

A million thoughts went through her mind as the lift made its climb to the top of the mountain. What if they couldn't find the girls in time? With the weather conditions worsening by the minute, they wouldn't last long in this cold. Stephanie knew Ashley understood basic survival skills, as she'd insisted that Ashley take a junior mountain-survival class last year when the child had pleaded with her, telling Stephanie she was old enough to ski the green runs alone. They'd compromised. Ashley took the class and was allowed to ski certain green runs, but she had to take Stephanie's cell phone with her. Why hadn't she thought to get the girls phones of their own? They could have called for help. The reception on the mountain was excellent, so there wasn't an issue about lack of coverage. Why in the world hadn't she provided both girls with such a necessity? She remembered when she first arrived at Hope House. Grace had insisted she take a cell phone, saying she gave them to all the women at Hope House just in case they needed to dial 911. Why, why, *why* had she been so irresponsible? Money, she thought as she shivered in the bone-chilling air. She'd been so intent on giving the girls a home of their own, she'd lost sight of their other wants and needs. Ashley had asked for a cell phone months ago, and Stephanie had dismissed it, telling her she was too young for a phone of her own, saying it was an added expense that she didn't need. How she wished she'd given in! As they say, hindsight is twenty-twenty. Little good it did her to dwell on what she should've done. Now all she wanted was to find both of her daughters safe and sound. She gave a silent prayer. *Please let them be safe. I'll equip them both with GPS if I find them safe and unharmed.*

The lift came to a slow stop at the top of the mountain. Stephanie practically jumped out of the chair. She whipped down the trail, making the twists and turns from memory, as the snow was coming down heavier by the minute. She wiped her hand across her goggles just in time to get a decent look at the bowl where Melanie had last seen the girls. She knew the girls would never attempt to ski a black diamond trail, so she followed Melanie's route, hoping and *praying* that she would magically find her girls hiding behind a snowdrift, visible only to her. She'd bring them back to the Snow Zone, where they'd sip hot chocolate, warm their hands with the chemical hand warmers they sold at the shop, all the while relaying to Candy Lee how brave they had been. If only, Stephanie thought as she traversed down the last quarter mile of the run, with still no sign of her children. She stopped every few minutes to call out their names, only to have her voice drowned out by the turbulent sound of the wind as it whipped through the towering evergreens.

Tears stung her eyes, freezing against her windburned cheeks as she continued to ski in areas that she knew were off-limits for the girls, but at this point she'd have skied down Mount Everest blindfolded if she thought it would bring her girls back. The late-afternoon sky was overcast, the light flat and indistinct, the snowfall heavy and thick, making visibility almost nil. These were blizzard conditions, Stephanie thought. Why hadn't she paid closer attention to the weather forecast? Why had she even allowed the girls on the slopes, knowing how packed they would be? She was stupid, her skill as a parent equivalent to that of a teenage babysitter. Her throat was dry, and her heart pounded in her chest as she used every ounce of energy she had left to pole her way back to the lift. She'd seen the chairs as they hung suspended from the heavy-duty cables, empty of passengers. Knowing the lifts were closed wasn't going to stop her. She'd borrow a snowmobile from the ski patrol. She was not leaving this mountain until she found Amanda and Ashley.

Alive. The word skittered through her brain. *Alive. Alive. Alive.* From out of nowhere, Stephanie was filled with a complete and utter sense of peace and well-being. Without knowing why, she suddenly knew her girls were alive. And not only were they alive, but they were fine.

Somewhat shocked by the epiphany she'd just experienced, she debated her next move. With the temperature dropping into negative numbers, Stephanie stopped in the middle of the storm, took a deep breath, and prayed for a higher power to guide her in the right direction. As though controlled by an outside force, she pointed her ski tips in the direction of Snow Zone, where she saw a crowd gathered outside its doors. Briefly, she wondered how anyone could possibly shop when her girls were missing, but then common sense took over. These people had no idea where her children were. For that matter, Stephanie was sure they didn't have a clue about her or her life. And why should they? She was nothing more than a shop manager who couldn't seem to keep tabs on two small children.

Beyond cold and knowing she needed to check in with the ski patrol, Stephanie skied as far as the snow allowed before she stopped to remove her skis, leaving them in the middle of the parking lot. Not wanting to disturb the crowd gathered at the front door, she used the employee entrance. Inside, she hurried to her office, where she dialed the emergency number for the ski patrol. The line rang a dozen times before a recorded message told her to dial 911 if this was a true emergency. What the heck? Wasn't someone supposed to be there manning the phones in case of an emergency? Wasn't that the entire point of having a ski patrol? Were they out searching for the girls? She hit the END button on the phone, then saw her black leather, fur lined boots, which she'd tossed under her desk. She quickly pulled off her ski boots, changed out of her damp socks into a dry pair, and crammed her feet into her warm boots before heading to the front of the store, where dozens of people stood in a semicircle. She would ask Candy Lee if she'd heard anything, then she would go to the ski patrol office to see if there was anyone there with any news of the girls. This was beyond a nightmare. The girls should be enjoying their Christmas vacation. They'd been so excited about tonight's tree-lighting ceremony. How could a day that started out so perfect turn into one so horrid? It actually caused her physical pain to think beyond the *what ifs* and the *if onlys*. She couldn't even imagine life without her children.

She wouldn't go there! *She couldn't.*

Stephanie hurried to the front of the store, where she found Candy Lee and Melanie . . . *smiling.*

How could they even think about smiling at a time like this? She was about to ask that very question when she saw what or rather whom they were smiling at.

Her girls.

Sipping cups of hot chocolate.

Chapter Six

Stephanie was momentarily stunned when she saw Amanda and Ashley seated behind the counter. "Thank goodness you're both okay! What happened? Where, who?" Stephanie cried out. She glanced around her, only to discover Patrick, along with several Maximum Glide employees, grinning from ear to ear. Apparently the two mischief makers had a story to tell.

Overwhelmed by the sheer relief of seeing her daughters safe and sound, Stephanie forced her way behind the counter. Not caring that she was being watched by several dozen strangers, she wrapped an arm around each of her daughters. Tears of relief streamed down her face, and her heart sang with delight as she breathed in the scent she knew and loved so well. The sweet smell of Johnson's Baby Shampoo clung to their long, dark hair. Stephanie gloried in the moment as she recalled her vision of her daughters being alive and well. It had happened exactly as she knew it would. She would leave it at that. After all, it was Christmas, and she still believed in miracles.

Candy Lee handed her a wad of tissues along with a piping-hot mug of cocoa. "You're gonna need this," she said.

Stephanie wiped the tears from her eyes, then took a sip of her drink. "Okay, now I think it's time I heard exactly what happened out on that mountain today."

"Patrick saved us, Mommy! He really did, then he cried," Amanda said. "Right, Ashley?"

Those were the last words Stephanie expected to hear. She caught Patrick's gaze across the group that had gathered around the girls. He smiled. Sort of. Joy bubbled up inside her like an overflowing fountain. She smiled back.

"I don't think he was crying. I think it was just the cold air," Ashley stated matter-of-factly in the way that only a ten-year-old can.

Patrick edged through the crowd, stopping when he reached the girls. "Why don't you tell your mother what happened out on that mountain today. I think she'll be very proud of you two," he added. "And it might help to keep you both out of trouble," he went on, grinning from ear to ear.

Amanda spoke up, "Are we in trouble? I sure hope not 'cause I still want to go to that tree-lighting thing. We can still go, right, Mommy?"

Using a firm-yet-gentle tone, Stephanie explained, "A lot of people were worried about you two today. Right now, I want to know what happened, then we will think about the Christmas tree lighting."

Ashley started to speak, then hesitated as the crowd gathered closer. Suddenly, she seemed bashful, almost as though she were afraid.

Patrick observed her hesitancy. In a boisterous voice, he spoke directly to the group. "I think Ashley feels a bit overwhelmed. If you're not here to shop, why don't we give the little lady a few minutes with her mother. As most of you know, these children have been through quite an ordeal." Patrick paused as he waited for the crowd to disperse. At least two dozen people left the shop, but not before wishing the girls good luck and congratulating them on a job well-done. The remaining few were Maximum Glide employees. Patrick turned to Stephanie. "If you don't mind, a few of my employees would like to stay and hear the rest of the story since they were part of the search party."

Stephanie looked at Ashley. "Only if you're okay with this?" If she didn't find out soon what her daughters had been involved in, she would take them to her office, where they could have a few moments of privacy.

"I'm okay with it, Mom," Ashley replied.

"Then spill the beans because I don't think I can wait another minute. I've been beside myself with worry the past hour," Stephanie said, in hopes that this would hurry along what was becoming quite a lengthy process.

"We were waiting for Melanie at the sign, but then me and Amanda heard this really loud crying sound. It was by that building where they keep those giant machines that smooth out the snow." Ashley smiled. "Then we just followed the crying. It was inside the building, so we weren't really cold, but Amanda had to use the potty in the corner."

"And there wasn't anyplace to wash my hands either, so I just . . . didn't," Amanda offered.

Laughter pealed from the employees as they listened.

"Go on," Stephanie encouraged.

"We heard where the crying noise came from." Ashley looked at Patrick. "She's gonna be okay, right?"

"Thanks to you and your sister she is," Patrick said. "Now don't keep your mom waiting any longer."

"Once we were inside the building, we just followed the cries. And that's when we found the mommy dog. She was so sad, her eyes had that look you know? So we just waited for her to stop crying, but then I saw a little baby puppy, and there was another one that was trying to . . . get out of the mommy's belly. That's why she was crying 'cause it was hurting her so bad. Amanda covered the baby pup up with her ski jacket."

"And I rubbed her head, too," Amanda informed them.

Ashley laughed at her little sister. "And the

puppy was fine. But the mommy was still crying, and that's when I helped her out, sort of."

Stephanie wasn't sure what was coming next, but something told her it was about to make her day.

"I watched those little tiger cubs on Animal Planet. That man helped take the cubs out with his hands, so I just did what he did, and another puppy came out, and the mommy stopped crying. She licked the puppy, and we gave her our granola bars. Amanda and me melted some snow and gave it to her to drink. So once the mommy had both of her pups, she just licked 'em, then she fed 'em. We put our jackets on them, so they wouldn't freeze. I wanted to leave to find Melanie so she could help us with the dogs, but when I peeked out of the shed, I didn't see her anywhere. The snow was really pouring out of the sky by then. And I remembered what I learned in my survival class. They taught us to stay where there was shelter, and, well, that's what we did." Ashley told the story as if it were something a ten and seven-year-old did every day.

The employees applauded loudly, some calling out to Ashley "Way to go!" "You're a hero!" "You can ski with me anytime!"

Ashley appeared surprised by all the attention, so she just smiled as some of the employees stopped to give her a hug before they left. Stephanie watched in amazement as her daughter accepted their thanks in stride as though this were a normal, everyday event.

Stephanie wasn't sure exactly what to think right then. How was it possible that her ten-year-old daughter had delivered a puppy? And not only that, she remembered what to do in an emergency situation while in a snowstorm. Tears pooled once again. She was extremely proud of both girls for using their heads in this situation when most children their age wouldn't have had a clue as to what to do. And where and how did Patrick fit into the picture?

"I can't tell you how proud I am of you both. I'm sure the dog was grateful you two showed up when you did, but that still doesn't get either of you off the hook for not waiting for Melanie. She was worried about you, and so was I. You both know how I feel about knowing where you are at all times, right?"

The girls nodded in unison.

"But what about helping others? Didn't you tell us that's what good, decent people do?" Ashley asked, a puzzled look on her face.

Oh boy. Stephanie didn't think now was the time to get into the moral of this lesson. She would wait until they were home, where they could discuss this in private. For the moment, she was simply relieved that they were alive and didn't seem to be fazed in the least by their experience.

Stephanie needed to know Patrick's role in finding her daughters. Since it didn't appear as though he wanted to tell his side of the story, she turned to face him. For a second, she was flustered. He was so sexy, with his wind-blown raven black hair just a shade too long.

And those blue eyes. Well she knew she could drown in them if given the opportunity, but it wasn't the time. "How did you find the girls? And before you say anything, let me say thank you."

Patrick chuckled. "It was by sheer luck, trust me. When Candy Lee called me and told me they were missing, and with the storm worsening by the minute, I didn't want to take a chance on using the snowmobiles. I took the lift up to the garage, where we store the Snow Cats. I found them there caring for the dogs. I loaded the pups and the girls into the cab, and brought them here before dropping the dogs off with a friend of mine who's a veterinarian. I stopped back by to make sure you'd found them. End of story."

"I can't thank you enough. I was beside myself with worry," Stephanie said, then stopped. "I know you don't have children, so you probably haven't a clue what it feels like knowing you might not see them again, so thanks, Patrick. You can't imagine how much this means to me."

"As long as you don't get any funny ideas about the future," he said.

Shock at his remark yielded quickly to anger. Not caring that he was her boss, and not caring that he was the man who'd just saved her daughters from being stuck out in a blizzard, Stephanie found she was practically breathless with rage. How dare he? And in front of her daughters, Candy Lee, and Melanie! She swallowed the vile words she wanted to sling at him before she made a fool of herself. Taking a breath, as much as she was able to, Stephanie spoke, letting her eyes convey the outrage and fury she felt. "Mr. O'Brien, trust me, any 'funny ideas' I may have had about you have been completely erased from my memory. If you don't mind, I'm going to take my girls home so they can change their clothes, then we're going to the Christmas tree lighting." She walked to the front of the store, where she flipped the OPEN sign to CLOSED.

"You can't do that! We've got two more hours before it's time to close up shop. In spite of what you may think, there are people still out there who might want to visit the shop before they call it a day. You can't just leave. There is money to be made, and I expect you to stay here and do your job. Or else," he added.

Knowing Patrick had about as much tact as a rattlesnake didn't excuse his smart-ass comments, and for once in her life, Stephanie refused to allow a man to browbeat her into submitting to his demands. Without giving it another thought, she shot back, "Or else what?"

She knew her remark caught him off guard just by looking at him. His nostrils flared like those of an angry stallion. She was familiar with Patrick's reputation as a tough and demanding boss, but that didn't prepare her for the words that spewed from his mouth.

He rubbed the dark stubble on his chin and lowered his voice. Standing as close to her as possible, he said, "Or else this. How about you take the next four weeks off work. Spend some quality time with your children."

Stephanie felt the blood rush to her head, settling in her temples only to pound like a jackhammer.

Before she even had a chance to respond, Patrick leaned next to her, and whispered in her ear, "Without pay."

Chapter Seven

As though she were on autopilot, Stephanie hastily took her daughters' hands and practically pulled them off the stools they were sitting on as she raced to her office. Rage consumed her, then the feeling left as quickly as it came, humiliation coming in its stead. She'd lost all her wind, all of her spark, in less than a few seconds. Like a deflating hot air balloon, every emotion, every word, every thought drifted out with each exhalation.

She removed her purse from a bottom drawer and grabbed her car keys from a hook on the wall. She quickly scanned the small space, searching for anything of value she might be leaving behind. Fortunately, her pride was visible only to her.

"What just happened out there?" Melanie whispered.

Stephanie shook her head. "Not now. I have to get out of here."

"You want me to take the girls?" Melanie asked. Realizing the enormity behind the innocent comment, Melanie swallowed. "I mean I can take them to the Christmas tree lighting with you, help out."

"Thanks, but I'd like to spend the evening with just the girls. I'm sorry, it's not you, it's . . ." She looked down the hall at the front of the store, where Patrick could be seen bossing Candy Lee around.

Melanie followed her gaze. "I see. Then I'll just go on. You call if you need me for anything, no matter what, okay?"

Melanie's words jolted her back to reality, the reality that she really did need a friend right now. "No, don't, I mean don't go off by yourself. Come with us to the Christmas tree lighting. I think I might need a friend tonight." There, she'd said it. She'd actually taken Grace's advice. When you need help, a friend, a hug, ask for it.

Melanie instantly brightened. "I was hoping you'd say that. I don't want you and the girls to be all alone tonight."

Stephanie nodded, then walked to the employee exit, Amanda and Ashley trailing behind. "You want to ride with us?" Stephanie asked as she stepped out into the frigid evening air. Snowflakes swirled in the bluish glow beneath the lights in the parking lot. Icy wind whipped the ends of her hair as she walked across the almost empty lot to her car, a car in such pitiful condition, it almost made her smile. She'd scrimped and saved for three long months so that she could have a car of her own. She and the girls had used the public bus system, but the buses didn't take them through the drive-thru at McDonald's, nor would a bus be there when they had the sudden urge to go out for ice cream. She'd been so proud of herself when she bought the car, her first major purchase with money she'd earned on her own. But as she fumbled through her pockets for the keys she'd placed there minutes ago, she saw the vehicle for what it really was. An almost-twenty-year-old hunk of junk just barely making it. Sort of like me, she thought as she unlocked the back door for the girls.

Surprisingly, neither girl had uttered a word since they'd witnessed Patrick whisper those harsh words to her. Then it hit her! They weren't talking because they were *afraid!* Even though they hadn't actually heard his words, they knew their import from the way in which she was behaving. How could she be so blind? They'd spent so many years living on pins and needles with their father that it was second nature for them to behave this way when they saw a man and a woman together who didn't appear to be on the best of terms!

For this, she was mad. Madder than she'd been in a very, very long time. Anger pulsed through her veins, throbbing with each thought that raced through her head. Thankful no one could read her mind, she took another deep breath before getting behind the wheel. It wouldn't do for her to be distracted in this weather, especially with the girls in the car. She looked in her rearview mirror. "Are your seat belts fastened?"

They nodded.

Melanie slid into the passenger seat, and Stephanie was glad she'd invited her, or rather that she'd accepted Melanie's offer to come along. The younger woman reached across the seat and clasped Stephanie's cold hand with her gloved hand. "We can talk later," Melanie said.

Stephanie gave a slight nod.

"Let's get these future veterinarians home so they can change clothes. Then I think we should all go out for pizza after the Christmas tree lighting." Stephanie glanced in the rearview mirror again. Both girls were smiling, and in that very second all was right in her world.

As she pulled out of the parking lot, Stephanie's thoughts drifted to the enormity of what had just taken place at Snow Zone. This was the worst time in the world for it to happen, but she'd try and put it out of her mind for the rest of the evening. She owed it to the girls to at least try to act as though everything were normal. It wouldn't be hard, as she was an expert at that type of behavior.

Amanda was the one who broke the silence. "Mommy, can we go to Burger King instead of having pizza?"

Kids, Stephanie thought as she carefully guided her old Ford down the narrow road that led off the mountain. "I think you should ask your sister."

"So do ya?" Amanda asked Ashley.

"Mommy, tell her she needs to speak in complete sentences. When you're in fourth grade, Mrs. Yost won't allow you to speak that way if you're in her class. Right, Mom?"

"I suppose that's true. But you didn't answer Amanda's question," Stephanie said in a teasing tone, amazed that she could still banter back and forth with her girls given the dire situation Patrick O'Brien had just put her in.

"Burger King is fine, but the only reason Amanda wants to go there is so she can get that Dora the Explorer toy they're putting in the kids' meals," Ashley explained. "She's too big for that stuff."

"And you're too big to sleep with that crummy old rabbit that you've had forever. Right, Mommy?" Amanda asked. She was at the age where she needed her mother's approval for almost everything she said. Most of the time, it was funny, but at that moment, Stephanie was trying to drive carefully in near-blizzard conditions, and it wasn't funny.

Melanie leaned over the front seat. "Let's allow your mom to concentrate on her driving. Okay, girls? The roads are very slippery right now."

"Is that right, Mommy?" Amanda asked.

Stephanie couldn't help but laugh. "Yes, Melanie is right. How about we play the quiet game until we get home. Whoever wins gets a double-dipped chocolate-covered ice-cream cone."

She was met with silence. She smiled at Melanie. "Both of them always win this game," Stephanie explained.

She knew the girls wanted to talk, but they were also very competitive. They'd bite their tongues if they had to.

The rest of the drive to the garage apartment was made in silence. Stephanie wanted to enjoy her night with the girls because, from the look of things, it might be a while before she had a free night. Since she was out of a job, she would have to hustle to find something so late in the season. While she had her savings for her down payment on the house, she didn't want to dip into them unless she absolutely had to. She still had high hopes of giving the girls a home of their own for Christmas. She might have to sacrifice the white canopied bed, but that would be okay, as long as they had a home of their own.

Stephanie parked the Ford Taurus next to the outside stairs that led up to their apartment. The girls knew the rules of the quiet game. Once they were inside the house, they could talk all they wanted. Both shot up the stairs like bolts of lightning.

"I think the quiet game is about to officially end," Melanie said as she waited for Stephanie to unlock the door. Both girls barreled through the door.

"I am not too big to sleep with my bunny

rabbit. Mommy said she slept with a stuffed Tasmanian Devil until she was fourteen, so there!" Ashley said in a huff.

"Well, then, it's okay if I want the Dora Explorer prize in the kids' meal."

In response, Ashley rubbed Amanda's shoulder. "I guess it's okay. I was just teasin' with you anyway. I like Dora, too, just don't tell anyone at school. Pinkie promise?" Ashley asked.

Both girls locked their pinkies together, then shook their hands. "Okay, so let's go change. I want to see the tree, but first I want something to eat. We never had lunch today," Ashley explained to her mother.

"I'm sorry. We'll make up for it at dinner, now both of you change into something warm and brush your teeth and comb your hair before we leave. You've got ten minutes, or we'll miss the Christmas tree lighting."

They ran inside their bedroom, slamming the door behind them.

Out in the galley kitchen Stephanie poured glasses of Coke for her and Melanie.

"Want to tell me what sent you racing out of Snow Zone today? I know that conceited idiot said something to anger you," Melanie said before taking a sip of her Coke.

Stephanie debated not telling her, but she needed a friend. Even though the girls had managed to get away from her today, she trusted Melanie to the nth degree. "He told me to take the next four weeks off. Said I needed to spend the time with my kids. Then he added that my extended leave of absence would be without pay."

Melanie's mouth opened and closed several times before she was actually able to form words. "That sneaky, low-life creep! How could he?"

"He's the boss, something he seems to like to remind me of all the time, that's how." Stephanie took a long pull from her glass of Coke. "I used to think he was a really nice guy, just a little rough around the edges. Now I think he's a mean, hateful SOB who needs to get a life."

"I can't believe he would do that to you, especially this time of year. Not only is the Snow Zone going to be swamped, but you have two children to buy Christmas gifts for."

"Yes, your thoughts mirror my own. But you know what angered me more than anything?"

"You're gonna tell me," Melanie stated.

"The girls were afraid. They knew that I was upset after speaking to that self-important jackass. It was like old times. When their father started ranting and raving, they would always clam up, hoping not to anger him. That's the exact way they acted today when Mr. Patrick O'Brien got up on his high horse and gave me the boot. He can fire me, give me a leave of absence, whatever he wants. He's the boss. But what he can't do is frighten my girls! I won't allow it, and I don't care if he fires me for leaving early today. They've seen enough already."

"Do you think you should bring Max in on

this? After all, he is your real boss, and Patrick's, too. He *owns* Maximum Glide, and I bet Grace would have a thing or two to say about Patrick's pissy managerial skills, not to mention his treatment of you."

"No, I don't want to do that. Besides, I think this is personal. You know Patrick and I went out a few times; it didn't work out for whatever reason, and it's as though he's had it in for me ever since. I don't want to involve Max, and certainly not Grace, in her condition. I will handle this, but thanks for offering. It's nice to have a friend go to bat for me." Stephanie put a finger to her lips, stopping further conversation. The girls were waiting at the front door.

"We brushed our teeth and our hair just like you said," Amanda informed her.

Stephanie bent over to give each of the girls a kiss on top of their shiny brown, nicely combed hair. "You're good girls," she added. And they were. Other than an occasional disagreement over something inconsequential, the girls got along remarkably well.

"Then I say it's time we go to see that giant evergreen that is going to light up Maximum Glide. Are you two ready?"

"Yes, yes, yes!" Ashley cried as she stomped down the stairs.

"Be careful, those steps are slick," Melanie said, then took Amanda by the hand and walked with her to the bottom of the stairs before she slipped and fell. That was the last thing Stephanie needed at this stage of the game.

Once they were loaded back in the Taurus and the girls were safely buckled in their seats, Stephanie relaxed. She knew how much the girls had been looking forward to this night. No matter what issues she had to deal with after the day's events, she was a mother first. A fun night out with the girls would make what she knew she had to do much easier.

Chapter Eight

Patrick sent Candy Lee on her way along with the rest of the Maximum Glide employees. He'd already been there for over an hour, and from the looks of things, it appeared that the weather had driven away whatever onslaught of customers he had expected. Stephanie had been right about closing Snow Zone even though her reasons for doing so weren't. She couldn't just take off whenever she felt like it. She had a responsibility to Maximum Glide and to him. While it wasn't he who signed her paychecks, without him she wouldn't have such a cushy position at the resort. It usually took an employee years to be promoted to a management position. And because she was good at her job, he'd given her the benefit of the doubt, and after last year's screwup, he hadn't demoted her. She was loyal to a fault, always on time, and never complained when he asked her to do things that normally a stock boy or girl would do. She did an excellent job no matter what he asked of her. She even cleaned the employee bathrooms every evening before she left.

He was still kicking his own rear end for the comment he'd made about her getting any "funny ideas" about their future. Where the hell that had come from, he didn't know, but he'd kick his own butt a hundred times if he could take back those words. Stephanie hadn't even hinted that she wanted anything to do with him after their last movie date. It was *he* who'd decided she wasn't top-quality pickings on the meat market. Patrick sighed. If his mother or his three sisters even had an inkling that he'd referred to a woman as meat on the market, all four of them would string him up like cattle, then use a cattle prod on him. He didn't really think of women as "meat." It was just something the guys said when they were trying to be macho. And he always wanted to blend in when he was with the guys. Max was the only one who really knew him, knew that he was more than the image he presented to the world. He was educated and quite brilliant, but that didn't always work on the slopes, though he had to admit it had been a blessing dealing with suppliers and a few angry guests. He knew what worked financially and what didn't. Max trusted his judgment, but he knew Max would be mad as a hatter if word of how

Patrick had treated Stephanie got back to him. As much as he hated to eat crow, he was going to have to serve himself a very large portion and swallow every bite as though it were the rarest of caviar.

He hadn't planned on attending the Christmas tree lighting, but knowing that Max and Grace would be there, not to mention Stephanie and her two kids, he figured it wouldn't look good if the manager of the resort didn't put in an appearance for what was widely billed as the kickoff to the Christmas season at Telluride. Plus, he didn't want to give Stephanie the opportunity to corner Max and Grace, not before he had a chance to explain to them what had happened.

Knowing another hour wouldn't make or break the day's sales, he quickly went about the business of closing the shop. Candy Lee had restocked all the shelves before she left, telling him that someone had to do it if Stephanie wasn't there. She went on to tell him what a great manager Stephanie was and that she wouldn't blame her one little bit if she just up and quit. Someday he was going to tell that kid to keep her thoughts to herself. But he liked her, she reminded him of Shannon back in the day. Candy Lee had . . . *moxie,* and he liked that about her. He secretly wished some of it would rub off on the store's manager. She was just a little too compliant at times. Not that he would admit it, but today she'd really surprised him when she walked out in the middle of her shift. Took a lot of guts for her to do that. He probably would've done the same thing had he been in her position. Which he reminded himself he wasn't. He'd had a job to do, and he did it. He could've left out that part about the future, but it had just rolled off his tongue. Why it had rolled off his tongue was something he did not want to think about. No how, no way. He liked his life as it was. No complications, no children to complicate the complications, certainly no children to break his heart into a million tiny pieces the way Shannon's death had left Colleen, Mark, and Abby. That was just too much pain for one man to tolerate.

He turned off the computer systems, did a batch report on the credit card machine, and counted out the cash, checks, and traveler's checks. After that was finished, he tallied up the day's total sales and was extremely impressed. Stephanie usually made a bank deposit on her way home from work. He'd do it because he felt he owed it to her. Once he had all the required checks stamped with the account numbers on the back of them and deposit slips made out, he stuffed them into the bank bag.

Since all the normal closing duties were finished for the day, Patrick walked back to the office just to make sure there wasn't anything there that needed his attention. He opened the door, peered in, and saw nothing out of the ordinary. He ran his hand along the length of the wall searching for the light switch when the flashing green button on the answering machine caught his eye. Dammit, he couldn't leave without listening to the messages. They might be important, and with Stephanie not there to take them, he'd have to intercept them in case there was something that needed his immediate attention. He pushed the PLAY button. A monotone female voice said, "You have fifteen messages."

"What the hell?" He hit the FORWARD button several times as most were calls from suppliers, customers, and other departments at Maximum Glide. He was about to click the STOP button when he heard a soft, but businesslike voice speak as though the woman were in the room.

"Hi, Stephanie, it's Jessica Rollins. I have some good news. I'm pretty sure the owners on the Placerville property are going to accept your offer. If Lady Luck stays on your back, I might be able to close this deal before the end of the year. Call me as soon as you can. I think you and your daughters just might have a Merry Christmas after all. Oh, before I forget, the bank wants to verify your employment. Talk s—"

The machine stopped.

Patrick flicked the light switch back on. He opened a drawer in search of something to write on when he was completely taken by surprise. In the top drawer was a pile of gold ribbon, and a movie ticket stub. He picked it up to read the title of the movie. He let the soft gold silk run between his fingers, then dropped the two items back in the drawer where they belonged. This wasn't good at all. Really it wasn't. Though he broke out into a grin as wide as the bunny run. She'd kept the ribbon from the box of candy he'd bought her, and the tickets from the movie they'd attended on their last date. It was *that* movie that sent him running for cover. She'd probably put these things in the drawer the next day and forgotten about them. Women did that. Saved things that had no meaning or value whatsoever. Stephanie must have forgotten she'd left them there. Should he take them to her, or should he just leave well enough alone? He didn't want her to think he'd been prying through her desk drawers, but he'd needed something to write on so he could remember Jessica Rollins's message. He found a blank Post-it. He played the message once more, wrote it down as best he could, then crammed the paper in his pocket. This Jessica hadn't left a number, but Patrick figured if Stephanie had been dealing with her, then she already knew her phone number. He closed the drawer again, turned off the light, and left through the employee exit.

He'd left his jacket in the Snow Cat; hopefully, one of the guys would remember it belonged to him and return it. Those Spyder jackets cost big bucks. The parking lot was completely covered in snow. What he wouldn't give for a snow tube just right then. He'd sail across the parking lot like a bat out of hell. He had a quick flash of two little girls in bright yellow ski jackets and wondered if they'd ever experienced the pure joy of sliding in a parking lot on fresh-fallen snow. Something told him they hadn't had much fun in their lives. It caused a lump to form in the back of his throat. *Damn! I'm not cut out for this.*

Yeah, those girls were as sweet as hot cocoa laced with the finest whipped cream. When he'd heard they were missing, he about jumped out of his skin though he didn't tell that to anyone. Riding the lift up to where the Snow Cats were stored had been his first priority. He knew if he took a Snow Cat out, first he would be in an all-terrain vehicle that would take him to any part of the mountain, double black diamonds and all. Also, it was equipped with bright lights and had a kick-ass heater. Lucky for him and the girls, and the dogs—he couldn't forget the mother and her pups—he hadn't had to go far. And now it seemed all was as it should be.

He jumped into the Hummer, cranked the heat up as high as it would go, then carefully made his way out of the parking lot. The snow was still falling, but it wasn't nearly as thick as it had been earlier that afternoon. He needed to go home for a quick shower and a change of clothes. He'd make sure to give Stephanie the message from her realtor friend, then he would apologize, tell her how sorry he was for being such an . . . a dope, then he'd tell her she could come back to work first thing in the morning. Once that was out of the way, he could breathe freely again. Hell, he might even ask Stephanie and the girls out to a movie. There were all kinds of G-rated movies out at Christmas. Maybe he would take Megan's boys along. One big happy family.

He shook his head as he traveled down the salt-covered road.

One big happy family!

He couldn't believe a thought like that had even entered his head! *What the heck is going on here?* It must be the holidays. Maybe he was supposed to enjoy them this year. It was just so hard without Shannon. When his family was together, it was so obvious a link was missing. Shannon was the first grandchild, the first niece. She was just the first. And, sadly, she was the first to die.

Tears filled Patrick's eyes, blurring the road in front of him. *Damn!* He wanted to be happy; he just didn't want all the pain that came with it. Knowing he couldn't have one without the other, Patrick figured he would always be the uncle, the good friend of a friend. He didn't have what it took to be a father figure. To anyone's child. He didn't know a diaper bag from a baby bottle. Well, yes he did, but it wasn't something he wanted in his daily life. That was all. Or was it? And was he just afraid to take the leap?

Chapter Nine

The crowd gathered smack-dab in the middle of Maximum Glide. Hundreds of people had faced the cold weather to attend the Christmas tree lighting. A thirty-foot evergreen was placed directly in front of the main offices, the site of most of the day's comings and goings. Ski lessons could be arranged in the building to the right of the giant tree. To the left, children under the age of three could be left in the capable hands of Bunnies and Babies, the day care offered by the resort. North of the tree was The Lodge, where one could eat breakfast or lunch, or simply sit by the raging fire that never seemed to burn out in the giant fireplace. South of the tree were the ski lifts that took men, women, and children to the other forty-six lifts that covered the mountain.

Tonight was like a scene from a Charles Dickens novel. Snow twirled like tiny ballerinas in the chilled night air. Mock gaslights wearing bright red bows flanked the main street on both sides. The shops stayed open, all displaying brightly colored lights and Christmas trees decked out in all the finery of the holiday season. The odor of mulled cider emanated from several of the shops, along with the earthy smell of burning wood.

Stephanie held her daughters' hands in hers as the three of them walked through the festive village that made up Maximum Glide. Melanie walked alongside them. The four were silent as each took in the fairy-tale-like images that lit up the resort like something right out of a magical storybook.

As expected, it was Amanda who spoke first. "Mommy, this is the most beautiful place in the whole wide world! I never want to leave here. I bet when Santa comes here, he doesn't want to leave either, right?"

They all laughed.

"I'm sure he doesn't, but he has many places to go all over the world. Still, I'm sure it hurts him just a tiny bit to leave this very special place," Stephanie said, as they continued their leisurely stroll down the main street, taking in all the brightly decorated windows and people dressed in their warmest, most colorful outdoor wear. It really was beautiful, Stephanie thought. It would be equally beautiful in its raw form, too. No lights, no flashy decorations, just the tall trees with the scent of evergreen perfuming the air, along with the clean freshly falling snow. Yes, she mused, that would be just as beautiful.

"What time do they light the tree?" Ashley asked excitedly. "I can't wait. I know it's just a tree, but it's so big!"

Stephanie and Melanie looked at one another over the girls' toboggan cap-covered heads. They laughed. "Seven o'clock, right on the dot. And it's ten minutes till, so we'd best hurry over so we can get in as close as possible. I don't want you two to miss anything."

"We don't want to either, Mommy. Right, Ashley?" Amanda singsonged.

"*Right,* Amanda. You know what I'm going to wish for when they light up the tree?" Ashley asked in a firm voice.

"I haven't the first clue," Stephanie said. "Why don't you tell us."

"I'm going to wish that Amanda would stop saying, 'right, Mommy,' 'right, Ashley,' 'right, Melanie' all the time."

Stephanie looked at Melanie, who could barely contain her laughter. Amanda, on the other hand, looked as if she was about to cry.

"It's okay, honey. Your sister is just doing what big sisters do." Stephanie fluffed the ball on top of her toboggan cap, hoping this wouldn't turn into an all-out verbal war between the two.

"Santa Claus doesn't tell me what to say, right, Mommy?" Amanda asked in her squeaky-I'm-about-to-cry-voice.

"Of course not. You're the only one who can

decide what words come out of that sweet little mouth of yours. Look"—Stephanie pointed to the tree a few yards ahead of them, hoping to distract her younger daughter—"they're about to light the tree. Come on, let's hurry."

Without another word, the quartet weaved their way through the throngs of people clustered around the giant tree's perimeter. They were able to find a spot about six feet away. Stephanie figured that was as close as they could get without actually trampling on toes, strollers, and, looking down, the largest boot she had ever seen. Her eyes followed the boot to the calf, then the knee, all the way to the thigh. Why did this look familiar to her? Before she knew what was happening, the boot man snatched Amanda right out of her grip and hoisted her on top of his very broad shoulders.

Patrick!

"If you'll follow me, I've got the perfect place to view the tree," he said.

Stephanie was about to tell him to back off when Melanie shook her head and pointed to the girls. They were so excited, the sparkle in their eyes could light up half the giant tree if needed. She mouthed okay and inched behind Patrick, with Ashley sandwiched between her and Melanie.

Patrick guided them through the crowd without too much pushing and shoving. On the opposite side of the street, Stephanie spied what she knew to be a giant boom lift, or a cherry picker as some referred to it. She couldn't help but grin. She glanced behind her at Melanie, who wore a grin as big as the tree. Ashley hadn't said a word since Patrick had come in and literally swooped Amanda onto his shoulders. Not that she could've been heard through the sounds of excitement coming from the groups gathered around the center of the resort.

"Let's hurry, we have about two minutes to climb up in this thing," Patrick said.

"This will hold our weight?" Stephanie asked cautiously. Up close, the machine didn't look that big or steady.

"I'm one hundred percent sure," Patrick attested. "I wouldn't risk it if I wasn't."

Was that supposed to be a dig of sorts, she wondered, as Patrick opened the glass door. Did he think she'd taken too big a risk when she'd allowed Melanie to take her girls skiing on the mountain? She figured if he had, too bad. It wasn't his concern how she raised her children. She told herself if he really knew her, he would know the last thing she would do would be to place her children in danger. A small voice reminded her that this was exactly what she'd done when she'd remained married to an abuser. *But that's for another time. Tonight, I simply want to enjoy being with my daughters and Melanie.*

Trusting he knew what he was doing, Stephanie allowed Patrick to lift Amanda inside the boom. Ashley wasn't nearly as excited as her sister about climbing into the small bucket.

"Mommy, is this safe?" she asked.

"Absolutely," Stephanie replied in her most reassuring voice. "I would not allow you inside if I thought otherwise," she added.

"Well, okay then," Ashley said, allowing Patrick to assist her.

Patrick placed Ashley next to Amanda on a small seat. He grabbed Stephanie's hand to help her take the giant step leading to the inside of the bucket. Sparks shot up and down the length of her arm as he held her for what she thought was a minute too long. She felt out of sorts for a few seconds. She stood behind the girls, then Melanie climbed in. Once they were all securely in position, Patrick spoke up.

"I'm going to be operating this thing. It'll only take a minute to reach the height you'll need to view the lights. Just try not to jump around too much, okay?" Patrick said.

"You're not gonna watch the lights with us?" Amanda asked.

"I'll see them from below, kiddo. Now let me close this door and get all of you ladies up in the air," Patrick said. He gave Stephanie a small smile before closing the door.

She wondered if this was his way of making up to her for the way he'd talked to her at Snow Zone. She wasn't sure, but again, for the girls' sake, she wouldn't question it, at least not just then. There would be plenty of time later for her to think about and rehash the day's events.

Before any of them could utter a word, they were lifted in one giant swoop. Patrick had positioned the boom so that they were able to view the tree at its midpoint. They could look up and down, yet they weren't so close that they couldn't see the people below them, too.

"Oh, Mommy, this is the best fun ever," Amanda said.

"Okay, let's watch," Stephanie said.

Within a matter of a few seconds, the giant evergreen lit up . . . just like the Christmas tree in Rockefeller Center!

Hundreds of red, green, blue, and white lights clung to the tree's branches, illuminating the entire perimeter around the tree. From somewhere there was a drumroll, then a giant silver star as big as a car tire sparkled, completing the ceremony.

"Wow," Ashley said. "This is so way cool from up here."

"And I'm not even scared, right, Mommy?" Amanda informed them.

"See, she's doing it again!" Ashley pointed out.

"Girls, now isn't the time. Let's just enjoy the view before Patrick puts us down."

A few minutes later, Patrick lowered the boom to the ground. Once they stopped, he stepped out of the cab, opened the door, and let them out into the frigid night air.

"That was the coolest thing ever, thanks," Ashley said.

"Yep, it sure was. Mommy thinks so, too, right?"

"Amanda," Stephanie chastened, "it was wonderful. Now, what do you girls say to Mr. O'Brien?"

Quizzingly, Amanda said, "That we want to do it again."

They all burst out laughing, even Stephanie.

"That's not what I had in mind," she said as an afterthought. Her girls knew their manners. Or at least she thought they did. Apparently tonight, that knowledge had taken a leave of absence.

"Thank you, Mr. O'Brien. That was very thoughtful of you to think of us," Ashley said in her most prim and proper voice.

Again, the adults laughed.

"You two are very welcome. That tree sure is a sight to behold, huh?" Patrick said as he gazed up at the rainbow of colors.

"Do you wanna go to Burger King with us?" Amanda asked. "We didn't have lunch today when we were with the pups. I am starving, and Mommy says we both can have double-dipped ice-cream cones because we didn't talk on the ride home."

If there had been a giant hole somewhere, Stephanie wished it would swallow her up right then and there. She was really going to have to start explaining to Amanda exactly what social manners were. She realized her daughter was only seven, but she had to learn sometime, and it might as well be now, before she totally humiliated Stephanie.

For once, Patrick saved her from Amanda's eagerness. "I'd love to, but I need to go to Claude's to see how the pups are doing."

"Oh, I want to go with you," Ashley said.

"I've been so worried about them. Can I go with Patrick, Mom? Please?"

Stephanie wasn't sure exactly what had gotten into her girls, but she was really going to have to sit them both down and discuss manners with them.

"No, you may not. And please don't assume that Mr. O'Brien has to invite you just because you want to go. That is very rude."

"I tell you what I'll do if it's okay with your mom," Patrick said to both girls. "As soon as I leave Claude's, I will call your mom with a pup report. Maybe later this week, if it's all right with your mom, I can take both of you girls to see the pups." Patrick looked at Stephanie, shot her one of his killer smiles, and her heart turned to mush, but only for a second. She remembered just how hateful he had been to her that afternoon.

"I'll think about it. I'll certainly have enough time on my hands to do so," Stephanie said directly to Patrick.

Patrick looked at his big brown boots. "About what I said today—"

"What's done is done, Mr. O'Brien. Thank you for offering the pup update. You can call my cell as soon as you have word of their condition."

With that, Stephanie took both girls by the hand and led them away from Patrick, his promises, and whatever it was he had been about to say.

Chapter Ten

Two Weeks Later . . .

"Well, I for one think he owes you at least a bit of loyalty. You've worked your rear off at that place for two years, and this is what you get? Laid off during the holidays?" Melanie took a sip of her coffee. "I still think you should have told Max and Grace at the tree lighting."

"I know you do. It stinks, but it is what it is. I didn't want to spoil their evening. I'll be fine as long as the deal on the house goes through. I've already filled out all the paperwork; the deposit is being held in escrow; now all I'm waiting on is the bank. And you know how banks are. They take their good old easy time. Jessica said if I was lucky, I'd be moved in before the end of the year, but I don't see that happening. Not with the holidays coming up."

Stephanie and Melanie had just returned from walking the girls to the bus stop. Since her forced leave of absence had begun, they had spent almost every day together. If anything good had come out of her layoff, it was her close friendship with Melanie. They'd taken the girls to the movies twice, three times to McDonald's, and once they'd gone out for pizza at a new pizza parlor in town called Izzy's. Melanie wanted to take them to see a Christmas play in Denver this weekend, but Stephanie really couldn't afford the tickets. Melanie had told Stephanie it was her treat, but Stephanie, who had no idea just how well-off her friend was, said that was too much. Instead, the four of them were planning to see *A Christmas Carol* at the high school in Placerville. It was free to anyone, and Stephanie knew the girls would get a kick out of it. Ever since Grace had taken them to see *The Nutcracker* at Eagle Valley High, they'd fallen in love with live performance of any kind.

"I know you can't wait to get out of this little place, but I think I will miss it when you and the girls leave," Melanie said as she gazed around the three-room garage apartment.

"Then you should ask your parents to rent it to you," Stephanie teased. "I'm sure they would give you a decent rate. Not that they haven't given me a good rate. I didn't mean to imply that they hadn't. I know what they could really get out of this place if they wanted to rent it as vacation property."

"I don't see that happening. They've loved

having you and the girls here. I don't think the place has ever looked quite as homey."

Stephanie had tried her best to make the small, cramped area into a home. She'd painted the walls a warm butter color and sewn cream-colored drapes to cover the large picture window in the living area. She'd spent two weekends putting new tile in the one and only bathroom. She'd been quite proud of herself, too. She'd taken a course on installing ceramic tile offered at the local hardware store and found it really wasn't all that hard to do. She'd borrowed the wet saw and cutters from Max, and the tiles she'd chosen, a creamy beige, were on sale. She'd asked permission first, and, of course, she'd been given complete and total discretion over the apartment. She was told to make it her own, and that was exactly what she'd done.

The kitchen wasn't much bigger than a closet, but Stephanie had left her mark there, too. She'd wallpapered the one wall with tiny butterflies, bought an inexpensive set of pale yellow canisters at a discount store, and added a sheer yellow curtain over the window above the sink. The table had been there when she moved in. Stephanie now knew that it had been a tenth-anniversary gift from Melanie's father to her mother many years ago. Solid hard rock maple with four matching chairs. She'd purchased yellow checkered cushions and matching place mats after she'd polished the deep honey-colored wood to a mellow shine. It was homey, just as Melanie said.

Stephanie had been hesitant about putting

up a tree that year, hoping by some sheer force of magic that she would be in the new house, and they would have Christmas there, but she hadn't told the girls about the house, so she'd had to decorate the small artificial tree she'd purchased the first year they lived there. The apartment couldn't hold much more than that, but she and the girls had decorated wherever possible. They'd tied red and green ribbons on all the doorknobs, and on the handles on the kitchen cabinets. They'd strung cranberries and popcorn on thread and draped it on top of the curtain rod in the living room. Baskets of pinecones they had gathered covered every available surface. Amanda had cut out shapes of stars and Christmas trees from red and green construction paper and taped them all over the walls. Not to be outdone, Ashley had used all the aluminum foil in the house making angels and taping them to the ceiling. That had been quite the task, but they'd all enjoyed themselves. And now their little place sparkled and shone, ready for the holidays.

Though it was expensive and not in her budget, Stephanie had bought the girls each a cell phone for Christmas. Remembering those few hours of fear on Black Friday had left her shaken, more so than she'd let on. She'd purchased cards with a limited number of minutes and would instruct the girls that the phones were only to be used in case of an emergency, but she didn't see that happening, at least not with Ashley. She was starting to talk on the phone with her school friends, and Stephanie knew she would want to fit in with the rest of her classmates by texting and talking on her new cell phone. When Grace and Max had asked what they could give the girls for Christmas, she'd told them to buy them minutes for their phones.

"Thanks, we love it here, it's just not big enough. You know what it's like when three girls share a bathroom?" Stephanie teased.

"I've witnessed it with my very own eyes," Melanie informed her.

"Yes, I suppose you have. I'm just lucky they're still young. Can you imagine what it would be like if they were teenagers?"

Melanie laughed. "I don't even want to think about it."

They chatted for a few more minutes. As Melanie was getting ready to leave, the phone rang. Stephanie hoped the girls were all right. She still didn't feel one hundred percent secure when they were out of her sight.

She raised her index finger to Melanie, indicating for her to wait a minute.

Melanie stood by the door.

"Hello," Stephanie said into the phone, her voice tinged with a bit a fear. "Jessica! It's great to hear from you." Stephanie paused, then nodded to Jessica, who, of course, couldn't see her. As though she were moving in slow motion, she sat down on the kitchen chair.

"That's not true," she cried vehemently. "I don't understand," she trailed off, her voice laced with disappointment. "Yes, of course. I don't know what to say except it's simply not true. I'll have to call you back," Stephanie said as she tossed the phone on the table.

Melanie walked across the small living room back to the kitchen. She sat down in the chair she'd just vacated. "You don't look so hot. Are the girls okay?"

"I hope so. That was Jessica Rollins on the phone. She said she just got off the phone with the bank." Her eyes pooled with unshed tears. "They've denied my loan."

Melanie reached across the table for Stephanie's hand. "How can that be? Jessica said the hard part was over. I thought they'd already approved the loan, that it was simply a matter of signing the final papers at the closing." Melanie appeared to be as dumbfounded as Stephanie. "Did they offer an explanation? Did Jessica say what happened to change their minds?"

Crestfallen, Stephanie nodded. "Jessica said banks don't give loans to people who are unemployed."

Chapter Eleven

"Out of a job? What is she talking about? You're not out of a job," Melanie said again, as though saying it would make it so, at least as far as Jessica Rollins and the bank were concerned. "I don't know where they got their information, but I sure hope you find out."

Depleted of whatever energy she'd had, Stephanie got out of her chair and stood at the sink looking out the window that overlooked the long, winding driveway leading to her apartment. She cleared her throat and wiped her eyes on a tea towel. "I know where it came from. It's obvious."

"You think Patrick is behind this?" Melanie stated the obvious.

Stephanie turned around to face her. "Who else would stoop so low as to do something like this? I think he's still upset at me for not allowing the girls to go to Claude's with him to see the puppies."

"I don't think he's that vindictive, or juvenile. I know he's not the most classy guy in the world, but I really don't believe he would stoop to this sea urchin level."

Stephanie sniffled into the tea towel, not caring that she'd painstakingly embroidered the butterflies on it late one night when she'd had a hard time going to sleep. "You don't get it, Melanie. The guy has it in for me. He thinks women like me are nothing but trash. I know what I'm talking about, trust me."

"Well, I never trust anyone who says 'trust me,' but I can tell you this; whatever makes you think you're trash and whatever 'women like me' are, I would be honored to walk in your shadow, Stephanie Casolino-Marshall. What you are is a decent hardworking woman who wants nothing more than a better life for her two daughters than she had. What you are is a loving, giving, caring mother and friend. Now I know you're not going to like this, but in this instance I'm going to tell you, too bad. I'm calling Max myself. This childish behavior from his manager, and I use that word loosely, has to stop." Melanie reached for the phone in the center of the table.

Stephanie placed her hand on top of Melanie's. "I really don't want you to call Max or Grace. It will seem as though I'm taking advantage of their friendship. And thanks for saying all those nice things about me. You're a good friend, you know that, right?"

"Yes, I know that, and thanks. But friends don't sit by and allow their best friends to get kicked in the butt when they're already down." Melanie held her hand up as if to ward off any further comments from Stephanie. "Go take a shower, wash your hair, and put on some make-up. Not that you need it with that peaches-and-cream complexion, but do it anyway. Then when you're finished, get that black pant suit out of the back of your closet. The one you wore when you applied for your mortgage. No, on second thought forget that. Get the tightest, sexiest pair of jeans you own and top them with that bright red sweater I gave you." Melanie was on a roll. "Don't say another word because I'm not listening. Go on, get in the shower. You have one hour to sexy up."

"Sexy up? That's a new one," Stephanie said.

"Yes it is. And that's because I just made it up. It's mine, an original, so don't think I'm going to let you take credit for it. Now get in the shower, or I will toss you in there myself."

"I'm not sure if I like you this way. Bossy and all."

"If you don't get out of here and get in that shower, I will show you what bossy is. Now *git*, and I don't mean perhaps. Now! Remember, you've got exactly one hour."

Stephanie gave up. "Okay. I guess I need to shower, but for the record, I want you to know that I will be okay with this."

Melanie shot her arm out like an arrow pointing toward the bathroom.

"Okay, okay," Stephanie whined before locking herself in the bathroom.

Melanie waited until she heard the shower running before she picked up the phone. She knew that Stephanie's pride was on the line, but right then she didn't care. What she cared about was that someone had caused her dear friend to lose out on her dream. Whether it was intentional or not didn't really matter at that point. It only mattered that Stephanie had worked harder than anyone she knew just to save a few thousand dollars for a down payment on a home for her and her children. In today's fast world of give or I'll take, Stephanie was a rare breed. And what was a huge sum to Stephanie was chump change for Melanie, who had way more than enough to make a real difference. For the first time in her twenty-four years, Melanie felt like this opportunity, to do something really, really special for people she loved, was a gift to herself, not the other way around.

She hit *69 on the phone to get the last incoming number. She scribbled it down on a magnetic pad stuck on the front of the refrigerator.

"Jessica Rollins, please," she said when a young woman picked up the phone. "And tell her it's a matter of life and death."

"Oh my gosh," the young woman said, "I'll take this call to her myself."

Melanie thought the girl deserved a raise.

"Thank you," she said.

A minute later, Melanie had Jessica Rollins on the phone. She made quick work of telling her what she needed and when she needed it. The woman was more than willing to jump through a few hoops to make her wishes come true. When they finalized their plans, Melanie dialed the number to the office at Maximum Glide.

A voice she didn't recognize answered the phone. Melanie wasn't sure if it was a male or a female either.

"Mr. Edward Patrick Joseph O'Brien, please. Tell him it's a matter of life and death." Melanie liked this new role of taking charge, sort of like kicking ass and taking names later.

Two seconds later, the man himself was on the phone. "This is Patrick."

Melanie rolled her eyes. She was sure the man deliberately downplayed his intelligence.

"Patrick, this is Melanie, and we have a problem." Just for meanness, she waited a few seconds before continuing. Let him wiggle in his britches.

"Is it Stephanie, or the girls?" he asked.

More meanness. "All of them."

"Tell me where they're at, and I can be there in minutes," he replied anxiously.

Again, she let him stew. She knew it was mean, but it was her way of getting even over his putting Stephanie on that unpaid leave of absence.

"Melanie, tell me what's wrong. Please!" He

shouted so loud she had to hold the phone away from her ear.

"I need you to listen, and I don't want you to interrupt me. Is that clear?"

She heard an intake of breath over the phone line. "Okay. I'm listening."

Melanie made fast work of telling him what she wanted and when she wanted it. He complied as fast as Jessica Rollins had. *Maybe graphic design isn't my calling after all.*

Thirty minutes later, Stephanie was showered, dressed, and looking like a million bucks.

"Now, I want you to get in my car. We're going out for lunch."

"Melanie, I know you're trying to cheer me up, and I really do appreciate it, but I have to be here when the girls get home." She looked at the clock on the stove. "And that's in two hours. I don't see how we can go out to lunch and actually enjoy ourselves in such a short period of time."

"Did I say we were going to enjoy ourselves? Hmm, I don't believe I did. Now go."

"Well, I hope you know I feel like a fool, all dressed up, looking so silly, just to eat lunch. And we'll have to go to a fast-food place because that's all I have time for. And I won't take no for an answer, not where my girls are concerned," Stephanie said adamantly.

"I've arranged for my mother to be here when they get home." She really hadn't, but she would. "You have way too much blusher on. Go wipe some off before we leave. You look like Ronald McDonald."

"I *really* don't like this side of you."

"Tough. Go wipe your cheeks. Now."

Stephanie turned around and headed for the bathroom.

Melanie called her mother and explained the situation. She was more than willing to help out. She said she would be waiting at the bus stop for the girls and from there she would take them to Chuck E. Cheese, if Stephanie didn't mind, of course. Melanie assured her she wouldn't but reminded her mother not to forget to take her cell phone, because Melanie knew Stephanie would want to call and check on the girls.

Stephanie came out of the bathroom as soon as Melanie hung up the phone.

"If I didn't know better, I would think you were up to something. But I don't know better, at least not today. So let's just have lunch and enjoy ourselves before the girls come home. It might be fun just the two of us for a change. We can order junk food."

"Yes, and we will as soon as you get in the car." Melanie practically shoved her out the door. "I told you my mother would be here just in case we ran a little late, and you're going to have to trust me on this one."

"And you want me to trust someone who says she doesn't trust people who say trust me?"

"Did I say that?" Melanie asked, as they loaded into her Lincoln Navigator.

"Yes, you did."

"Well, I'm telling you now that you have to

trust me. You don't have to like me, just trust me."

Stephanie took a deep breath. "Turn the heat on, it's freezing. I really wish you would tell me what's going on. I don't like surprises."

"Tough," Melanie said as she maneuvered down the long, winding drive. Evergreens topped with a heavy layer of snow flanked the sides of the drive. It never failed to remind her just how beautiful Colorado really was.

Exactly twenty minutes later, they pulled into the main parking lot at Maximum Glide.

Stephanie looked as though she were ready to do battle. "What are we doing here? This is the last place I want to be right now."

"Tough. It's where you need to be. There is someone here who wants to talk to you. Now get out, or I will carry you over my shoulder like a sack of potatoes."

"I'm not sure I want the girls to see you like this. It might scare them," Stephanie teased.

"Right! They love me any way I am, and we both know that."

"Yes, they do."

As they trudged across the parking lot, snow crunched against their boots, the sound barely audible over the crowds on the mountain. The previous week's blizzard conditions were long gone. In their place the sun was as bright as butter, the sky as blue as a robin's egg, and the snow as white and clean as freshly beaten cream.

They hurried inside the main offices because even though the sun was out, the temperatures were still in the teens.

"We're having lunch in Patrick's office. I told him to order in from The Lodge," Melanie explained.

"I don't know why I agreed to this, but remind me when we leave to wring your neck."

Melanie tapped on Patrick's door, then opened it before he had a chance to tell them to come inside.

Just as she had commanded, there was a table set for *two*, an exquisite crystal vase with one single yellow rose, and a bottle of Cristal chilling in a bucket of ice.

Stephanie glanced at Patrick, then back at her friend turned harridan. "Tell me this isn't what I think it is."

"It isn't," Melanie said. "Enjoy lunch."

She hurried out of the office before Stephanie even had a chance to ask what was going on. She saw the table, the rose, and the champagne.

"Please, come in and have a seat." Patrick motioned to the chairs, which Stephanie recognized from The Lodge.

"Just so you know, I'm not here because I want to be. Melanie seems to think this is . . . I don't know what she thinks, but let's just get this over with."

"You sound like you're headed for the guillotine."

"It's probably not as bad," she responded, then sat down in the chair Patrick pulled out for her. Surprise, surprise. She didn't know he had manners.

"You can tell me that when I'm finished

with what I have to say. I took the liberty of telling Jack to wait on our food. You might not want to be in the same room with me when I say what I need to say, something I should've said a long time ago, and I would have if I'd had the guts to admit it to myself. But better late than never, so here it is."

"Look, if it's about my job, I probably shouldn't have walked out the way I did. I was just so worried about Amanda and Ashley, then you made that comment about . . . well, you know what you said. I was embarrassed and just wanted to leave. So if you're going to apologize, then fine. I accept."

"Actually, this isn't about your job at all. As a matter of fact, it has nothing to do with this place." He took a deep breath, raked his hand through his dark locks, then took another deep breath. "I come from a very large Irish family. I have three younger sisters and four older brothers, and my sisters have three sons and two, uh, one daughter. My brothers have a number of children also, but this is about my sisters and their children and me. About how it's my job to protect them."

"Okayyy," Stephanie said, still unsure what this was all about.

"This is hard, okay?"

"Sorry."

"Two years ago, my sister and her husband lost their daughter, Shannon."

"I'm so sorry, Patrick, I had no idea." Stephanie still didn't know where this was leading, but she was calmer, knowing it had something to do with his family. Family she could handle.

"She was seventeen. . . . She had this rare blood thing called TTP. She died the day she was supposed to graduate from high school. Our family hasn't been the same since. *I* haven't been the same since. It's been a nightmare for my sister, and their younger daughter, Abby. It took about a year before the shock wore off. I . . . This isn't coming out the way I want it to."

Patrick reached for her hand, and her first thought was to pull hers away, but when she saw the look in his blue eyes, she stopped herself. Sadness blanketed his face.

"I swore that I would never allow myself to get in a situation that would make me suffer a loss as great as Shannon's death. I saw what my sister went through, what she'll go through for the rest of her life, what I couldn't protect her and my oldest niece, my parents' oldest grandchild from, and I decided that wasn't the life for me. If I didn't get too close to anyone, I wouldn't get hurt. Typical cliché, but true. Then you and your girls came along. I tried not to like you, I tried not to like your daughters, but that's impossible. I've been trying to figure out a way to tell you this without putting my foot in my mouth, or ticking you off, and as luck would have it, Melanie called and told me what I knew but wouldn't admit to."

"When did Melanie become such an authority on everyone?"

"She's observant, and she's smart. A little mouthier than usual, but I'm glad she chose me to use as an example. What I'm trying to say is I have very, very strong feelings for you, and your girls. Do you think it would be possible to give me another chance to do things the right way?"

This was the last conversation she'd ever expected to have that day. And with Patrick, of all people. So there was a heart beating inside that massive chest after all. Stephanie grinned.

"I suppose I could, but there would have to be conditions."

"Anything you say," Patrick agreed, then squeezed her hand.

"Anything?" Stephanie asked.

"Whatever it takes," he said, his eyes boring into her as though it were the first time he'd actually looked at her.

"Let's hit the double black diamonds, first," Stephanie said, feeling more lighthearted than she had in years. She actually felt like having fun for a change. She didn't worry about the girls because she did trust Melanie even though she had told her she shouldn't. That day Stephanie was simply going to enjoy being in the company of a man she thought was the sexiest boss alive.

Patrick stood up, pulled out her chair, then took her in his arms. "I haven't even kissed you."

"Then let's not waste another minute," Stephanie said just before his lips met hers.

Epilogue

Christmas Eve

The knock at the door sent both girls racing to answer it. Melanie was stopping by to bring them their gifts. They'd been acting like two Mexican jumping beans ever since she told them.

"Girls, let's remember our manners," Stephanie said.

Both girls slowed down and opened the door.

"You're not Melanie," Amanda said.

"Amanda, that's rude!" Ashley said, stepping aside to allow Patrick to come in out of the cold. "We're trying to teach her manners, but I think it's going to take a long time."

"I'm still learning myself. It just takes some people longer than others," Patrick replied.

"Patrick, I thought you were Melanie," Stephanie said, though she wasn't unhappy that it was him. They'd been out four times in less than two weeks. He wasn't the man she'd thought; he was more. Loving, funny, and kind. He had the patience of a saint where the girls were concerned. She'd never been happier.

"Yeah, speaking of Melanie, she called me and told me she couldn't make it until later, something about her car. Said she wanted me to give you this." Patrick reached inside his leather jacket and pulled out a thick manila envelope.

"Oh, that must be the gift she wanted to give to the girls."

"I'm sure of it. Why don't you open it?" Patrick asked as he invited himself to sit at the small table in the tiny kitchen.

"Well, it's not for me," Stephanie said. She was surprised that Melanie hadn't wrapped the girls' gifts since she knew how much they loved shiny paper and fancy ribbons. But maybe she hadn't had time.

"Actually, Melanie said it was for you *and* the girls, so I think it's okay to go ahead and open it."

By that time both girls were hanging all over Patrick. He lifted Amanda onto his right knee and Ashley onto his left. "Go on, Mommy, open it!" Amanda said.

"Oh, all right, but I wish she hadn't . . . Well, okay, I'll just open it." Stephanie had knitted a sweater and matching scarf for Melanie and a

hat and gloves for Patrick. She had been hesitant to dip into the deposit money, which had
been returned to her after the purchase of the
house fell through, so gifts from her this
Christmas were handmade.

She used a fingernail to open the top of the
envelope. She pulled out several official-looking
papers. She skimmed through them, looked
over at Patrick, who had her girls sitting on his
lap as though they'd been doing that their entire lives.

She looked at the papers again. And again.
Then it finally hit her.

Melanie's gift to her. Tears filled her eyes
and coursed down her cheeks like a waterfall.
She could hardly speak. She thought she must
be dreaming. But it was what it was. She didn't
know how it was possible, but somehow, some
way, Melanie's gift to her and the girls was the
deed to an unencumbered piece of property,
the little house in Placerville.

"This is the best present we've ever gotten,
right, Patrick?" Amanda asked.

They all laughed as the girls told their
mother about Melanie's surprise and how it
was possible. And how Melanie had said that,
for the first time in her life, she knew the true
joy of Christmas giving.

And a surprise it was, a complete and utter
surprise.

For the first time in her life, Stephanie and
the girls would truly have a home of their own,
thanks to the incredible generosity of a loving
friend.

Fern Michaels Talks About Christmas

Recently, Fern Michaels took time out of her busy day to chat with her editor at Kensington and share her thoughts with you about Christmas—why she loves writing stories set during the holiday season, and some of her own memories and cherished traditions from Christmases over the years. We hope you enjoy getting to know a little bit more about one of America's most beloved storytellers, Fern Michaels.

Fern, you have written at least a dozen Christmas novels and novellas over the years. Is there something about this particular holiday that especially inspires you?

I've always thought Christmas was the happiest time of the year, not just the one day but the entire Christmas season. Everything is so fes-

tive, so colorful, and people just seem to treat each other nicer. And of course the kids—that's what makes Christmas Christmas . . . the joy in their eyes, the excitement. I remember when I was little I would get so excited I'd make myself sick. My mother used to block off the days on the calendar so I wouldn't know exactly which day it was. And of course there is the spiritual side to Christmas that I truly enjoy. Personally, I couldn't ask for anything more perfect.

Do you have a favorite Christmas story?

No, sorry to say I don't have one single favorite. However, I do love the poem "Twas the Night Before Christmas," by Clement Clarke Moore. I used to know the words by heart. Somewhere in my attic I have my first coloring book set to the words of "Twas the Night Before Christmas." It was a sorry mess because I wasn't old enough to color inside the lines. Does that count?

Ha! It sure does. Does it help to write holiday fiction around Christmastime, or can you write it anytime of year?

No, I can write it anytime. I usually burn a balsam candle and if I'm writing it in the summer I play Christmas music. Sometimes it helps and sometimes it doesn't. But you know, when the publisher wants the manuscript, I have to make it happen!

That's true, and we sure do appreciate it! How is writing a shorter story or novella different from writing a longer, full-length novel?

Ohhhh, I find it much harder to write short stories. I'm a wordy person and it's hard to condense everything I want to say into shorter paragraphs and still get it all out. I'm not good at it and it takes me twice as long to do a novella than it does an actual novel, believe it or not.

At least two of your holiday novellas involve skiing. Are you a skier, or does skiing just make for a good wintertime story element?

I love to ski. But that was back in the day. I have arthritis now and no longer do it. My kids all go to Utah and other places to ski, so I live vicariously through them with their tales. I do miss it, though, more so now that I live in a warmer climate with no snow.

Your holiday novel Christmas at Timberwoods *takes on the darker side of Christmas, with a disgruntled mall Santa and his plans to wreak havoc at a busy shopping center. Was there a specific incident or news story that sparked this idea?*

There was, but for the life of me I can't remember what it was at this moment. I might remember around this time next year. I seem to recall plucking something from the headlines at that time. But it only takes the smallest hint of an idea to send my imagination off and running—so the story I end up with doesn't bear any resemblance to whatever the story was that inspired it.

There's often a romance or romantic element in your holiday fiction. Why does Christmas tend to bring couples together?

That's true, but I don't have the answer. I think people are more giving of themselves during the holidays, thinking about others, thinking about family. There's something magical about Christmas—hopes, dreams, sugarplums, mistletoe, that kind of thing. Maybe the word I'm searching for here is it's a time of expectation. And if you're single, the expectation may be to find someone to love.

What do you remember most about your own childhood Christmases?

Snow up to my knees, sled riding, a Christmas tree so fragrant you could smell it all the way upstairs, trying to find where Mom hid the gifts. The excitement of trying to guess what would be under the tree. Oh, so many memories . . .

Did you often receive books for Christmas as a child? If so, do you remember any favorite titles?

Yes! I got so many books. Nancy Drew and the Bobbsey Twins, along with the Hardy Boys and Cherry Ames. I saved them all, and then at some point my mother gave them all away. . . . Then one day I got an e-mail from some lady who said she was the one my mother gave the books to. She asked me if I wanted them back. I would have driven night and day to get them back, but she was kind enough to send them to me. I wish you could see my signature inside. Made me laugh for days.

Are there traditions from those Christmases that you still keep today?

No, not really. We made up our own as we went along. We do Christmas Eve as opposed to Christmas Day. We all go to midnight mass, have the big dinner, the gift opening, check out everyone's special ornament on the tree, go down memory lane with all the macaroni ornaments that are basically just glue holding them together. I wouldn't part with any of them for the finest blown-glass ornaments. We laugh a lot and sing "Jingle Bells," all off-key, of course, and the dogs go running to hide.

Are there things from your childhood Christmases that you deliberately changed for your own children?

No, not deliberately. I sort of let them find the way each year, and our own traditions developed gradually with all the kids' different personalities. With five kids it was really interesting.

Can you tell us about how you and your family celebrate Christmas today?

Oh, dear, that's a tough one. Actually, we now go away. My youngest daughter died the day after Christmas unexpectedly several years ago and none of us could bear to be home with all the memories. We've been talking about maybe trying to do it at home this coming year. As the time grows closer, we will decide.

Do you often give books as Christmas presents?

Absolutely. I am the booksellers' best customer. People get them whether they like it or not.

The holidays are oftentimes stressful for people. How do you balance writing, holiday preparations, shopping, and family celebrations at this busy time of year?

It used to all just somehow fall into place. These days I don't do that much, to my own sorrow. Perhaps this year. I just don't know. . . .

We understand you are an excellent cook. Do you have any favorite holiday recipes you'd like to share with your readers?

I like to think I'm a good cook. I took a gourmet cooking class years ago and tried everything out on my kids. The end result: This is okay, but don't make it again. We have pretty plain palates. Okay, rum balls are my specialty, and no, I am not going to give out this recipe!

Ooh, we're going to keep after you for that one! Thanks so much for sharing your time and thoughts about Christmas. We wish you and your family a wonderful holiday season, and please keep writing the stories we love to read!

*In a heartwarming novel of secret wishes and
family lost and found, acclaimed New York Times
bestselling author Fern Michaels creates a timeless
Christmas story to cherish . . .*

HOLLY AND IVY

The flames of memory always seem to glow a
little brighter during the holidays. Perhaps
that's why this time of year is so difficult for
airline heiress Ivy Macintosh, as she faces
thoughts of yet another festive season alone.
Since the plane crash that claimed the lives of
her husband and two children eight years ago,
she's been submerged in grief.

When eleven-year-old Holly Greenwood
knocks on her door, lost and frightened after
a forbidden visit to her singing teacher, Ivy's
self-imposed exile is shattered. Holly has an
extraordinary voice, and wants nothing more
than to perform in an upcoming Christmas
musical. Holly's father, Daniel, doesn't allow
music in their home, refusing to give a good
reason why, yet Ivy is drawn to the warmth she
senses beneath his gruff exterior. As Christmas nears, their shared concern for Holly be-
gins to draw Ivy back into the world again . . .
and toward a family who may need her just as
much as she needs them . . .

*A Zebra mass-market paperback and eBook
on sale now.*

Keep reading for a special look!

November 2016

"You're too young to be hanging around with a bunch of old ladies. You need to be with girls your own age," Daniel Greenwood explained to his eleven-year-old daughter, Holly.

"Well, you work around those 'old ladies,' and I think you need to be around women *your* own age. You will never find a girlfriend at The Upside, now, will you? And I do have friends my own age," Holly countered as she spread Skippy extra-crunchy peanut butter across a slice of bread. "I'm getting bored with peanut butter sandwiches, too. Can't you get some turkey or ham at the grocery store next time? Besides, Miss Carol asked me if I could help out with their Christmas musical production this year." Holly slipped that last bit in because she knew that her dad wasn't very hip with her participating in The Upside's Christmas *anything*, especially since it involved music. He was worse than Scrooge, and she'd told him that every time she thought she could get away with it.

"Holly, that's enough. The subject is closed. Finish making your lunch before you miss the bus. Again."

Tears welled up, but *no way, José,* was she going to cry in front of him. He would just tell her to toughen up and get over it. He was mean sometimes, and she wished she had someone she could talk to about her dad. She knew he loved her, but he wasn't a very nice dad the way her friends' dads were. All he did was work and come home, read the papers, throw something in the microwave for dinner, then shut himself up in his den for the rest of the night. He didn't even bother telling her good night on most nights. She'd tried her best to be cheerful and nice to her dad, but he would always come back with something snotty like, *"Don't you have homework or something to do?"*

"Get a move on, Holly. I don't have time to drive you to school today. And make sure you come home as soon as school is out. No stopping at The Upside." He gave her that dad look over his shoulder.

She rolled her eyes as soon as he looked away and stuffed her peanut butter sandwich and an apple in her lunch bag. Remembering that she'd forgotten something to drink yesterday, she grabbed a bottle of water and tossed it in her backpack.

Hoping he might be in a better mood this evening, she smiled, then said, "Sure, Dad, see you tonight. Have a good day at work." She had every intention of getting off at the bus stop three blocks from The Upside. She'd promised Miss Carol she would bring her a list of songs they could practice.

He waved her off without saying a word, his usual form of good-bye.

Holly slung her backpack over her shoulder and headed out the front door, making sure to slam it behind her. This was her way of letting her father know he had failed her again. She never said that to him, but it was exactly what she thought. She ran the two blocks to the bus stop, where Kayla and Roxie were waiting for her.

"We thought you were gonna miss the bus again," Roxie said, when Holly all but skidded to a stop.

She leaned over, her elbows on her knees, as she tried to catch her breath. "Almost, but I ran all the way. Dad's gonna kill me if I miss it again. That's, like, five times in three weeks."

Holly had been friends with Kayla and Roxie since kindergarten. They were always together at school, and this year, for the first time since first grade, they were all in the same classroom together. It was Ms. Anderson's fifth-grade class. When they had learned this at the beginning of the school year, they had made a pledge to never, ever let anyone come between them. They'd termed themselves *the three girl musketeers.*

The orange-yellow bus ground to a noisy stop. Holly was the first to hop on the bus, and she hurried to the much-coveted seat in the rear before anyone else noticed it was empty. She slid all the way over to the window, making room for Kayla and Roxie. They dropped their backpacks on the floor, using their feet to keep them from rolling forward when the bus took off.

"So," Roxie said after they were settled in their seats, "did you tell your dad about the Christmas musical?" Five-foot-four Roxie was the tallest of the trio. Holly thought that with Roxie's long blond hair, which reached all the way to her waist, and her clear blue eyes, Roxie was the prettiest girl in their fifth-grade class. Kayla, on the other hand, was a tiny little girl with short, curly black hair and eyes to match. Holly thought that both of her best friends were extremely pretty, and told them so often.

Holly was polite, friendly, helpful to anyone who asked her. She did her best to make good grades in school and succeeded pretty well except for math, where she barely managed a B minus. Ms. Anderson told her she would do better if she studied harder at home, and she'd even offered to come over to her house and tutor her, but her dad went into a rage when she told him what Ms. Anderson had offered. And she really tried, but math was never going to be her best subject.

Her dad was really good with numbers, and she'd asked him more than once to help her, but he'd told her no, she'd have to learn on her own or else she'd never get it. She wanted to tell Ms. Anderson that her father wouldn't

help her with math no matter what, or any
homework for that matter, but she didn't want
to make her father look bad. He had never
been really friendly to her, and she still didn't
understand how her own dad could treat her
like she was nothing more than a piece of
yucky old furniture. So many times, she had
wanted to tell Kayla and Roxie, but she suspected they knew that she didn't have the
nicest dad in the world because they had been
to her house lots of times, and her dad rarely
acknowledged them when they were there.
Sometimes she thought he was mad at her because of her mother, but she figured she was
too young to understand that part of her dad.
She wished her mother were still alive. It would
make her dad happy again, she assumed,
though she didn't actually have any real memory of his being happy. Every time she asked
him about her mother, he would get so angry
at her, so she had decided never to ask about
her mother again. There was no one else to
ask, either. Her dad had no brothers or sisters,
no living parents. His parents had died when
he was only a teenager. Holly's mom wasn't
even thirty when she died. She kinda thought
she remembered her mom, but she wasn't really sure. She had one picture of her mother
that she'd sneaked from beneath her dad's
pile of underwear when she was seven. If he
missed it, he'd never said anything, and she
wasn't going to tell him. Her mom was so
pretty, with deep, reddish-gold auburn hair

like hers. Her eyes were a clear gray, and Holly sometimes thought they kinda twinkled back at her whenever she took out her picture, even though she knew that pictures didn't smile or twinkle at people. It was wishful thinking, and she was smart enough to figure that out.

"I told him Miss Carol wanted me to help out with the music, but all he heard was The Upside and music, then told me I needed to hang out with girls my own age. I told him that I would come straight home after school." Holly hated dishonesty. "I crossed my fingers, you know, just so I could, well . . . lie." She smiled, and she knew that her best friends would get what she meant.

She had another secret that was ready to burst from her mouth, but she had promised Maxine she wouldn't tell a living soul. *Still, it is the coolest thing ever. If it really does happen.* She quickly pushed those thoughts aside before she revealed their secret.

"I don't see why it's such a big deal. It's not like you're hanging on the street corner with drug addicts," Roxie said with all the knowledge of a street-smart eleven-year-old.

"She's right," Kayla added. "Your dad should be glad we're such nerds."

They all laughed.

"I don't think he even knows what a nerd is," Holly said with a bit of sadness in her voice.

Roxie wrapped her right arm around Holly. "He knows, he's just mad at the world. At least that's what my mom says."

Holly jerked to attention. "How would your mom know? She hardly knows my father," Holly said.

Roxie seemed slightly uncomfortable. "I know, but she told me once that she knew your mother." She'd never said anything about this to Holly because she knew it would just raise more questions that she probably wouldn't have the answers to.

"How come you're just telling me this now?" Holly asked.

"I didn't want to hurt your feelings is all," Roxie said quietly.

Holly nodded. "Sure, I know. I'm sorry. I just . . . Well, I've never really talked about my mother. It just seems weird, you know? Maybe someday I could talk to your mom about her."

"Maybe," Roxie replied.

Kayla spoke up. "You guys are way too serious today."

"Sorry," they both said at the same time, and they all laughed.

"Two more stops," Roxie said, as though Holly and Kayla were suddenly clueless. They had been riding this same bus, the same route, with most of the same kids who'd lived in the same houses, since they were born.

Billy Craydell and Mandy Simpson hopped on the bus at the next-to-the-last stop, followed by Terri Walker, whom most of the fifth-grade boys called *Street* Walker. Holly felt very bad for her because she was a nice girl, just shy. She'd make a point to say hi to her today. Ms.

Anderson once told the class that it took little effort to be nice; every Friday in class, she'd ask if anyone had had occasion to put her advice to use. Holly would this week.

The bus clanged to a stop in front of the two-story redbrick building that housed grades one through five. Kindergarten classes were held in the cafeteria, and Holly never really counted that as a real grade, though she supposed she should. Holly remembered attending kindergarten classes in the cafeteria and thinking she was so grown-up. If only she was an adult, she thought now as she waited to exit the bus.

Inside the school, the hallways were packed with kids lugging backpacks and lunch bags. Most of the older kids deposited their cell phones in their lockers. A new rule required that they not be carried. She had never given much thought to that rule, since neither she nor Kayla nor Roxie had one. She'd planned to ask her dad for one this year for Christmas. She knew he'd tell her no, but she thought it was still worth a try. Kayla and Roxie were asking for cell phones, too, though their parents would probably decide it was time for them to have cell phones, since both girls were about to turn twelve.

Holly spent the morning in Ms. Anderson's class, and at noon they broke for lunch. She found her table and saved places for Roxie and Kayla. She couldn't wait for this day to end. She had so many things to tell Miss Carol when she stopped at The Upside on her way home.

Just the thought brought a huge grin to her face.

Roxie plopped down beside her. "What's so funny?"

"Yeah," Kayla parroted, "why the humongous smile?"

Holly's eyes twinkled with mischief. "You'll just have to wait and see."

Connect with Us

Visit us online at
KensingtonBooks.com
to read more from your favorite authors, see books
by series, view reading group guides, and more.

Join us on social media

for sneak peeks, chances to win books and prize packs,
and to share your thoughts with other readers.

facebook.com/kensingtonpublishing
twitter.com/kensingtonbooks

Tell us what you think!

To share your thoughts, submit a review,
or sign up for our eNewsletters, please visit:
KensingtonBooks.com/TellUs.